The Master of Shilden

LUCINDA CARRINGTON

Black Lace novels are sexual fantasies.
In real life, make sure you practise safe sex.

First published in 1997 by
Black Lace
332 Ladbroke Grove
London W10 5AH

Typeset by CentraCet, Cambridge
Printed and bound by Mackays of Chatham PLC

ISBN 0 352 33140 2

The Master of Shilden

Chapter One

When Ralph finally answered the door he was dressed in a silk bathrobe and his thick blond hair was damp and tousled. He had obviously just come from the shower. Elise imagined his muscular body under the cascade of water, his skin shining. They had never showered together, but maybe this weekend they would. There were lots of things she wanted to do with him this weekend. She was so pleased to see him that it took her a few moments to realise that he did not look equally pleased to see her. His eyes moved quickly from her face to the bulging carrier bags she was holding.

'Elise?' He did not smile. 'What are you doing in London? I thought you were going to visit your parents?'

'I changed my mind,' Elise said. She let her eyes stray downwards. It always gave her pleasure to see him semi-naked. Hard muscled from a careful exercise programme, tanned from a sunbed, his body excited her. The bathrobe had fallen open to his waist, and clung to his thighs in a way that made his partial erection quite obvious. The battering of the water had aroused him. Maybe later she would repeat the process, she thought.

First the shower, and then my mouth. She smiled. 'Do you always answer the door without any clothes on?'

He took a step back and she followed him. 'I've got clothes on,' he said.

She glanced down at him. 'Well, sort of,' she agreed. 'Just don't answer the door like that if you've got a postwoman! Here, take these.' She handed him the bags. One of them clinked. 'Wine,' she explained. 'And there are some interesting tins as well. We needn't go out again this evening.'

She walked past him into the small kitchen. It was gleaming and immaculate. Sometimes his extreme neatness irritated her. His clothes were always on hangers, or folded, and never flung over chairs or on the floor. His hi-tech glass and chrome rooms could have been illustrations in a design magazine. They always looked perfect and quite unlike her own colourful, untidy bedsit.

'You're staying?' He sounded worried. 'Staying the night?'

Elise dumped her bag on the stainless steel kitchen table and thought: I've upset him by arriving unexpectedly. She knew Ralph arranged his life as precisely as he arranged his too perfect apartment. Appointments were all planned in advance and noted in his electronic diary. She often wondered how he listed their meetings. Make love to Elise: 7.30pm to 8.15pm. Eat meal. Make love again. It would be typical of Ralph to have everything neatly listed. She wouldn't have been surprised if he had added: orgasm lasted one minutes and two seconds precisely!

She also knew they were an unlikely couple. While trying to survive as a theatrical designer she had taken a temporary job as a receptionist at Sellicks. And she had met Ralph Burnes. He had attracted her from the start. It was not only his beautifully proportioned body, his wide shoulders and narrow waist, and his pale golden hair. It was his attitude. He came across as a man who was in control of his life, in control of himself. Quite unlike the disorganised art school students she had known before.

Immaculately tailored, he could have stepped straight out of a glossy photograph in a quality fashion magazine. She had used this compliment to open a conversation with him. He had seemed flattered, and she played on it. In fact, she remembered guiltily, in an effort to hook him she had rather exaggerated the extent of her own contacts in the modelling world. Well, maybe exaggerated was putting it mildly. She had lied! He had seemed more that casually interested and had questioned her repeatedly about it since. Now she gazed at his worried face, well aware that something was very wrong.

'I'm sorry if I've upset your schedule,' she said. 'I thought you'd be pleased to see me. You always said we should spend more time together; that I could stop over for the weekend. Well, now I'm going to.' She paused. 'Unless you want me to leave? You've only got to say the word.'

'Of course I don't want you to leave.' He fidgeted with his bathrobe. 'But it's ... well ... it's a bit awkward. I'm – I'm going out.'

'I'll come with you,' she suggested.

'No,' he said, quickly. 'You can't.'

'Why not?'

'Don't hassle me, Elise.' He turned away from her. 'It's a stag party.'

'Anyone I know? Someone from Sellicks?'

'No. An old school friend of mine.'

It sounded too slick. And Ralph looked positively nervous. She was not sure whether she really believed him, but decided to give him the benefit of the doubt. 'Well, I wish you'd told me in advance,' she said. 'I've brought all this food.'

'It'll keep,' he said. 'I'll put it in the fridge.'

She followed him out into his open plan living area, watching the movement of his tight buttocks under the clinging silk. 'Have you arranged a striptease for your friend?'

'I haven't arranged anything,' he said. 'The others have done all that.'

'Maybe a strippergram? That's traditional, isn't it?' She moved closer to him. 'And after the groom has been sufficiently embarrassed, he goes off with the girl.' Another step and she was practically touching him. 'Won't you be jealous?'

'No,' he said.

'You can have your own girl,' she murmured. 'Your own stripper. All to yourself.' She reached out and stroked one finger down the front of his robe. She moved her hands over his chest and felt his nipples, hard and erect under the sleek wine-coloured cloth. 'Wouldn't that be more fun than a stag party?'

He stood still. Her exploration reached his waist, and continued downwards. She knew exactly how to tease him. She knew precisely the moves she had to make. She would cup her hands under his balls and massage them gently, then stronger, making him groan. She would rub her thumb up the length of his swelling erection, circling and pinching, harder than she would have thought comfortable, exciting him even more.

She knew that he enjoyed rough handling. It aroused him much faster than the gentle caresses she had given him during their first love-making session. His needs and reactions were predictable. It had surprised her at first. And disappointed her. She liked variety, the unexpected. Ralph responded to one set of caresses and never seemed to want any variations. Sex was to be as precise and ordered as all the other parts of his life. She obliged him, because she wanted to give him pleasure. At least

4

it made it easy for her. Success was guaranteed. She always knew exactly what to do.

The trouble was he thought she was equally rigid in her needs. He established a pattern and, because it seemed to work, he never varied it. He stroked her back and spine (but never long enough) then moved to her buttocks, massaging them strongly. Moved up again to her breasts, kissing them (and again never spending enough time on them) before sending down exploratory fingers to feel if she was already wet and ready for him. Because she found the sight of him, and the scent of his skin, and the closeness of his superb body, sexually exciting, she usually *was* ready. But she found herself frequently wishing that he would startle her with a new technique; a new position. He never did.

Maybe she would suggest it later, she thought. But not now. She did not want to start an argument, or indulge in a discussion. He was tense enough as it was. Now she just wanted to enjoy him, explore him, relax him. Make him want to spend time with her. Make him forget whatever other appointment or activity he had planned for that weekend.

'I'm going to give you the best orgasm you've ever had,' she promised huskily. 'Come into the bedroom. All you've got to do is lay back and enjoy it.'

'No,' he said. 'I have to go out. I've got to dress.'

But he allowed her to back him into the pale and spartan bedroom, with its lightly-polished wooden floor; a room dominated by a low, double divan. She noticed that there were no clothes laid out for him to change into. He always laid out his clothes in advance if he was going to shower and change. From his underpants to his tie, everything arranged in a neat line. She put one hand on his bare chest and pushed him backwards. 'On the bed,' she said. 'That's an order.'

He sat down, slowly. She knew his resistance was weakening. She ran her hand over his chest, bent forward and closed her lips over one nipple while playing insistently with the other. She heard him groan a protest: 'Please, no. There isn't time . . .'

It did not sound very convincing. She fastened her teeth on him, and nipped his flesh. He groaned again, this time with inarticulate pleasure. She pushed him and he sprawled back on the bed. His silky robe fell open. Kneeling over him she admired the hard ridges of his abdominal muscles, a tribute to the hours he spent in the gym. She moved her hands over his chest again, downwards, smoothing them along his inner thighs, forcing his legs apart, her fingers tickling the softness of his balls and stroking his swelling cock.

As she did so she could not help wishing the positions were reversed. That he was exploring her body, lightly at first, then harder, handling her with possessive authority. Making her feel irresistible. She sucked on his nipple again, wishing his mouth was performing the same action on her. Then, his thick penis rose fully from its bed of golden hair. Her fingers circled it, and she began to stroke and tug.

'No,' he protested, weakly.

She felt him tremble. 'You don't mean no,' she whispered. She leant over him, her tongue flicking. His body shuddered. She knew his nipples were as sensitive as her own, and she took full advantage of it. 'You mean yes, please.'

'I've got to go out,' he groaned.

She slid her tongue down his chest, played around his navel for a moment, then moved on. She shifted her hand from his penis to his balls, massaging them with increasing speed and pressure. 'You prefer a stag party to me?'

'No. But I promised . . .'

'Phone up and say you can't make it.'

She took his cock between her teeth, nipping him roughly, knowing how this excited him. He writhed on

the bed, almost out of control. She loved this feeling of
power over him. Loved the idea that she was the one
who could do this to him. His hips began to thrust
towards her, pushing himself more deeply into her
mouth. She drew back, suddenly.

'Of course,' she said, with mock concern, 'if you really
want me to stop, I will.'

'No,' he pleaded. 'You know what I like. Make me
come. Please.'

She ran her tongue up the length of his erection and
flicked the sensitive tip. 'If you're sure we've got time?'
she teased.

For an answer he grasped her head with one hand
and pulled her down. His other hand guided his penis
back into her mouth. She closed her lips around him,
and began to work on him again, sucking hard. He
opened his legs wider for her.

'Do it,' he muttered. 'You know what I want.'

She reached out to the immaculate white bedside
cabinet and pulled open the top drawer. Her hand
closed over the vibrator. She switched it on and shifted
her position until she was sitting between his legs. He
took hold of his erection and continued to excite himself.
She ran the vibrator along his inner thigh, then circled
the opening that he wanted her to penetrate, teasing
him with the shivering tip, touching him and withdrawing, tormenting him until his body writhed with delight
and need.

'Put it in!' he gasped. 'Now! Hard!'

And the doorbell chimed.

'Oh God, no,' he moaned in frustration.

'Don't answer,' she said. She touched him with the tip
of the vibrator, pushing against his anus, feeling him
respond. 'They'll go away.'

The bell chimed again.

'They won't.' He tried to sit up, and she tried to push
him back, still thinking that this was part of the game.

Surely he did not have to answer the door? No one important called in the evenings. It was probably a salesman. Or a Jehovah's Witness. They struggled briefly. Ralph won. The bell sang out again, twice. Ralph got to his feet and pulled the edges of his robe together. His erection was still visible, thrusting against the clinging silk.

'You can't answer the door like that,' she giggled.

'I can.' He sounded irritable now. 'You stay here. I'll see who it is and get rid of them.' He paused at the door and repeated his instructions, insistently. 'Stay here, Elise.'

She lay back on the bed and closed her eyes. She heard the door open. Heard Ralph's voice. Heard a female voice, angry, raised in argument. She sat up. Who was Ralph talking to? Why did he have to argue with a casual caller? Curiosity got the better of her and she went over to the bedroom door and peered out.

A young woman was trying force to her way into the flat. Her dark, smartly tailored suit was almost masculine in its severity: a double-breasted jacket and straight skirt that skimmed her knees. But her shining, shoulder-length hair, long slim legs and stiletto-heeled shoes made the suit look unexpectedly sexy. Ralph was resisting her attempts to push past him.

'Stop playing games, Ralph.' Her voice was sharp and authoritative. 'I've dressed up just for you, and I'm damn well coming in.' She managed to get round him, saw Elise, and stopped. They stared at each other for a long moment. 'Well.' The woman's voice was brittle. 'No wonder you wanted me to come back later!'

'I can explain,' Ralph said, weakly.

'I'm sure you can.' She flicked his robe open and inspected him. His erection had not subsided. Her red-nailed fingers caught hold of him, none too gently. 'You can explain this too, I suppose?' She twisted her hand and he yelped.

8

'Jemma, you're hurting me, damn it.'

'Sure I am,' she agreed, letting him go. She smiled. 'And you're loving it, aren't you? Well, there's more to come, when we're on our own.'

'Ralph?' Elise stepped forward. 'Who is this woman?'

'I'm Jemma Harrisford.' A pair of cold brown eyes surveyed Elise. 'And I think I know who you are. Elise something-or-other, the little theatre groupie.' Jemma's dark fall of hair swung as she turned her head. 'Ralph, just what are you playing at?'

'I can explain,' Ralph said.

'Theatre groupie?' Elise glared at Jemma. 'That's rich – coming from a tart!'

Jemma Harrisford's face changed. She confronted Elise aggressively. 'Me, a tart? Oh, very funny! Just what were *you* doing before I arrived? Or did Ralphie get that hard-on by using his imagination?'

'I can explain,' Ralph repeated.

'You'd better,' Jemma agreed. 'This was supposed to be our long weekend, right? I mean, I know you've been fucking this person for a reason, but I don't really fancy a threesome. What's going on?'

'What I do with my boyfriend is my affair,' Elise said furiously.

'Boyfriend?' Jemma laughed harshly. 'Grow up! Just because Ralphie gets it up with you once in a while doesn't mean he's your boyfriend.'

'Ralph,' Elise said, surprising herself by keeping her temper under control. 'Tell this . . . female to leave.'

'That's right, Ralph,' Jemma mimicked. 'Tell me to leave! And if you do, you can be sure you'll never see me again.'

'Great,' Elise said, tightly. Jemma stood watching her, smirking. Elise could have cheerfully punched her. She waited. 'Ralph,' she repeated. 'Tell her!'

'I can't,' Ralph said, pathetically.

'Of course you can't,' Jemma purred. 'You take orders,

Ralphie, you don't give them.' She turned her bright red, insincere smile to Elise. 'You haven't worked that out yet, have you, darling? A bit thick, aren't you? I'm amazed Ralphie could actually get it up with you, but I expect the idea of that modelling contract he thought you could get him turned him on. He always did fancy the idea of his pretty face, and his pretty body, spread all over the glossies for everyone to admire.'

Elise turned to Ralph. 'You believed I could get you a modelling contract?'

'Of course he did,' Jemma said. 'So I thought, well, if he has to fuck you to get what he wants, I'll put up with it. I knew you didn't actually mean anything to him, or I wouldn't have let you near him. But it doesn't look as if you're going to deliver, does it?' Her red lips twisted into a sneer. 'I don't think you really know any fashion photographers. I think you're just a silly failure with a big mouth. And I also think it's about time Ralphie gave you the push.' She glared at Elise, hands on her hips. 'You're getting to be a nuisance, darling. If Ralph gets a hard-on in future, it's going to do me some good, not you!'

Elise turned to Ralph, silently willing him to protest. To argue. To support her. But she knew he would not do it. He stood with his head bowed, unable even to meet her eyes. And she realised that now everything made sense. No wonder he looked dismayed to see her. He had no intention of going out to a stag party, or anywhere else, come to that. He had his weekend's entertainment arranged – and she did not figure in his plans at all.

'There's the door,' Jemma pointed. 'Out!'

Elise considered smacking Jemma across the face. It would have certainly relieved her feelings. But she suspected that Jemma would hit her back – and Ralph might just enjoy seeing a cat fight. She did not intend to provide him with any more entertainment. Instead, she marched into the kitchen. She certainly wasn't going to let either of them enjoy the tinned caviare and exotic fruits she had chosen so carefully. She grabbed the bags, contemplated smashing a bottle of wine and dirtying Ralph's pristine kitchen, then thought better of that, too. Be dignified, she told herself. That'll annoy Jemma, the bitch! Why should I give her the pleasure of seeing that I'm hurt and furious?

'Good riddance!' Jemma called after her, and she stalked towards the door. Before it had even closed behind her, Elise heard Jemma's harsh voice giving Ralph orders: 'Get stripped, you disgusting wimp! And get on the floor. You owe me an apology, and it better be good. You're going to crawl, starting now!'

'Well, I think it's the best thing that could've happened to you,' Jannine insisted, as she sat opposite Elise and munched a beanburger. 'He was so wrong for you, it just wasn't true. I don't know what you saw in him. I mean, talk about boring. All he was interested in was himself. I can only assume he was hot stuff in bed.' She gazed quizzically at her friend. 'Was he?'

'No, he wasn't,' Elise said. 'It's just that I fancied him like mad. That made it good.'

'Fatal attraction,' Jannine nodded. 'That's where they get their power from, the bastards. I was like that with Brett. It really screwed up my life. He knew I'd do anything he asked, and boy, did he keep asking.' She took another bite of her beanburger and licked some ketchup from her fingers. 'You've got over it, I hope? You don't dream about him, or any crap like that?'

'Of course I've got over him,' Elise said, sharply. 'He was just using me. I'm well rid of him.'

'You'll find someone else,' Jannine said. 'Try to play it cool this time. Have fun, but don't get involved.'

'I'm not sure I want to find anyone else. What I want is another job, a long way from London.'

'Jobs aren't that easy to find, especially when all you've got to offer is a bit of paper that says you're a stage designer or an actress. Don't we both know it? Sellicks has to be better than bloody waitressing. Stay there.'

And see Ralph every morning, smart and elegant in his expensively tailored suits, Elise thought. And know that he was going to bed with the appalling Jemma Harrisford and not me? She did not want his infuriatingly attractive image cluttering up her imagination for months. She did not want to be constantly reminded of him.

'I'm fed up with Sellicks,' she said. 'It's not exactly creatively stimulating, sitting there with a smile pinned on your face, saying good morning and good-bye all day.' She opened her copy of *Plays and Players* and pointed to the small ads. 'Look at that. The one I've ringed. What do you think?'

'Designer wanted to help refurbish castle in Northumberland,' Jannine read. 'If you're creative and imaginative phone us now.' She looked up at Elise. 'A castle? In Northumberland? You're joking, of course?'

'No, I'm not. It sounds great. It'd be a nice long way from London. And Ralph.'

'It's a nice long way from civilisation, full stop,' Jannine said. 'And you're a stage designer, remember? That can't be what they're looking for. You won't even get an interview.'

'Why put the ad in a theatre magazine?' Elise challenged.'

'Because they're crazy?' Jannine guessed. 'Because it's a hoax? Because it's one of those mysterious messages spies write to each other?'

'Because they want someone creative and imaginative,' Elise corrected. 'Because they don't want a run-of-the-mill boring interior designer. They want someone to make their castle look exotic and beautiful. I can do that.'

'Just suppose, by some wild and improbable quirk of fate, you actually got the job,' Jannine said. 'Do you really want to emigrate to the north? Anyone with any sex appeal probably moved to London years ago. Do you want to be surrounded by a lot of nerds with funny accents, wearing cloth caps and mufflers? You'll hate it. There won't be any dishy blond actors to cheer up your love life. You'll be bored to tears.'

'I'm bored to tears now,' Elise said. 'Doing up a castle sounds fun. I'm going to ring for an interview. They can only say no. And as for men, I don't care if I never see another dishy blond male in my entire life!'

But it wasn't strictly true. Ralph had come dangerously close to her current physical ideal. When she fantasised, she always imagined a man with a golden tan and golden hair. When she dreamt, her dream men always looked like Ralph. And she dreamt that night. He was standing in front of her, immaculate as ever in his business suit. Then he began to strip. It was something she had always wanted him to do in real life. The idea of a man slowly removing his clothes, knowing that he was being watched, playing up to it, excited her. But she had always felt slightly embarrassed about asking him to perform for her.

Now he behaved exactly as she had always wanted. He slipped off his coat and dropped it on the floor; something he never would have done in real life. He unbuttoned his shirt and threw that down, too. His skin was glowing from his weekly sessions under the sun lamp. He did not have much bodily hair. His nipples were small and tight. She watched as he slowly unfastened his trousers and stepped out of them. He was wearing close-fitting black briefs that stretched across his hips; briefs that emphasised his now bulging, trapped erection.

Very slowly, he pushed his hands under the waist-band and eased the briefs down. But just as he was about to expose his considerable sexual equipment, he turned, sliding the dark, stretchy material over the curve of his buttocks until it contracted into a black strip. Then, as he pushed further, it became a band imprison-ing his thighs. She admired the taut muscles of his bottom, hardened by hours of regular exercise. He bent over, still with his back to her, and stepped out of the briefs. He posed, casually, flexing his shoulders, parting his legs, tantalising her with brief glimpses of his cock and balls until she wanted to scream at him to turn around and display himself properly.

The dream shifted. She was naked. His hands were roving over her body. She felt his erection throbbing as it pressed against her; felt her breasts tingle as his mouth excited them, his lips sucking and teasing; felt him explore between her thighs. First his hands, and then –

She jerked awake with a start. The sensation of being entered was so strong that for a moment she thought Ralph was there with her. Her hands slid down and she touched herself urgently. The dream had aroused her so fully that she shuddered to an orgasm almost at once. And afterwards she drowsed back into a satisfied, restful sleep.

But when she remembered the dream in the morning she was less pleased. She did not want Ralph's image haunting her. She wanted to forget him. She would never see him tantalising her by slowly removing his clothes, although she realised now that she could have made him do just that. She could have made him do anything. The super efficient, outwardly macho Ralph Burnes, with his sculpted muscles and his outdoor-man tan, really enjoyed being bossed about by a woman.

Elise had never even guessed it, because she wanted

a strong man. If she had acted more like Jemma Harris-ford, would he have stayed with her? Could she have acted like that all the time? She did not mind the occasional role reversal but she doubted if she could have played the dominatrix on a permanent basis. Sex games were about give and take, but Ralph had never shown any inclination to find out what turned her on. She had instinctively known he was happy when she was doing things to him, and so she had gone along with it. While she had secretly hoped that he would fulfil her fantasies by playing the dominant partner, she had always ended up fulfilling his needs instead.

It was easy to look back now and see how easily he had duped her. No wonder he was so meticulous about arranging their dates; so insistent that he only saw her when he chose. He had been juggling his time with Jemma Harrisford. Jemma had probably arranged his timetable for him! He's welcome to his dominatrix girlfriend, she thought. I hope she beats him up every night. He's a selfish pig. A wimp! Once he knew she was not going to give him any contacts in the fashion world he had let his bossy girlfriend order her out of his flat without even a word of protest.

The trouble was she still felt a thrill of sexual pleasure when she thought of him. His Chippendale physique, moving with muscular efficiency under the smooth lines of his tailored suit, suggested hidden power, hidden strength, and even though she now knew he had not the slightest desire to exploit this aspect of himself, it still excited her.

She did not want to see him again. And if she stayed at Sellicks she would probably see him every morning, walking across the foyer to the stairs. Every morning she would have to remember what had been, and what she had hoped could have been. She did not need that kind of trauma in her life.

She knew that Jannine was right, jobs were hard to

find, and she had a suspicion that if she simply went from Sellicks to another receptionist's job, or something similar, she would find herself seduced by the comfort of a regular weekly wage and her career as a designer would go no further than producing sets for the local amateur dramatic company. Not that there was anything wrong with that, but it was not the way she had intended to organise her life. She needed a creative challenge, and 'refurbishing a castle' sounded promising. She had been brought up in the country. The thought of leaving London did not really bother her at all.

Her phone enquiry was answered by a girl's bright voice giving her an address and telling her to send a CV. Apart from some unpaid theatre work, and her college projects, Elise did not have much to put on a CV. She thought about lying, and decided against it. Instead she wrote a covering letter, explaining how keen she was to branch out into interior design. After she had sent it, she wished she had not been so honest. There were probably hundreds of qualified interior designers around, all eager for a chance to decorate a castle. She did not expect to receive a reply. The curtly typed note inviting her to an interview came as a complete surprise. The note was signed by proxy: Max Lannsen.

She took a long time deciding what to wear for her interview, unsure whether to go for an arty look, with a long skirt, dramatic make-up, her favourite Tibetan jewellery and her burnished auburn hair worn loose, or a more conventional approach: one of the smart suits she had bought to wear at Sellicks, a plain silk blouse and her hair neatly swept back into a loose French pleat. In the end she settled for convention, but wore an unusual silver brooch (designed by a friend) as her concession to creativity.

If the offer of an interview had surprised her, so did her final destination: a large, detached Victorian house

16

on the outskirts of London. Set back from the road, it was hidden behind trees and hedges that needed cutting. The gravel drive and overgrown flower beds also looked in need of attention, and the huge windows appeared to be uncurtained. The dense shrubbery cloaked any traffic noise.

Elise hesitated before putting her finger on the bell. What was she getting herself into? She had expected to be interviewed by a design agency, but now she realised that the advert had probably been placed by a private individual and, judging from the state of this house, one without much money. How could such a person afford to 'refurbish a castle'? Whose castle was it, anyway? Was this even a genuine job offer?

There's only one way to find out, she thought. She pressed the bell and heard it jangle loudly behind the paint peeled front door. The door actually creaked as it opened. She half expected an ancient butler in an evening suit to shuffle out of the darkness. Instead, she saw a young girl with a blonde bob, wearing a tight pink sweater and a miniskirt.

'Hi!' The girl gave her a cheerful smile. 'Come for an interview, have you?'

'Yes,' Elise said. It was almost a disappointment. Behind the girl the hall was bare and uncarpeted, but brightly lit by an unshaded bulb. It led to a large room, sparsely furnished with two cluttered tables and a battered filing cabinet. There were posters of pop stars on the wall. A kettle and a jar of coffee stood on a box. Another girl, also young, looked up from her old-fashioned typewriter and grinned cheekily.

'Another one to see Count Dracula?'

'Count who?' Elise stared at them both in surprise.

The first girl went behind one of the tables and shifted a pile of papers. 'It's just Kelly's daft joke,' she said. 'She really fancies Max Lannsen like crazy.'

'I do not!' Kelly tugged the sheet of paper out of her

typewriter, screwed it up and threw it in the wastebin. 'God, I hate these antique machines. Why can't we have a word processor?'

'They don't have them in Transylvania,' the blonde girl said. She turned to Elise. 'Are you Veronica Barclay?'

'Elise St John,' Elise said.

'Ann's really efficient,' Kelly said with friendly sarcasm as her friend searched though a drawer. 'Give her about ten minutes and she'll find your CV.'

'Why Count Dracula?' Elise persisted.

'It was a compliment really,' Kelly said. 'I mean, lots of people think vampires are sexy. Would you say no to Tom Cruise?'

'I would if he had those fangs in,' Elise said. 'And a blond vampire doesn't seem quite right, somehow.'

'Then you're going to love our charming Max Lannsen,' Kelly said. 'There's nothing blond about him. He'd look really sexy in a long black cloak.'

'Mr Lannsen might be sexy, if you like that sort of thing,' Ann said, 'but charming he is not.' She turned to Elise. 'I don't think he even likes women. One of the girls he interviewed came out in tears. He's not exactly friendly to us, either, but we don't care 'cos we're only here for a couple of weeks anyway, just until he finds some staff for this castle. If he ever does.' She pounced on a sheet of paper. 'Here's your CV. Take it in with you, will you?'

'Hasn't Mr Lannsen read it yet?' Elise asked.

'He may have done, when it first arrived,' Ann said vaguely. 'After that we lost it.'

'Does Mr Lannsen own this castle in Northumberland?'

'I think so,' Ann replied. 'I think he inherited it, or something.'

'Why does he want it decorated? Is he going to live there?'

18

'No idea.' Kelly shrugged. 'We're just part-time temps. No one tells us anything. The Count isn't exactly chatty. Ann says she's lucky if he says good morning. And he certainly never says good-bye.'

The intercom on Kelly's desk buzzed noisily. 'Has Miss St John arrived yet?'

It was a cool voice, and not particularly welcoming. Elise tried to imagine a face to fit it, and could not do so.

'She's waiting out here, Mr Lannsen,' Kelly said.

'Then send her in,' the voice said, impatiently.

Kelly clicked the intercom off. 'Good luck,' she said to Elise. 'It's the second door on the right.'

With her footsteps sounding loud on the uncarpeted floor, Elise walked down the hall. She reached the second door and paused, wondering whether to knock or walk straight in. She shook herself, irritated. Max Lannsen had got to her already, and she hadn't even met him yet. She wondered suddenly if she really wanted to work for someone who apparently hated women and reduced interviewees to tears.

Was he gay? She had known quite a few gay men at college. A couple had been bitchy, but most had been fun. Far from disliking women they had enjoyed female company. She remembered swopping make-up ideas with Paul, who told her: 'Why shouldn't we get on well with women? We've got lots in common. We all like men!'

She knocked briskly and pushed open the door. The room seemed dark because its large, uncurtained window over-looked a walled garden full of trees. An old-fashioned desk stood in a central position. There was a padded chair behind it and a single upright chair in front. Elise was uncomfortably aware of the sound her heels made on the bare wooden floor. It seemed a long way to the desk.

A man was standing by the window, looking out.

19

When he turned, she experienced an almost physical jolt of shock. He was the opposite to everything she believed she would find attractive. She liked her men more obviously muscular than this slim, tall figure. Blond and golden, not dark suited and dark haired. She understood exactly what Kelly had meant with her Count Dracula analogy. Max Lannsen had slavic cheekbones and slanting eyebrows that gave him an almost devilish look. She found it difficult to guess his age. Maybe thirty, she thought. He would certainly have looked at home in a long black cape. With a red lining. Blood red. There was a hint of the unknown about him; slightly foreign and definitely sexually attractive.

'Sit down,' he said.

His voice had no trace of an accent, and not much expression either. She sat down. After a moment he did the same. He stared at her silently. With his back to the window he was still in shadow, a dark, almost sinister figure. Then he reached out one hand and she noticed how long and slim his fingers were. An artist's hand, she thought. But he did not look like an artist. She could not imagine him in any profession. He was a mystery.

'Has that idiot girl found your CV at last?'

Elise stopped day dreaming. Flustered, she handed over the sheet of paper she had been carrying. He gave her a long steady look and then started to read. He's already made me nervous, she realised, crossly. One up to him. But that's the only advantage he's going to get.

'Why have you applied for this job?' he asked, abruptly. 'You haven't any experience in interior design.'

She felt like saying: you knew that, but you still asked me to come for an interview. Instead she found herself on the defensive. 'My college course included interior design – ' she began.

'You're supposed to be a stage designer,' he interrupted her. He glanced at her CV again. 'You don't seem to have done much of that, either.'

'I only left college six months ago,' Elise said. 'It's very difficult to get theatre work.'

'Then why choose it?' He was still watching her with disconcerting intentness. 'Did you think it would be easy to find a husband with all those handsome actors around?'

His hostility actually made Elise feel better. It gave her something to react to. He has no intention of offering me a job, she thought, so I don't have to be polite to him. He's an arrogant sexist bastard who likes putting women down. To hell with him!

'It may surprise you to learn that finding a husband is very low on my list of priorities,' she said coolly. 'Practically non-existent, in fact. Finding an interesting job is much more important to me.' She stood up. 'Obviously I'm in the wrong place for that!'

He stared at her for a long moment. She knew she should have turned and stalked out; that was what his attitude deserved. Instead, she found herself hypnotised by his unflinching, angry gaze. Then his eyes shifted to the portfolio she was carrying.

'I suppose I could take a look at your work,' he said ungraciously.

Elise felt like refusing. She dumped the portfolio on his desk, silently fuming. If he expected her to open it and talk him through her college projects he could think again. She wasn't going to encourage him at all. He opened the portfolio and took his time leafing through it.

'Imaginative,' he said, at last.

'I could be equally imaginative with your castle,' she said.

For a moment she thought she saw a brief smile touch his mouth. 'Maybe you could.' The smile disappeared. She wondered if it had really been there at all. 'You know where the castle is? If I employed you, what guarantee would I have that you wouldn't get bored in a week or two and head back to London?'

Because she had convinced herself that he had no intention of offering her a job the question took her completely by surprise. 'Why should I get bored?' She returned his look, coolly.

'Maybe you'd miss all the partying and dancing?' he said, equally cool. 'That's what you women enjoy, isn't it?' There was a definite sarcastic edge to his voice now. 'A full social life, I believe it's called.'

Elise met his eyes and held them. 'I enjoy being sociable,' she agreed. 'But I don't let it interfere with my work. If you offered me this job I'd be happy to sign any kind of contract . . .'

'Contracts can easily be broken,' he interrupted her, abruptly. 'Women are particularly good at it, I've noticed.' Before she could react to that he reached out and one slim hand pushed her portfolio back across the desk. He spun the chair round, got up, and walked over to the window again. With his back to her he added: 'Make sure that those inefficient females who call themselves secretaries haven't lost your address. I might want to contact you again.'

Elise realised that she had been dismissed. She wanted to say: wait a minute, I have some questions. It's no good contacting me unless I know more about the job. And the wages. And the living conditions. And the starting date. But one look at the tall brooding figure by the window convinced her that she would not get any answers from Max Lannsen.

Kelly seemed surprised that she had been asked to confirm her address. 'No one else has had to do that,' she said. 'Perhaps the Count is really thinking of offering you a job.'

'If he does, perhaps he might find that I don't want to work for him!' Elise said, tartly.

22

But it was not true, and she admitted as much to Jannine the next day. Her friend was unimpressed.

'He's a sexist bastard, and you want to get involved with him? First that two-timing creep Ralph Burnes and now Count Dracula's brother? Are you a closet masochist, or what?'

'I don't want to get involved with him,' Elise protested. 'I said I wouldn't mind decorating his castle, or whatever it is he wants. If only to prove to him that I *can*.'

'Why should you want to prove anything to him?' Jannine challenged. 'Why care? Ask yourself that?'

'Professional pride,' Elise said.

'Crap!' Jannine retorted. 'Listen. It's obvious you fancy him like crazy. You see him as a challenge. You want to impress him. And that's the road to disaster, believe me.'

'He's the last man in the world that I'd fancy,' Elise said. 'He's simply not my type.'

But, later that evening as she prepared for bed, Elise remembered those words and wondered if they were true. Did she really fancy Max Lannsen? No, she didn't, she decided. It was just that he was – unusual. Striking looking. Dramatic. She liked her men more obviously muscular; sun-gilded. Like Ralph, she thought – and then dismissed the painful memory quickly. And Max Lannsen's attitude was infuriating. Supercilious. Condescending. That was partly why she wanted to go to Northumberland. She wanted to prove to him that, despite her lack of hands-on experience, she was quite capable of fulfilling whatever plans he had for his castle.

She slipped into bed and pulled the lightweight duvet over her. Her mind wandered sleepily. What kind of castle was it? Had he really inherited it? Did he intend to live there? She imagined a craggy outline, stark against a stormy sky. Towers and castellated walls. She added an atmospheric roll of thunder and some light-ning. Then, framed in an open window, a tall figure, a black cloak swirling round him like a pair of dark wings. This should have been Ralph, but she knew it was Max Lannsen. Damn him, she thought. I don't need this. I don't want to think about him! She banished the theatrical images and let sleep overtake her.

She was in a stone-walled room, and the window was there again, opening on to a stormy sky. She was naked, stretched out on a wooden framework like a medieval rack. But she was totally comfortable with her position; excited even. She knew there was someone else in the room with her, but she did not feel threatened. Manacles circled her wrists and ankles like a welcome embrace. She wriggled in anticipation.

A man walked towards her. He wore a black mask that covered his head and eyes, and pair of tight, knee-length black breeches. He moved silently on bare feet. She admired the golden gleam of his muscles, his broad chest and narrow hips, and the way his sexual equip-ment was bulging against the restraining cloth of his trousers; cloth so taut she felt that a single finger nail, pushed against it with sufficient force, could rip it open and display his clearly outlined balls and obviously erect penis for her appraisal. He turned. The breeches looked as if they had been sprayed over his buttocks. Each muscular cheek was clearly defined, as was the deep cleft between them. She wanted to dig her fingers into their jutting shape and feel the firm flesh. Pull him towards her.

The man stood over her, and she saw his eyes glitter behind the mask. They were blue, like Ralph's. He let his gaze wander slowly over her body, admiring her breasts, her stomach, her thighs. She lay back, pulling and twisting seductively against her restraints but she had no desire to escape, and they both knew it. She saw him smile. Ralph's mouth, smiling. He reached out and allowed his hands to follow the path already taken by his eyes.

Here the similarity to Ralph ended. Ralph's caresses had been fast and perfunctory, a necessary means to an end, essentially boring because they were so predictable. This was a lingering, but demanding, inspection. The dream creation behaved as she had always wished Ralph would behave. With her arms stretched back, and her body arched, she was deliciously helpless and unable to resist.

He touched her nipple, lightly at first. He bent his head and his mouth found hers. His tongue moved in rhythm with his fingers. Ripples of increasing pleasure made her tremble. Fingers and tongue grew more insistent, seeking out the special places that excited her. He knew them all. He varied the pressure of his touch, sometimes moving fast, sometimes slow, arousing her in ways Ralph had never imagined, and her body responded with equal passion.

She moaned and gasped as the tip of his tongue circled her navel, touched the soft inner skin of her arms, searched her ear and traced delicious patterns on her shoulders and in the hollow of her throat. Lingering caresses, like those of a lover who knew her intimately, knew exactly what she wanted, and was willing to take the time and trouble to fulfil all her needs. She felt the restraints pull at her wrists and ankles as she writhed under his expert hands. This man was enjoying his mastery over her, but she knew that he found her sexy and desirable. His fingers twisted into her hair, pulling her as far into a sitting position as her chains would allow. His mouth nuzzled the side of her neck, his tongue flicking, while his free hand massaged her shoulders then moved downwards to her breast.

Then he abandoned all pretence at gentleness. He shifted position and circled her nipple with his lips, sucking hard, pinching the other nipple with his fingers,

25

handling her with an erotic roughness that made her feel both used and wanted. She pulled against the chains, but it was a token gesture. Having her hands and feet secured gave her the freedom to enjoy what was happening to her without the need to do anything in return. She did not have to worry about pleasing him or turning him on. All she had to do was let him please her. And he was certainly doing that.

'That's right.' The masked man's hands moved between her parted thighs, his fingers working expertly, stroking faster. 'Dance for me. Dance!'

But it was not Ralph's voice. It was not the man who was now astride her, suddenly naked, his body gleaming and oiled, as beautiful as a classical statue, still masked. This man was smiling. This man was still massaging her breast with one hand while with the other he stroked his already erect penis. The voice came from the shadows. Someone was observing them both.

Suddenly, being chained no longer had any erotic appeal. She struggled, with a genuine desire to get free. She was being used. Someone was watching her, enjoying her erotic writhing. She saw the window gaping like a blank eye, and a tall figure, a dark silhouette. She knew who it was. She did not need to see his face. 'Dance,' the voice said. 'Dance. That's what women enjoy.' Her frustration turned to anger. She wrenched her hands upwards and the chains snapped.

The action jolted her awake. The room disappeared. She lay in bed, unfulfilled and angry. She had not had such a pleasantly sustained erotic dream for some time, and Max Lannsen had ruined it. The idea of providing him with a voyeuristic thrill infuriated her. She was even more infuriated to realise that she still felt sexy. She wriggled under the duvet and tried to recall the dream's imagery. She remembered the muscular figure who looked like Ralph but behaved so totally out of character. She tried to re-create the scene: the delicious and unthreatening feeling of helplessness; the way the masked man had aroused her, first gently and then with increasing dominance; the sensation of his hands as they searched her body.

She let her own hands stray, and felt herself shiver as her fingers brushed her nipples and then slid down over her stomach, between her thighs. She was already damp and swollen. She touched the aching tip of her clitoris and stroked gently. She imagined the eyes behind the black mask watching her. Her hand increased its pressure and speed. Now she was the captive on the rack. It was not her hand, but the masked man's. Her body trembled. Her hand moved faster.

'Dance,' a voice said. A cool voice, inside her head. 'Dance!'

She had a brief vision of Max Lannsen's shadowed face, his eyes dark and unreadable. He's watching me, she thought. Her fingers moved expertly. The thought came, unbidden: he's touching me! And then she came, with a shuddering intensity that surprised her. Her body jolted in the kind of orgasmic spasm that she had never experienced with Ralph. She gasped, and felt her heart pound.

As the sensations subsided she relaxed and waited for her breathing to steady again. Damn you, Lannsen, she thought. Get out of my dreams. She felt foolish and embarrassed, as if she had really made love in front of him. As if she had really let his long fingers trigger her orgasm. I was thinking about him before I fell asleep, that's all, she comforted herself. I was angry at the way he treated me. Things that have been on your mind during the day often surface in dreams. There's nothing more to it than that.

'Dreaming about Max Lannsen?' Jannine searched the bottom of her Coke can with her straw, making a noisy slurping sound. 'That's interesting. Dreaming about

27

Ralph I can understand. You're still a teensy bit in love with him, right? And he does have the kind of body a Chippendale would die for. But Dracula's brother? That's something else. Are you kinky, or what?'

'I'm not in love with Ralph,' Elise said. 'I'm not sure now that I ever was.' She added defensively: 'And as it happens, Max Lannsen is quite attractive. He's just not my type, that's all.'

'So you *do* fancy him? That makes your dream easy to suss out. You were annoyed because your Transylvanian mystery man appeared to reject you. Your subconscious was saying: look, if you don't want me there are plenty of others who do. This great big blond masculine hunk, for starters. Just watch!'

Elise laughed. 'Rubbish. I don't care what Max Lannsen thinks. And I certainly wouldn't make love in front of him.'

'Not for real,' Jannine agreed. 'But this is dreamland. You should listen to your dreams; they can be fascinating. You've already told me this masked man was Ralph. Obviously you've always wanted him to strip you and tie you up. Why didn't you ask him?'

'I never even thought about it,' Elise said. 'And he certainly wouldn't have obliged.'

'No, I suppose not,' Jannine agreed. 'He'd have preferred it the other way round.' She paused. 'Did you?'

'Did I what?'

'Ever tie him up?'

'Of course not.'

'Pity,' Jannine said. 'You probably should have.'

'He never asked me.'

'You should have sussed it. That's what we're supposed to be good at. Feminine intuition. You should have tied him to the bed and gone to work on that gorgeous bum of his.' She thought about it for a moment. 'With a nice flexible riding crop. Or a slipper.

28

Or a brush. Or even your hand. He'd have loved it, and you'd probably still be together.'

'It never occurred to me,' Elise said. 'And even if he'd asked me I don't think I could have done it.'

'You could. You'd have enjoyed it.'

'I'm not into those kind of games,' Elise said. 'I'd have felt silly.'

'Darling, with the right guy you can get into any kind of games,' Jannine said. 'And you wouldn't feel silly, you'd feel great. Dishing it out or taking it, if you're both enjoying it, it can be a real turn on, believe me.' She grinned suddenly. 'One of my boyfriends did it to me once. With a cane. I didn't think I'd like it, but I did.'

Elise stared at her in surprise. Jannine stared back.

Well, go on,' Elise said. 'You know you're dying to tell me about it.'

Jannine's grin widened. 'You mean you're dying to hear! If you must know, it was all quite casual and unplanned. I was with this guy I hadn't known for very long. We were fooling around a bit and he told me to behave, and I said "make me", or something like that, and he said OK, and went over to a drawer and took out this cane and started swishing it about.'

'Well, he'd obviously planned it,' Elise said. 'You don't just have a cane in a drawer.'

'Well, maybe,' Jannine said. 'Anyway, I said something like "you wouldn't dare", rather hoping he would. And he did.'

'And you liked it?'

'It turned me on,' Jannine said. 'The idea of being held captive, you know? By this big, strong attractive male. And he didn't actually hurt me. It stung, but even that was sexy. And he must've felt the same, because we made love afterwards and he had the biggest hard on I'd ever seen, and we both came almost at once. I remember thinking we'd have to do it again. In fact, I was quite looking forward to it. I even thought it would

29

be fun to dress up the next time, and make a little fantasy drama out of it.'

'And did you?'

Jannine shook her head. 'No. Never. The next time we met he was all sheepish and apologetic, and said he didn't know what had come over him. I kept saying it was OK, and he kept telling me that the cane belonged to a friend of his, and he wasn't really into that kind of thing. I felt like asking him how he managed to get such a huge erection if he was hating every minute of it, but he looked so embarrassed, I didn't have the heart. And I certainly didn't dare suggest any play acting. The next time we made love it was a disaster. And that was that. End of relationship.'

'And you haven't tried any game playing since?'

No. I've never had any hints from anyone else that they might enjoy it. I do seem to pull boring men! But if I picked up the right signals, and I trusted the guy, I'd go for it. I'd dress up, too. I'd be a maid, or a schoolgirl, or whatever. Why not? Wouldn't you?'

'No.' Elise said.

'You would,' Jannine said. 'Forget Northumberland. Forget Drac's cousin, forget goddamn Ralph. All men are bastards, but what the hell? Stay in London. Find yourself another guy. Be a bastard back. Live a little. Have fun.'

'I have forgotten Ralph,' Elise said. She knew it wasn't true, but her mental image of him was changing. The golden muscled body was still there, but the face was fading. 'And I don't want another boyfriend,' she added.

'Liar!' Jannine accused.

'I don't,' Elise said. 'Not now. Not yet.'

'But later? Like tomorrow?' Jannine predicted. 'Well, that's a comfort. I couldn't stand having a celibate friend. It would make me feel too damn guilty.'

No, Elise thought, not tomorrow. Or next week. Or even next month. Ralph hurt me. It's going to take time to get over it, and I'm going to be more careful in the future. I'm not going to be used. If anything, I'll do the using. For starters I'll use Max Lannsen to get me away from London. Northumberland sounds fine. I doubt if I'll meet any would-be male models up there. If I get a letter offering me a job I'll take it – even if the wages are terrible!

But when the letter came it contained no mention of money. Elise was making her first cup of morning coffee and sorting through her post, separating the letters she knew she wanted to read from the ones she suspected were bills or junk mail. The foolscap envelope with her name and address typed by what was obviously an ancient machine that needed its keys cleaned did not fall into either of those categories. She opened it.

It was brief and to the point, suggesting that if she was still interested in the possibility of assisting with the interior design work proposed for Shilden Castle, Northumberland, she should visit the castle for a first-hand assessment the following weekend. Her travelling costs would be reimbursed. She could stay overnight at Shilden if she wished, and would she please telephone to confirm her acceptance. Once again she noted that Max Lannsen had not bothered to sign the letter personally. That really makes me feel wanted, she thought.

But she did not care. A photocopied portion of an Ordnance Survey map of the area was also enclosed. A yellow highlighter marked her destination. She studied it and realised that if she wanted to get away from town life this looked like the ideal answer. That evening she began to pack a small case. That night she dared either Max Lannsen or Ralph to disturb her dreams.

Neither of them accepted her challenge.

Chapter Two

*U*nwilling to trust her elderly Mini, and encouraged by the letter's promise that expenses would be paid, Elise hired a car for the weekend and headed north, accompanied by music from her favourite cassettes. There was a mobile phone in her bag, on loan from Jannine. She had tried to refuse it, saying, 'They *do* have telephones up North, you know!'

'They might not have them where you're going,' Jannine said. 'Some wreck of a castle, God knows where.'

'I know where,' Elise said. 'I've got a map.'

'Listen,' Jannine said. 'I'm serious for once. What the hell do you really know about Max Lannsen? Not a goddam thing. Take the phone, and check with me once in a while. I want to enjoy this weekend, not have to spend it worrying in case you've been shipped off to a white slave market as bargain of the month.' When Elise laughed she added crossly: 'OK, so the image is out-dated, but women still disappear, even if they don't end up in some eastern potentate's harem! Take the mobile.'

To keep the peace, Elise obliged. But as the hired car smoothly ate up the miles, and the motorway signs announced less familiar names, she began to feel grateful for her friend's concern. And she had to admit that Jannine had a point – she *was* taking a lot on trust. She thought it safe to assume that Shilden castle would not be a ruin, or Max Lannsen would not be planning to have it decorated, but for her it was still only a highlighted mark on a map, in the middle of open country. She knew nothing about it more than that.

And what did she know about Lannsen? Had he really inherited the castle, as Ann had claimed? If he had, it implied that his family had ties with the area. But his name did not sound English, although his voice was accentless. And what was his occupation? She could not begin to guess. He had the arrogant manner of a man who did not have to waste time being polite to anyone he did not like, and the look of someone who was used to getting his own way. But Jannine was right, she did not know a thing about him.

Was he a businessman? There was nothing very business-like about his handling of her own employment. It was as if he did not care much who he employed. He seemed angry, she remembered. And he obviously doesn't like women. Or doesn't trust them. Or both. She tried to smile at the thought of him as a white slave trader. She knew it was an outdated image, and in reality it was sordid and unpleasant: women as merchandise, to be sold for a profit? For sex? But she still let her imagination wander. As a fantasy it had distinct possibilities.

She recalled Max Lannsen's dark figure standing by the window of his house. Would a white slave trader check out his goods before sending them off to exotic secret destinations? She imagined a crowd of women – herself included – waiting for him to summon them for inspection. What a humiliating idea, she thought, secretly rather taken with the fantasy.

There was very little traffic on the road. Sitting

33

comfortably in her lane she pictured the kind of room her imaginary overseer would occupy, furnishing it with a polished wood floor, and chairs upholstered with leather. A darkly masculine room that smelled faintly of expensive cigar smoke. And the man? Maybe he would be an Arab, in an elegant suit. A man with shadowed face and a neatly cut beard.

Her own mental picture startled her. This was supposed to be a personal fantasy. Why was she imagining someone directly opposite to the type she usually found sexually attractive? Because you're trying to exorcise Ralph Burnes, she told herself. Your subconscious is telling you that a golden-haired man has hurt you, so try a different design. Or may it's just that you've seen too many daft silent films at the college film club? Handsome sheiks galloping about on white horses. Grow up! Change your storyline! There's nothing sexy about the slave trade in real life, and a real slave trader would probably be as ugly as his profession. She suddenly realised that the music had stopped. She clicked the cassette player on again, rewound the tape, and let the sound of Queen clear the fantasy out of her mind.

After twenty minutes she turned off the dual carriageway. From then on the road wound through open countryside and she began to think she was the only car in existence. The entrance to the castle was so badly signposted that she drove past it and had to brake and reverse, finally turning into a private drive lined by trees. This green tunnel led her to a sweeping expanse of smoothly cut grass. And finally to Shilden itself.

Her first impression was that, despite its name, and despite the two round towers and castellated grey stone walls, this building was really a large house. Difficult to date, it had huge Gothic-style windows with leaded glass, and tall decorative chimneys which looked Elizabethan. Her second impression was that it was obviously in excellent repair. Her third was that it was deserted.

The paved forecourt was clean and the borders weeded. A flight of wide steps led to the massive double front doors which, Elise discovered when she finally reached them and searched, had no bell or knocker, or any note pinned on them to tell her where to go. As she stood wondering what to do, the wind blew around her and whipped her long red hair into wild strands. She shivered. Although the sun was shining, she felt chilly.

Because she disliked tracksuits she had travelled wearing a pair of loose black trousers and a silk kaftan-style tunic top that a friend had made for her, the collar edged with an embroidered border she had salvaged from an old jumble sale dress. The outfit had been comfortable in the warmth of the car, but now the brisk wind moulded the thin material to her body, and she realised that her nipples had contracted with the cold and stood out sharply, pushing against the pale silk. Suddenly, she felt naked and vulnerable. The idea of the slave market came back to her, unexpectedly. She even looked round quickly to see if anyone was watching her, and then, just as quickly, told herself not to be an idiot. There wasn't anyone here. That was the problem.

This is ridiculous, she thought. What exactly is Max Lannsen playing at? She had paid out more than she could really afford to hire a car, made a long journey when she could have happily spent the weekend in London with friends, and now it seemed that she had wasted her time. She began to get angry. I'll take a look round, she decided, and if I don't find a way into this place, that's it. I'm going home. And Max Lannsen will get a bill for my expenses!

She went back to the car to fetch her cloak, and coiled her windblown hair into a loose bun. A friend had once told her this style made her look like a red-headed Brigitte Bardot. She had enjoyed the compliment, although she did not really believe it. She decided to walk right round the castle. Before long, she realised that extensive renovations had already been carried out. A large area had been cleared and was being used as a temporary builder's yard. Several skips, full of old pipes, cables, glass and rubble, stood waiting to be collected. The surrounding countryside was green, wooded, unspoiled and peaceful. Wrapped in her cloak, she could appreciate the clean coolness of the air. I could get used to living up here, she thought suddenly.

'I suppose you must be one of the London ladies?' The sharp voice, with its lilting northern accent, startled Elise. She turned and saw a middle-aged woman in a white overall watching her from a small side door. The woman's face looked far from welcoming. 'Well, you had better come in.'

'I'm sorry,' Elise said, once she was inside. 'I wasn't snooping. It's just that I haven't any idea where I'm supposed to go.'

She was rewarded by a disapproving sniff. The woman walked quickly down a dark passage. Elise followed and found herself in an old-fashioned, but very clean, kitchen warmed by an Aga cooker. The woman turned and stared at her again.

'Come to be checked out by Mr Lannsen, have you?' The emphasis on 'Mr' was clearly not intended to be polite. Elise could smell coffee and would have loved a cup, but the woman did not look inclined to offer her anything. 'You'll be wanting to see Miss Lorna what's-her-name, no doubt?'

'Is that Mr Lannsen's assistant?' Elise asked.

She saw the woman's mouth tighten. 'Maybe that's what she calls herself.'

Elise felt her temper slipping. 'I don't really care who I see,' she said sharply, 'as long as they can give me some explanations.'

'What is there to explain?' There was undisguised

contempt in the older woman's voice now. 'You know why you've been asked to come here.'

'To decorate the castle,' Elise said. 'If I get the job.'

The woman took a few minutes to digest this. She gave Elise, who was still wrapped rather dramatically in her cloak, a quick inspection. 'You're some kind of artist, I take it?'

'An interior designer,' Elise said. 'Elise St John.'

'A designer?' The woman's voice was slightly less hostile now. 'Well, I'm Mrs Stokes. I've been the cook here for twenty-eight years. Not that Mr Lannsen would care about that. Why should our lives interest him?' She stared challengingly at Elise. 'You note that I don't call him master. And never will.'

'Why should you?' Elise asked, mystified.

She received another stare. 'You know nothing about Shilden, do you? But then, you're a southerner.' For a moment Elise thought Mrs Stokes was going to smile. 'Well, you'll learn. *If* you stay. Come, I'll take you to Lorna what's-her-name.'

Several dark passages led to a wide, light corridor with uncurtained windows on one side. Elise was surprised to see that the decorations looked recent and fresh and, she thought, rather unimaginatively pale. The air still smelled faintly of emulsion. The floor was carpeted.

'Second door,' Mrs Stokes said, and disappeared back into the darkness again.

Elise spent a few minutes by the door surveying the corridor, imagining how much warmer she would have made the colour scheme, then knocked. A cheerful female voice answered, inviting her in. The room was large and light and furnished as an office. Like the corridor it had been decorated in unimaginative colours. The young woman who came towards Elise had an English rose complexion and a mass of pale brown curly hair. She wore an old-fashioned lace-trimmed blouse

37

with a high frilled collar, and a long skirt that reached the top of her Victorian-style ankle boots.

'You made it, then? Super.' Her accent was definitely London; Sloaney, in fact. Her smile was wide and friendly. She held out her hand. 'Just remind me of your name?'

'Elise St John,' Elise said. She shook hands, and wasn't surprised at the girl's firm grip. That Victorian lace is just a disguise, she thought. I bet your hobby is galloping round the countryside chasing foxes. 'You're Mr Lannsen's PA?'

The girl laughed. 'I'm his dogsbody. Lorna Chorley-Smythe. Do tell me how you found your way in? Has someone actually put up some signs at last?'

'I met the cook,' Elise said.

'Oh, God,' Lorna said sympathetically. 'Poor you! Do sit. I'll sort out your details.' She began to stab at the computer keyboard. The computer beeped irritably. Lorna sighed. 'The wretched thing's gone on strike again. I really believe it doesn't like me. But you don't really need a print out, do you. You know why you're here.'

'Hopefully, to decorate this castle,' Elise said.

'Well, part of it,' Lorna nodded. 'You're going to make the boring old east wing into a house of pleasure, aren't you? Paint the walls with gold leaf and load the ceilings with reinforced chandeliers so that people can swing on them. I'm sure it's going to look absolutely super.'

'House of pleasure?' Elise repeated.

Lorna looked suddenly uncomfortable. 'Isn't that what you were told?'

'I haven't been told anything,' Elise said, honestly.

'Well, I'll let Max give you all the details.'

The familiar use of Lannsen's name startled Elise. Was this Victorian Sloane Max Lannsen's girlfriend? It would explain what she was doing as his assistant. She clearly did not have any office skills. Elise had a brief mental picture of Lorna's pale, English rose beauty teamed with Max Lannsen's satanic darkness. The image was surprisingly erotic. But was it really likely? Lorna's next comment answered her question.

'What do you think of Mr Untouchable Sex on Legs, then? Exciting, isn't he?'

Masking her surprise, Elise said coolly: 'He's not my type.'

'Really?' Now Lorna sounded surprised. 'Sorry, but I just find it absolutely impossible to understand how anyone can look at Max without feeling horny.' She leant back and sighed. 'I'd just love to strip all his clothes off and then really go to town on whatever he's got underneath.'

'Well,' Elise said, even more startled, 'I wish you luck.'

'I'll need more than that,' Lorna admitted. 'I think he keeps his cock in cold storage.' She grinned wickedly. 'But I'm working on ways to thaw him out.'

'Perhaps you should start by calling him master?' Elise suggested.

Lorna laughed. 'You've been talking to Mrs Misery!' She suddenly did a very good imitation of Mrs Stokes's voice and accent: 'He can sack me if he wishes, but I'll not call him master. Never!'

Elise laughed too. 'But what is this master thing all about?' she asked.

'Master of Shilden?' Lorna shrugged. 'It's just some kind of honorary title the locals give to the owner of the castle, God knows why. Sounds kinky, doesn't it? But rather exciting, too.'

'You're sex mad!' Elise said, grinning.

'Can you blame me, with gorgeous Max around, all dark and mysterious?' Lorna sighed theatrically. 'Can't you just imagine him in riding boots and carrying a whip? The Master of Shilden, surveying his domain?'

'No,' Elise said, not altogether truthfully. 'But when did you first meet him, anyway?'

'He interviewed me in a grotty London house,' Lorna said. 'A really strange interview, actually. I warned him I wasn't terribly good with computers and things. Actually, I told him I wasn't qualified at anything at all – well, not anything secretarial, anyway. I fluttered my eyelashes like mad, but he didn't take the hint.' She sighed again. 'I wonder what turns him on? I hope he's not gay.'

'But you got the job,' Elise said.

'I think Max was interested in my contacts,' Lorna said. 'And my languages. Daddy dragged me round the world with him for a few years after Mummy dumped him. I just seem to pick up languages easily. And accents and things.' She finished vaguely. 'I suppose that could be useful here. International clientele, you know?'

No, Elise thought. I don't know. Why should anyone expect an international clientele to come to a remote hotel in Northumberland? Or would they be coming to a house of pleasure – whatever that might mean? And why had Lorna taken a job so far from London? She didn't sound as if she was running away from a broken love affair. Surely she had not really come all this way just to chase Max Lannsen?

'Aren't you bored up here?' she asked.

'Sometimes,' Lorna admitted. 'But there are advantages. Like plotting how to get Max Lannsen out of his expensive suits. And then there's the money. I mean, that's why we're both here really, isn't it?'

'No one's discussed money with me,' Elise said.

'Well, you're in for a nice surprise,' Lorna said. 'There's a lot of cash tied up in this project. The investors want everything just right – and they're willing to pay to get it.'

So why choose me? Elise thought. An inexperienced unknown. What kind of contacts did Lorna have that outweighed her lack of office skills and experience? All right, Master of Shilden – or whatever you expect to be called – I want some answers, and they'd better be good. I want to stay here. I want to work here. But if I do, I want to know exactly what's going on.

'When will I see Mr Lannsen?' she asked.

'He's gone into Alnwick,' Lorna said. 'I'll give you a ring when he gets back. You can wait in your room. The staff rooms are quite nice, actually. There's a television and coffee. If you've driven up here I expect you could do with a shower and a rest.'

The room was light and clean, economically but comfortably furnished, with a small private bathroom, and had a window that looked out onto a small internal courtyard.

'This is the staff wing,' Lorna explained. 'Or will be, when everything gets going.'

After making coffee and having a shower Elise relaxed on the bed. The long drive had tired her. A short cat-nap, she decided. Then she would be fresh for her meeting with Max Lannsen. She closed her eyes, but it was difficult to sleep. There were too many voices nagging her memory. Jannine's voice saying: 'White slave trade.' Lorna saying: 'House of pleasure.' Mrs Stokes's warning: 'I don't call him master, and never will.' And Lorna again, commenting: 'Can't you just imagine him in riding boots and carrying a whip?'

I can, Elise thought, but I'm not going to. She remembered her brief fantasy about the white slave trade. Men in boots and carrying whips would be quite at home in that scenario. But would she fit into it? Being used was the very thing she objected to. And no one was more of a sex object than a slave girl.

Try another kind of fantasy, she thought. But her tired mind had ideas of its own. Images crowded her thoughts. A dark figure seated in a leather armchair, legs stretched out in front of him, his face obscured by shadows. She dozed with the pictures still in her mind. Go with it, she thought drowsily. Relax. Fantasy never hurt anyone, politically correct or otherwise.

She imagined herself being pulled along a dark corridor by two muscular young men. One had short-cropped, dark hair, the other was blond. They wore T-shirts and tight, sun-bleached Levis. Her own clothing was loose and flowing: a short kaftan and harem-style trousers, and sandals with thin golden straps. The outfit covered her modestly, but she knew that the two men had already discovered that she was naked beneath the silky cloth. They were grinning as they manhandled her, making sure their hands explored her as they pushed her forward. She struggled, ineffectively. They both looked as if they spent all of their spare time in a gym, and had the strength to match their bulging muscles.

'A fighter. That's good.' The dark-haired one twisted her arms behind her back, just tight enough to be uncomfortable. 'The master likes them with a bit of spirit.'

'She's got more than spirit.' The blond moved forward, flexing his fingers. His face reminded her of Ralph. She tried to blur the image, making him golden skinned but anonymous. 'This one has a body even I'd pay to use. Keep hold of her. Let's have a quick sample of what the master will be getting.'

'It's forbidden,' her captor said, sounding nervous.

'Who's to know?' the blond man said.

'I'll tell,' Elise said, quickly.

The man grinned. 'What makes you think anyone will listen?'

He reached forward and cupped her breasts with both hands, forcing them upwards, kneading her flesh roughly. His thumbs searched for her nipples beneath their silky covering and he began to stroke them. Elise tried to evade him, but only succeeded in thrusting herself backwards. She felt her captor's swelling penis move against her bottom, and heard the quickening of his breath.

The blond man's fingers worked faster. She stopped struggling now. She was responding to his caresses, both in her fantasy and in fact. As she imagined the insistent pressure of his thumbs, her body reacted and her nipples hardened. He would be watching her, she thought, and once again she found herself thinking of Ralph's face. Then his hands dropped to the hem of her kaftan and he bunched the thin cloth, pushing it up, exposing her from neck to waist. She felt the warm air touch her skin.

'Enough!' The man who was holding her was shaking now, his erection pushing between the cleft in her buttocks.

'Enough?' The blond man objected. 'I haven't even started yet.'

'The master's waiting.'

'Let him wait.' The blond head bent towards her and she felt a tongue flick over her nipples, moving swiftly from one to the other. She let her own hands roam lightly, touching herself, mimicking his moist caresses. The tingling sensations of lust ran through her body.

'Look at them!' Her captor stood back for a moment and admired the tautly erect pink buds. 'Like ripe berries, ready to eat. And I'm going to do just that.'

His hands clasped her waist and his lips closed greedily over one nipple. She felt the tip of his tongue, circling, and the strong pull of his mouth as he sucked. The man who was holding her writhed in sympathy. He was watching the action over her shoulder, and the sight of the erotic foreplay was getting to him. Suddenly, she realised that although he was holding her, she could really control him. She deliberately let her body rub against him, seductively. She heard him make a strangled noise of protest, deep in his throat, but his hips jerked convulsively forward as they responded to her pressure. For a few moments she was sandwiched between the two of them, the blond man busy with his mouth and hands, the other one trying to hold back his imminent orgasm.

Then she was turned, spun round, and suddenly forced to her knees. The dark-haired man unzipped his jeans and pushed them down. He stood with his legs apart, his massive erection waiting for the relief he expected her to give him. The blond pressed his thighs against her back. He urged her forward. 'Please him!' His voice was hoarse. 'Let me see you do it.'

'No!' she said.

She had no objection to using her mouth. Imagining it now would probably give her a lot of pleasure. Her body was already uncomfortably aroused, and she pictured the dark-haired man's penis as enticingly attractive. But she knew that these two were the kind of men who, in reality, would have seen women as objects for sexual play, and sexual relief: a means to an end, nothing more. She glanced up at the man in front of her. The lines of his face blurred and he looked like Ralph. She turned her head. The blond looked like Ralph as well.

'You want it!' His lips were close to her ear.

'No,' she repeated. 'This isn't what I want. Not like this.'

'Look at you.' The kaftan had fallen back, covering her. The dark-haired man pushed it up again, deliberately brushing her hard nipples. Despite herself, she groaned softly. 'You want it!'

He knelt. His fingers slid down over the harem pants, searched between her legs, and felt the silky cloth was warm and damp. The edge of his hand pressed against her clitoris, rubbing. She groaned again. 'You want us both. First him, then me. Hurry!'

Were they right, these fantasy figures who had suddenly taken on a life of their own? Did she still want Ralph? Why did she keep imagining his face?

44

'No!' Suddenly she was on her feet again, and they were on both sides of her. 'The master's waiting. Or had you forgotten?'

The scene shifted. She was being pushed into a large room with a huge window; a chair was positioned close to it. A dark figure sat watching her, his legs stretched out. Thrust down to her knees in front of him she saw his booted feet inches from her face.

'This one's a vixen,' the blond man said. 'We had trouble bringing her here.'

'You mean you thought you'd try her out?' A calm, cultured voice. 'What happened?'

'She encouraged us,' the man said, virtuously. 'She begged us for it.'

'And you refused, of course?' Mild amusement now.

'We know your orders, master,' the blond man said.

The seated man put the toe of his boot under Elise's chin. She smelled the faint, and pleasant, tang of leather. He pushed her head up, not roughly, but insistently, so that she was forced to look straight at him. She glared defiantly from under a tangle of glowing auburn hair. She knew exactly who she was going to see. The same face that she had imagined before, although she had refused to admit it, even to herself. The face she previously had disguised with a different nationality – and a beard. Max Lannsen's face.

'What do you say to the accusations?' he asked her softly. 'Are they telling the truth?'

'They're both liars,' she said. 'They forced themselves on me. I fought them.' And added: 'Just as I'll fight you!'

He laughed softly, but he was looking at his two waiting servants. 'I might keep this one for myself,' he said. 'At least for a little while. Stand her up. And strip her. I want to inspect her properly.'

Before Elise could begin to struggle, the blond man grasped her tunic by the neck band and pulled it down her back ripping the material. She tried to wrap the tattered cloth round her body. The blond man spun her, grabbed at the ragged silk and tugged hard. The tunic came apart. He tossed the pieces away. The dark-haired man caught the waist of her harem pants and tried to slide them down. She kicked out at him. He let go of her and dodged back.

The man in the chair laughed softly. 'Do you normally take that long to undress a woman?' He stood up and walked towards Elise. His movements reminded her of a panther, stalking. 'Hold her,' he said sharply, and the blond man obeyed, pulling her arms behind her back, forcing her to arch her spine. Her breasts were pushed upward and forward.

The slave-master stood in front of her: dark, authoritative – and attractive. She wanted to imagine his hands touching and exploring her, his tongue exciting her nipples into further tension; the harem pants grasped and pulled down to her ankles, and expert fingers beginning to play between her legs, driving her to further heights of excitement. She wanted to imagine it in explicit detail, but she also wanted to prolong the erotic agony of expectation.

He stared at her, his gaze moving up from her feet, lingering on her thighs, and on the damp V between them. The blond man bunched the slack silk of the harem pants and tightened it against her legs, making her appear naked. The thought of the silk pressing against her clitoris made her feel uncomfortably sexy. She saw the master's eyes assess her lazily, and again expected his touch. But he simply said: 'Turn her round.'

She stood with her face close to the blond man's chest, her wrists captured by his hands. She felt someone grasp the waist of her harem pants, but she knew it was the slave-master's hands, and shuddered in anticipation. He pulled the pants down slowly, and at the same time he traced a line over her buttocks and her thighs with his thumbs, lingering behind her kneecaps, lightly drawing patterns on her calves. The thought of it was so unexpectedly erotic that she moaned with delight.

He knelt behind her. His lips touched the curve of her bottom, brushing the skin. The tip of his tongue circled the base of her spine, causing her to writhe forward against the blond man, who still held her. She felt his erection, huge and hard, pushing at her stomach, but it no longer interested her. She had decided he would not be allowed to relieve his sexual tension, unless he serviced himself.

Her dark tormentor, his fingers moving possessively under her buttocks, confirmed this. 'Get out, both of you.' As they backed away he added: 'And leave the rest of my merchandise alone.' Strong hands on her hips turned Elise round. For a moment she stared down at the glossy crown of the slave-master's head. 'A natural redhead,' he murmured. She felt his breath, warm on her thighs. 'Unusual. I'll be able to get a good price for you.'

She was tempted to imagine his mouth on her, tormenting her briefly, then giving her relief. But that would have ended the fantasy too soon. Instead she imagined him standing, going to his chair, relaxing with his legs outstretched, the bulge of his erection pushing against the tight white riding breeches. He looked at her with a lazy, sardonic smile. 'Seduce me,' he said. 'Show me just how well you can use that body of yours. And take your time.'

A shrill buzzing jolted her into reality. She opened her eyes and, for a moment, she could not remember where she was. She felt sexy and relaxed. Her mind was still filled with pictures: a darkly masculine room, a tall, slim, shadowed man in knee-high riding boots. A voice echoed in her head: Seduce me ... and take your time. She wanted to continue with her sexual adventure. The

47

buzzer grated through her head again. She groped for the phone.

'Max will see you in half an hour.' Lorna's voice sounded infuriatingly cheerful. 'He'll be in the east wing. Come to my office first and I'll tell you how to get there.'

'Thanks,' Elise said, briefly hating Miss Chorley-Smythe.

'Don't worry,' Lorna added, obviously mistaking her abruptness for nerves. 'You've got the job. This meeting's just a formality.'

Even if Lorna thought she had secured the job – and Elise was inclined to believe it herself, otherwise why else would she have been asked to come up and see the castle – she still dressed neatly and conventionally in her 'Sellick's suit', and folded her hair into a loose pleat.

She found her way to the east wing without difficulty. Max Lannsen was waiting for her by a large door. He had obviously come straight from a business meeting, and was wearing an elegant black suit. The memory of her erotic dream was still clear in her mind and she almost blushed when his dark eyes met hers. But there was no sexual interest in them when he looked at her. If he had any expression at all, it was one of slight hostility.

When he pushed open the door, she noticed that it was fitted with a very modern-looking lock. He let her precede him. Another corridor stretched in front of her. This one had obviously not been decorated for many years. The walls were stained and dusty. The windows blanked by layers of dirt. Their rather ugly wooden frames had rotted. The floor was stone but littered with plaster that had fallen from the cracked ceiling. The air smelled of decay. She heard the lock click. Startled, she turned quickly. Max Lannsen was close behind her. 'Is there something the matter, Miss St John?'

'You've locked the door,' she said.

'It locks itself.' He held up the key. For a moment she thought she saw something that could have been humour in his eyes. 'But I can let you out at any time.' The look disappeared, and she wondered if she had imagined it. He added: 'Domestic staff at Shilden are not permitted in the east wing.'

'Why not?' she asked.

'Because it's unsafe,' he said. 'Some parts of the floor still need replacing. The last thing I need is to be sued by one of the locals. Don't worry, everything will be finished by the time you start work.'

She walked ahead of him, her shoes stirring dust and fallen plaster. 'It's going to need a lot of work to turn this into a house of pleasure,' she said.

He stopped abruptly. 'What exactly has Miss Smythe told you?' His voice was cold.

The idea of using first names seemed to be solely Lorna's idea, Elise thought. 'Miss Chorley-Smythe hasn't told me anything,' she said, 'except that you want this wing decorated in a special way?' She glanced at him. 'A theatrical way?'

He gave her a long, cool stare. 'How much do you know about Shilden?' he asked. 'And my involvement?'

'Very little,' she said. 'I was told you inherited the castle, and I assume you're going to run it as some kind of commercial enterprise.' She paused. 'Your cook said there was a title involved: Master of Shilden?'

'You can forget that nonsense,' he said, irritably. 'That's a ridiculous local custom, and I certainly don't intend to use the title.'

Neither does Mrs Stokes, Elise thought, but kept silent.

'It's true I inherited the building,' Lannsen admitted. 'Unfortunately I did not inherit any money to go with it, and the legal position is so complicated I'm not able to sell. So I have to make it pay. As far as I can see there's only one way to do it, and that's to use the place as an hotel, or a conference centre – something like that.' He started to walk, swiftly, still talking, and not looking back to see if she was following. 'If some of the guests want to combine business with pleasure, they'll be able to do it here.' He pushed open a door and Elise saw a huge square room with a high ceiling and a massive fireplace. 'Discreetly.' He paused. 'I'm not suggesting anything illegal, but I take it you understand what I'm saying?'

Of course I do, Elise thought. If the guests want to bring their girlfriends or their secretaries for a dirty weekend, you'll provide them with privacy. And I've been hired to turn the rooms into a series of exotic love nests so that they can act out their fantasies.

'I understand perfectly,' she said.

'Your wages will be generous,' he added. 'And you'll live here while you're working. I have several investors involved in this project, and others are interested. Money is available. They want the best. They want imagination. That's where your theatrical experience, small as it appears to be, will come in useful.'

'Will I have a free hand?'

His dark eyes surveyed her. 'Not entirely. You'll be given some suggestions. That's not a problem, is it?'

'As long as they're workable.' she said.

'They will be.' He walked towards the window. His voice sounded curiously flat. 'You'll have some ... experts advising you.'

She sensed that he was angry. Angry but controlled. Inheriting this castle did not seem to have given him any satisfaction. She had the distinct feeling that he would have been happier if he had never seen the place

'Miss Smythe will give you all the details you need about your terms of employment.' He turned towards her again, his back to the window, his face dark. 'I suppose you'll have to work out your notice at your current job. How soon can you begin here?'

'I'm only employed on a temporary contract at Sel-licks,' she said. 'And I pay for my flat weekly. I could start in two weeks.'

'That will be satisfactory,' he said. 'If you want to carry on inspecting this wing on your own, you're free to do so. If you find locked doors, it means the rooms are currently unsafe. The top floor need not concern you at the moment. That will stay locked as well.' He paused. 'There is one other area I have to show you.' He turned abruptly and obviously expected her to follow. Her mind was already making plans. Each huge room could be treated like a stage set. With the right budget, she could have fun – and get paid for doing it. Max Lannsen stopped by a door. 'Down here,' he said.

A steep flight of steps led into darkness. He touched a switch and a single pale bulb illuminated the stairs. He went down ahead of her, disappearing into the darkness. She waited at the top of the stairs.

'Come down. It's quite safe.' His voice sounded irritated. She negotiated the stairs carefully. Suddenly a beam of light snaked out and she realised he had a torch. 'This was a wine cellar. You'll turn it into a dungeon.'

'A dungeon?' She was surprised. 'Whatever for?'

'For the guests to enjoy,' he said.

'I can't imagine anyone enjoying themselves down here,' she said.

The torch beam swept over the stained walls. 'That depends on your definition of enjoyment,' he commented, dryly.

She looked round, and suddenly remembered her fantasy of being tied on the rack. Would it be as exciting in reality? In a place like this? As she stood there, with the air smelling of damp, she wasn't too sure. But what if this cellar was warmed and redesigned, with flaming torches throwing exotic shadows on the walls? And what if her tormentor was a man like Max Lannsen?

She tried to imagine him in the same outfit that she had previously given to Ralph: tight breeches, leaving nothing to the imagination, his chest bare. She could not picture him dressed like that. He would more likely be standing in the shadows, cloaked in darkness, watching while a half-naked man tied her down. Only when she was secured would he step forward, inspect her body, spreadeagled and restrained, ready for him to use in any way he chose.

'I said, have you seen enough?' Lannsen's voice startled her out of her daydream.

'Oh, yes,' she said.

Standing with the torch he looked as delightfully sinister as the man in her fantasy. For a brief moment he held her in the beam, and she had a strange feeling that the atmosphere had changed between them. That he was looking at her as a woman, and not just a prospective employee. The beam wavered slightly then suddenly swept over to the stairs.

'I have work to do,' he said abruptly. 'Miss Smythe will give you any further information you need.'

He moved quicker than she expected, and she ran to catch up with him. As she did so, she tripped. She was not sure afterwards if she fell against him, or if he moved forward to catch her, and they collided. All she knew was that suddenly she felt the strength of his body next to hers, and the hard grip of his hands. Her breasts were against his chest and her thighs touching his legs. His mouth was very close to hers. She was both startled and excited by the physical contact. She did not want to move. And for a brief moment she had the distinct feeling that he felt the same way. Then he pushed her away, and none too gently either.

'You don't have to bribe me, Miss St John,' he said, coldly. 'I've already said you have the job.'

He was half-way up the steps before she realised exactly what his comment had implied. If he had still been standing there she knew she would have slapped him – and probably ruined her chances of staying at Shilden. As it was she followed him, seething. He was waiting for her in the corridor.

'Please feel free to explore the rest of the wing on your own,' he said. And paused. 'Unless you'd feel ... safer if I came with you?'

She had the strangest feeling that this was a challenge – and a test. She could say yes and see what came of it. Would he take her into an empty room and make love to her? If he did, what would it be like? An impersonal exploration of her body, his hands under her clothes, searching briefly, then a quick thrusting that satisfied him and left her feeling used? She did not want it to be like that; a joyless coupling or something he would have forgotten by the next day. And she did not want to believe that he thought she wanted it, either. If he did, it was an insult to her!

She stared at him, her green eyes meeting his dark brown ones. 'I'm sure I can find my way around on my own,' she said, her voice matching his in glacial temperature. And added: 'Please don't worry about me. I didn't hurt my ankle, when I *tripped* down there in the cellar.'

She saw the briefest trace of a smile touch his mouth. It wasn't a friendly smile, but it satisfied her, all the same. It was an acknowledgement of her small victory. She knew instinctively that she had won this round.

'Take your time,' he said. He turned away from her. 'And make sure you ask Miss Smythe to settle your expenses before you leave.'

'It's going to be a cat house!' Jannine said, delighted. 'A classy cat house for rich businessmen. And in Northumberland. I just don't believe it! You bet I'll drive you up there. I can't wait to see the place!'

'It'll be a fantasy hotel,' Elise corrected. 'With theme rooms.'

'Oh, for God's sake,' Jannine leaned forward, grinning. 'I'm your friend, not a spy from the vice squad. Tell me more.'

'There isn't any more,' Elise said. 'And I shouldn't have told you anything. It's all supposed to be very discreet.'

'I bet it is,' Jannine agreed. 'Discreet – and illegal.'

'There's nothing illegal about taking your secretary for a dirty weekend,' Elise objected.

'You don't believe that crap?' Jannine grinned. 'It all makes sense now. No wonder your Count Dracula didn't want to employ anyone with a professional name. He wants hard-up unknowns who'll do as they're told. He's bought you, darling – and aren't you lucky! For the kind of money you're getting, he could have me, too.'

'He's employing me,' Elise said firmly. 'I'm decorating the rooms. I'll be gone before they're actually used.'

'Like to bet?' Jannine grinned. 'It sounds to me as if they want to get the place up and running as soon as possible. I'll bet you won't have finished painting the mock dungeon or whatever before some randy businessman is banging on the door offering you five hundred pounds if you'll let him whip you.' She looked speculatively at Elise. 'Would you let him?'

'Certainly not,' Elise said.

'I mean whip you sort of – sexily?'

'No.'

'Suppose the guy who asked you looked like Ralph?'

'No. And I've never seen a businessman who looked like Ralph.'

'Suppose he looked like Max Lannsen?'

'No,' Elise repeated.

'You hesitated!' Jannine challenged.

'I did not.' Elise said. 'I wouldn't let anyone whip me.'

'Well, I would,' Jannine said, unexpectedly. 'I don't

54

mean your Count Dracula, in particular. But a client. If he wasn't too flabby and awful. If he gave me five hundred pounds. And if I was sure it was going to be ... well ... fun, you know? None of that heavy stuff, with real pain. Just sort of – play acting.' She stared defiantly at Elise. 'Don't pretend to be shocked. I'm an actress. I could do the frightened maiden bit. I think I'd do it rather well. It sounds a lot more fun than waitressing. When they start recruiting for professional virgins, drop me a line.'

'I most certainly will not,' Elise said. 'Isn't that called pimping? And you're not to say a word about this to anyone. I shouldn't have told you.'

'You'd have burst if you'd had to keep it all to yourself,' Jannine grinned. 'Are you sure you can't wangle me in as your assistant?'

'I've already been promised some experts,' Elise said. 'Whatever that means.'

'The way things are shaping up in darkest Northumberland,' Jannine grinned, 'I simply wouldn't want to guess. Make sure you keep me posted. I want to know *everything*, and the sexier the better!'

Leaving Sellicks was a relief, but Elise was touched and surprised when Frank, the doorman, presented her with a card – signed by far more people than she thought actually knew her – and a parcel. She noticed Ralph's name, in his precise handwriting, tucked away on one corner of the card. There was no message with the signature, but the parcel contained two books on design that she had always wanted and never got round to buying. Ralph was the only one who could have suggested the titles. A week ago, she thought, that would have meant something to me, tempted me to believe that Ralph still cared for me. I might even have changed my mind about going to Northumberland. But not any longer. I've shaken Ralph out of my life!

But what had she replaced him with? Daydreams about Max Lannsen? As she packed her belongings into a case and several boxes, Elise tried unsuccessfully to understand her new employer. Did he really believe she was the kind of woman who would literally throw herself at him, offer him a quick bout of sex as a thank you for being given a job? If he did, it was damned insulting. And was he really the kind of man who would accept? Is that what he thought of women? They were all easy? And if that was the case, why hadn't he already serviced Lorna Chorley-Smythe, who certainly wouldn't have said no?

At least she knew a little more about him now – although it wasn't quite what she had expected. She knew that Jannine's assessment was probably right. Max Lannsen's business enterprise at Shilden would involve a lot of sexy activity in fantasy theme rooms that she was being very well paid to design. Her job was to provide the scenery, not become a participant – she was easy enough in her mind about that – but it wasn't exactly the kind of thing she would describe in detail in her letters home.

Was it what she really wanted? Well, no, she thought. Her dream was to work in the theatre, as a set designer. However, it was better than sitting behind a desk at Sellicks, smiling at visitors and incoming staff. Did she really want to leave her friends and live so far away from London? Oh, come on, she chided herself, stop being so *southern*. Admit that you loved the unspoilt countryside around Shilden; the peace and quiet; the lack of traffic noise. And you love the idea of getting a fat wage packet for doing work that will be creatively satisfying. There's life north of London, you know.

And men? The hurt from Ralph was wearing off, but not the memory of the way he had used her. It wouldn't happen a second time. Not with anyone. Certainly not with Max Lannsen, despite the unexpected way he seems to have invaded her thoughts. For a moment, when she fell against him, she had honestly believed that something had almost sparked between them. But his reaction had proved otherwise. Well, at least he had shown himself in his true colours. She would go up to Shilden Castle with her eyes wide open. She was not going to be hurt again!

Chapter Three

'Well, it's a nice room,' Jannine said, dumping Elise's case on the floor. 'A bit spartan, but you can soon liven it up with a few posters. Or maybe take some snaps of Count Dracula and stick them on the wall. Am I going to get to see him, by the way?'

'Probably not,' Elise said.

'Oh, come on, you've got to introduce me,' Jannine insisted. 'I drove you all the way up here, didn't I? I want my reward.'

'Some reward,' Elise grinned. 'Max Lannsen doesn't like women, remember? If he saw you coming he'd probably walk the other way.'

'That could be a real challenge,' Jannine murmured. 'I bet it's part of the reason he fascinates you.'

'Nothing about Max Lannsen fascinates me,' Elise lied, coolly. 'I told you, he's not my type.'

'And I believe you,' Jannine nodded. 'Like I believe the moon's made of green cheese. That's why you spent most of the journey up here talking about him.'

'I did not. I was talking about the job.'

'Sure you were,' Jannine agreed. 'And what Max wants or doesn't want, and what he said or didn't say.'

'I've never called him Max.'

'All right,' Jannine said. '*Mr* Lannsen this, and *Mr* Lannsen that. Darling, you've got it bad. Why apologise? You're not married, or anything dull like that. You can have fun chasing your sexy vampire, if that's what you want. You and all the other beautiful women you're soon going to have around here.'

'I haven't come here to chase anyone,' Elise said. 'I've come to work. You know what that word means?'

'When you've looked two thousand dirty dishes in the eye, you know what that word means,' Jannine said. 'Come on, you've got plenty of time to unpack. Let's go and find Lorna whatsit. You know I want to see her before I go.'

'You don't, really,' Elise said.

'I do,' Jannine insisted.

She went out into the corridor. Elise followed her. 'I think you're being really foolish.'

'Darling,' Jannine said, 'you're stuck in a fifties groove. We're nineteen-nineties women, and we're in control of our own destinies, right? Our bodies are our own. We can sell them, or give them or trade them, and what the hell? And stop looking so prim. You're not exactly a blushing virgin, are you?'

They reached Lorna's office and found her drinking coffee and reading a paperback.

'Sorry if you're inundated with work,' Jannine observed, politely, 'but I've got to speak to you before I go.'

Lorna grinned and put the book down. 'I think I can spare you five minutes. Have you changed your mind? Are you going to stay the night after all?'

'I'd like to,' Jannine said, 'but if I don't visit my sister on my way back to the Smoke I'll feel guilty for the rest of the week. And I'm supposed to be at work tomorrow morning.' She smiled winningly at Lorna. 'That's what I wanted to see you about.'

'This has nothing to do with me,' Elise said quickly.

'Go polish your halo,' Jannine said. 'Leave us sinners to discuss business.'

'What kind of business?' Lorna sounded curious.

'Pleasure,' Jannine said. 'Pleasure *house*. Are we on the same wavelength?'

'Oh, you want to volunteer your body?' Lorna said, helpfully.

'Well, yes,' Jannine agreed. 'I'm an actress.'

Lorna searched round for a piece of paper and a pen. 'That could be useful. What are you willing to do?'

'Well – er – what do you want?' Jannine hedged.

'It depends,' Lorna said. 'We're hoping to arrange some theme parties, some banquets, some shows. Whatever our guests want, really. We'll probably need supporting players.' She stared up at Jannine. 'Plate carriers. That sort of thing.'

'Sod that,' Jannine said, crossly. 'I do that already. I was thinking of something more exciting.'

'And better paid?' Lorna nodded. 'Give me your telephone number. I'll be in touch.'

'Great,' Jannine smiled. She glanced at Elise. 'And you needn't look so disapproving, Miss whiter-than-white St John. I know for a fact you had several flings before you got stuck on your blond Mr Muscles.'

'But I didn't get paid,' Elise emphasised.

'None of those fellas bought you meals? Presents? A holiday?'

'That's different,' Elise said.

'Only to you,' Jannine argued.

Lorna grinned at Elise. 'What's this about Mr Muscles? You had an affair with a body builder? Is it true what they say about them?'

'What do they say?' Jannine asked.

'That they've got muscles everywhere but in the right place?'

'Ralph wasn't a body builder,' Elise said. 'He just liked keeping in trim.'

'And he liked being kicked around,' Jannine added. 'By big strong women.'

'Really?' Lorna sounded interested. 'I've never met a real masochist.' She turned to Elise. 'What's it like, beating a man up? Do tell!'

'I've no idea,' Elise said. 'Jannine's just a scandal-monger. I didn't do anything like that with Ralph.'

'You didn't spank him or anything?' Lorna sounded disappointed. 'Not even once?'

'Not even once,' Elise confirmed. 'I'm not into that sort of thing, and I didn't know he was either.'

'I would have thought that'd be the first thing you discussed,' Lorna said.

'We didn't discuss anything much,' Elise remembered.

'You just fucked?' Lorna nodded. 'Well, I must say I wouldn't mind a similar arrangement with gorgeous Max.'

'Hey, what's with this guy?' Jannine interrupted. 'He insults you, and you're all drooling over him?'

'All?' Lorna asked, curiously. 'I thought I was the only one. Who else has been drooling?'

'Elise,' Jannine said, ignoring her friend's furious look. 'All the way up here. And back in London. She even dreams about him.'

Lorna turned to Elise. 'You told me he wasn't your type.'

'He isn't!' Elise said, even more angry because she knew she was blushing.

'Not much!' Jannine agreed.

'Well, don't worry,' Lorna grinned. 'I'm willing to share.' She looked at Elise speculatively. 'Maybe we could end up doing a threesome? D'you think Max'd like that? Or we could do a show for him, just you and me?'

'Certainly not!' Elise said, her blush deepening.

'Well, don't sound so miffed,' Lorna said mildly. 'Lot's of people do the group thing. Three's company, so they say, and you don't have to be a lesbian to enjoy the occasional fling with a woman.' She paused. 'You mean if Max suggested that we both perform for him, you'd refuse?'

'Of course,' Elise said, quickly.

'Even if he promised to make love to you afterwards?' Lorna persisted.

'I'd still refuse.'

'I wonder?' Lorna grinned.

'I came here to work,' Elise said. 'And earn some money.'

'Didn't we all?' Lorna agreed. 'But that doesn't mean we can't have fun as well!'

Elise was looking at sketches for one of her final designs, described on the list she had been given as a 'space-age hotel room'. Deciding that a view of the rolling Northumbrian countryside would hardly be appropriate, she had begun by blanking out the windows. The centrepiece would, of course, be the bed. A huge bed, she thought, maybe a water bed, with a control panel that accessed the television and video, the music system, and the lights. Hidden lights, coloured lights, moving lights. A touch of a button would project them like confetti on the walls and ceiling, dim them or brighten them, concentrate them into a spotlight, blank them out altogether. She would line the room with reflective material to enhance the effect. What a pity there wasn't a way to make the lights tactile, she thought. The lovers in this room could excite each other with probes of colour. Would this be the remote control sex trip of the future? She certainly thought it sounded better than the virtual reality sex-suits she had seen in a magazine. The partners in that experiment had looked like a cross between bondage fanatics and scuba divers.

She let her mind wander, seductively. In her room of sexual pleasure one partner would be suspended, weightless, in a cube of glass, while the other would lounge outside, fingers on the control panel, sending his or her lover's body on a journey of erotic delight. She imagined what it would be like, imprisoned in the cube, floating on air, twisting and turning gently. Beams of light would touch her body, probing her, wherever her lover wished. There was nothing she could do to prevent it. She could kick and twist, but in this cube all movement would be in slow motion. She could not evade the lights, even if she wanted to. They would always find her.

What if each colour had a different psychological effect? She imagined blue like a cool breeze moving through her hair. Pink circling inside her ear like a warm tongue, smoothing the sensitive skin of her inner arms. Or stroking behind her knees, separating her toes and caressing the soles of her feet – something she had always enjoyed and something none of her lovers had ever really exploited. These would be preliminaries, used skilfully to induce relaxation. She would close her eyes and spin slowly, lulled by these softly erotic caresses.

And when her partner grew tired of being too gentle? What colour then? Red, maybe? She imagined the red beam, searching her. No longer light and playful, but hunting for more interesting areas to excite. Finding her nipples and teasing them like insistent fingers. The red beam tracing a line down her spine to the cleft of her buttocks. Pushing between them, bending her over as it explored and penetrated. She wriggled with delight, pretending to try and evade the intimate stimulation, but not really wanting to. Then another beam – white, maybe – took advantage of her upturned position and whipped across her naked bottom, several times, making her whole body tremble and squirm – not from pain, but from the erotic shock the unexpected action caused her.

The red beam withdrew and the white light stroked her upper thighs, coaxing them open. She spun, a captive toy in the weightless cube as it searched between her legs. The beam touched her clitoris, rubbing gently at first, and then harder and far more expertly than any of her previous lovers had ever managed. She arched backwards as it played with her, her body spreadeagled now, displaying her sex to her watching lover, knowing that he was enjoying her reactions as she gradually lost control. He seemed to know exactly how she liked to be touched. The beam was both fingers and tongue, exerting just the right amount of pressure. When it finally entered her she groaned with delight and need. Her daydream was so vivid, her body had responded and she squirmed uncomfortably on her chair. Her mind shifted to the man lying outside her glass-walled prison. The man enjoying the seductive dance he was forcing her to perform. A man whose body was dappled with subdued moving patterns of colour. A man with Max Lannsen's face.

The internal telephone on her desk trilled insistently. Startled, she came back to the present, and reached out for it.

'Welcome back,' Lorna's voice sounded cheerfully in her ear. 'Where have you been? In the loo?'

'Right here,' Elise said.

'I've been ringing for ages,' Lorna said. 'I've got super news. Gorgeous Max has sold that grotty house in London and he's moving up here full time. We could walk down the corridor and bump into him at any time. So no more slopping around in those arty kaftans. High heels, tight skirts and seamed stockings from now on.'

During the three months she had been at Shilden, Elise and Lorna had found themselves bound together both by a mutual need for friendship and by the insular and unfriendly attitude of the castle staff. Although Lorna had a fund of stories about the places she had visited and the people she had met, her conversation inevitably turned to men and sex – and Max Lannsen in particular. Elise had given up pretending that she did not find her employer attractive.

'I haven't time to plan any seductions,' she said. 'I'm much too busy.'

'I'm not,' Lorna said. 'And even if I was, I'd make time. And so can you. The pressure's off you a bit now, anyway. All those lovely designs of yours have been approved by the money men. You're going to get some expert help. Max wants to talk to you about it. And so does his . . . expert.'

It sounded slightly sarcastic. Elise remembered that Max Lannsen had already hinted there might be someone else involved in her design work. She had been working so hard she had forgotten about it.

'Who is this expert?' she asked, suspiciously.

'God knows,' Lorna said evasively and, Elise felt, not quite truthfully 'Someone from London, I think. Max will give you the details.'

'I'm not sure I want any help.'

'You don't have an option,' Lorna said. 'The Master of Shilden decrees it! And actually, you could do with a rest. You've been working flat out. It isn't good for you. You don't want to look all weary and fatigued with Max around, do you?'

Elise realised that Lorna was right. She had become immersed in her work. Anything she needed had been ordered by phone and delivered to her office. Despite the fact that her generous wage packet had enabled her to get a nearly new car, she had not been outside the castle grounds since she arrived. Not that there was anywhere to go. The village was a straggle of cottages and a small pub where Lorna had already told her she had received a very cool reception. ('They didn't think much of a woman coming into a pub on her own, and, once they knew I worked at Shilden the atmosphere was positively frosty.') If she wanted a change of scenery and some company, Elise thought, where could she go?

'Why not come to White Gates with me?' Lorna might have read her thoughts. 'You told me you've always wanted to ride.'

Elise remembered that Lorna had claimed White Gates had the best horses in the county. She had seen Lorna setting off in her bright red Mini, looking sexy and efficient in her glossy knee-high boots and tight breeches. She could not imagine herself in the same kind of outfit.

'I don't want to make myself look stupid,' she hedged.

'Do you think I'm going to stand around laughing at you?' Lorna said, exasperated. 'Or that anyone is, come to that? No one's born on a horse, you know. We all started as absolute beginners.'

Yes, but you probably started just out of the cradle, Elise thought. Plonked on a fat little pony by your doting mother. Young children don't have any fear of looking ridiculous. But the idea was attractive. And riding was an activity she had always wanted to try.

'I wonder if Max rides?' Lorna murmured. Elise had a sudden embarrassing picture of herself, lurching up and down like a total beginner on a bored looking horse while Max Lannsen cantered past, wearing the same kind of boots and tight breeches that she had dressed him in during her white slaver fantasy. My God, can't I think about the man without thinking about sex as well, she thought angrily.

'Just come with me,' Lorna suggested. 'You don't have to sign on any dotted lines. Just come and see what goes on. Agreed?'

'Maybe,' Elise said.

* * *

The voice in her ear sounded as cool and remote as Elise remembered it. 'Please come to my office, Miss St John. We have some problems to discuss.'

Elise put the internal phone down. She knew that Max Lannsen had already been at Shilden for two days. His old, but immaculate, dark green Mercedes estate was parked on the forecourt. But she had not seen him, and neither had Lorna. His apartment was in a wing of the castle only accessible through a door that was permanently locked. That morning she had looked out at the Mercedes to see a large black – and much more up to date – saloon version standing next to it. My 'expert help' has arrived, she thought. It looked like the kind of car a man would drive. In fact, she decided, with its tinted windows it looked like the kind of car the Mafia would drive.

As she walked down the passage to Max Lannsen's office, she wondered what problems he wanted to discuss. If her designs had already been approved, what was the point of this 'expert' adding his opinions? She formed a mental picture of her new collaborator: probably gay but, judging from the car, the kind of designer who wore conservative suits and silk ties rather than an arty type in a ruffled shirt.

When she opened the office door she realised that she could not have been more wrong. Max Lannsen, darkly elegant, was sitting behind a large, old-fashioned desk. He looked as attractive and unattainable as ever. His eyes, under slanting eyebrows, showed no sign of recognition or welcome. And yet she was suddenly reminded of the feel of his body close to hers during that brief moment of contact in the east wing cellar.

'So you're our imaginative designer?'

Elise pulled her gaze away from Lannsen. The woman sitting next to him had a hard-edged, glossy elegance. She wore an understated designer dress with simple, but obviously expensive, gold jewellery. Her hair and make-up were immaculate. She looked, Elise thought unkindly, as if she would despise men as weaklings but would use every feminine trick in the book to clinch a deal if she thought it would pay dividends. From insincere flattery to insincere sex.

'You liked my ideas?' Elise forced a friendly smile.

'Darling, I *loved* them.' The woman returned the smile easily. 'They were . . . sweet.'

Elise felt her temper bristling. She wondered why the woman was sitting so close to Lannsen. Her long legs were crossed, but her knees slanted towards him. She was leaning towards him too, her body language speaking of possession.

'Miss Altham has ideas for some additions to your various designs,' Lannsen said, in a neutral voice. His eyes fixed on Elise. There was no expression in them. He added: 'I warned you about this, if you remember?'

'Oh, Max – warned? You make me sound like an ogre.' The unwavering smile flashed towards Lannsen, who gazed sombrely back. 'And let's not be so formal.' The smile switched to Elise. 'I'm Petra. And you're Elise, aren't you?' Elise nodded. 'So unusual,' Petra murmured. 'Is it foreign?'

'It's short for Elizabeth,' Elise said. 'It's the way I pronounced my name when I was young. It just sort of stayed with me as I grew up.'

'How lovely,' Petra gushed. 'So *individual*.' Elise realised for the first time that her sketches and plans were in a folder on the desk. Petra's long fingers, with their beautifully manicured and varnished nails, tapped on the folder's cover. 'Now,' she said, her voice harder, 'let's go over a few points, shall we?'

For the next half an hour Elise submitted to having every room she had designed changed in some way by Petra Altham. Petra wanted colours altered so that they were 'more seductive'; mirrors fitted because guests would want to 'watch each other'; furniture removed to make way for pieces of equipment that Petra claimed 'guests would find exciting and stimulating'. The only room that Petra did not find fault with was Elise's space-age hotel room. She liked the reflective walls and the moving lights, but seemed at a loss to suggest a piece of equipment to make the room 'special'. Elise remembered her fantasy with the weightless cube but, as she knew it was not practical, she declined to share it with Miss Petra Altham. Throughout the conversation Max Lannsen kept silent, and Petra did not consult him. Elise had a strange feeling that he found the discussion faintly distasteful. In any event he seemed glad when it was over.

Elise was equally glad. She knew there was no friendship behind Petra's glossy smile. And she disliked the familiar way that Petra spoke to Max Lannsen, not to mention the way she pushed herself as close to him as possible without actually touching. And Lannsen, Elise remembered after she had left the office, had made no obvious attempt to move away.

'I suppose he couldn't really back off,' Lorna said, when Elise described what had happened. 'Not if that woman is supposed to be a business colleague. She sounds absolutely ghastly. Unfortunately I've got to work with her too. I can't say I'm looking forward to it.'

'What makes her an expert?' Elise asked. 'And an expert at what? She's certainly not a trained interior designer.'

Lorna gave her a quick, quizzical look: 'I didn't think she would be.'

'Then who exactly is she?' Elise said.

'A pain in the arse,' Lorna said. 'But one we've got to tolerate. Look, you're obviously fed up to the back teeth with everything at the moment. Come to White Gates with me this evening. You don't have to book any lessons. Just come for the ride. It'll do you good.'

* * *

White Gates was a rambling farmhouse set in acres of rolling green. Lorna's red Mini stopped close to a wall and Elise saw the entrance to the stable yard on her right. When the car door opened she smelt the pleasant scent of hay, leather and horses, and heard the clatter of hooves.

It was a warm evening and Elise, who was wearing a man's cream silk shirt like a loose tunic over her jeans, and faded pink canvas shoes, left her cloak in the car. Lorna, as always, looked demure and Victorian in her long skirt and a lace-trimmed, pleat-fronted blouse.

'There's a big indoor school here,' she explained to Elise, 'And one for individuals to hire out. There are some great bridle paths, too, if you want to go for a hack.'

They walked into the yard. It was clean and neat, and the paintwork on the stables looked new. Horses pushed their heads out curiously. Some whinnied and snickered, others surveyed the visitors silently, then decided they were not particularly interesting and disappeared inside again.

'They've got some really good horses,' Lorna said.

'Did you ever have your own horse?' Elise asked.

'Heavens no,' Lorna said. 'Don't I wish! We were never in one place long enough to even have a cat.'

Suddenly they heard a high-pitched whinny and a girl's angry voice: 'You great thick-headed bugger! Get in. Get in!'

'That sounds like Penny,' Lorna guessed.

She guided Elise through a gap between the stables. A young, slightly-built girl was battling to get a massive horse into a horse box. Clearly unwilling, the horse had braced itself obstinately at the foot of the ramp. The girl, her face red with frustration and exertion, looked up and saw them watching.

'Having trouble, Penny?' Lorna called cheerfully.

'You could say that,' Penny agreed. 'This great fat brute won't go into the sodding box!'

'Try bribery,' Lorna suggested.

'I've tried it,' Penny said. 'He ate the sugar, and he still won't move. He just doesn't like the box. He hates travelling.' She turned to the horse again: 'Get in there, you pig!'

Oblivious to the insults the horse shook its head, huffed gently through distended nostrils, and stayed where it was. The difference in size and strength between the girl and the horse was so great that Elise thought it was absurd to expect such a small person to manage such a huge animal. As they walked away, leaving Penny to resume her struggle, a man stepped out from behind the horse box. Tall and slim in tight riding breeches and boots, he wore a dark waistcoat over a white open-necked shirt. His sleeves were rolled up to the elbows.

'For God's sake, Penny, stop being so damned nice!' His voice had no trace of a local accent.

'You try getting this bugger to move!' Penny responded, exasperated.

For an answer the man went round to the driving cabin of the horse box, reached inside and came back again carrying a short riding crop. Without any warning he walloped the horse across its rump. The horse jerked in surprise and snorted indignantly. The whip struck again and this time the horse jumped forward. Its hooves slithered on the ridged surface of the ramp, but now that it had started moving it seemed to accept that it might as well carry on. Encouraged by Penny, it moved sedately forward and disappeared into the dark interior of the box.

'What a bastard,' Elise said furiously. 'I'd like to do that to him.'

Her voice was loud enough to carry across the yard. The man turned and walked towards her. Despite her

71

anger she could not help noticing the easy elegance of his stride. Stopping in front of her he stood with his legs slightly apart, tapping the whip gently and rhythmically against his boot. A pair of amused grey eyes surveyed her.

'Is that an offer?' he asked, politely.

'I'll report you to the RSPCA,' Elise said, still furious.

'The RSPCA would laugh at you,' he said. 'Isn't that right, Lorna?'

'Fraid so,' Lorna said. 'Don't worry, Elise. Hurricane probably thought he'd been bitten by a rather large horsefly, that's all.'

'A very vicious horsefly,' Elise said, still angry.

'You don't ride?' The grey eyes watched her. The whip still tapped.

'She wants to learn,' Lorna said, before Elise could answer. 'Elise, this is Blair Devlin, co-owner of White Gates.'

'I *thought* I wanted to learn,' Elise corrected.

'And I've put you off?' Devlin smiled. 'If you ride you'll discover that some horses need a firm hand.' The whip stopped tapping. He grasped it in both hands and flexed it gently. 'Just like some women.'

Penny had closed the horse box and came round to join them. 'The kettle's boiled. Anyone for coffee?' She smiled at Elise. 'Do you want to book a lesson?'

'She's not sure yet,' Blair Devlin said. 'First, we've got to convince her that this isn't a school for trainee sadists.'

Penny glanced first at Lorna, then Devlin, and then snorted with laughter. 'You're going to persuade her of that, Dev?'

'Certainly,' Devlin said. 'We don't punish horses here.' He slapped the whip against the palm of one hand. 'Do we, Penny?' he added, politely.

'Not horses,' Penny agreed, grinning. She winked at Lorna. 'Come on, we'll let Dev show your friend round while we satisfy our caffeine addiction.'

Elise was well aware of the implied sexual innuendo in Blair Devlin's remarks. And she realised, with surprise, that they excited her. He was a very attractive man. His face was tanned from the sun rather than a lamp, with features that were not quite regular enough to make him too pretty, and his thick brown hair had a golden sheen. It was windswept now, but she could see that it had been beautifully cut. There was a casual elegance about him. He was obviously a man who cared about his appearance, without going to narcissistic extremes. And he had the kind of self-confidence that she always found intriguing. He walked beside her with the whip looped over his wrist.

'How long have you been at White Gates?' she asked.

'Since leaving agricultural college,' he said. 'I did a comprehensive course in stable management – not that it taught me much I didn't already know – and then went into partnership with a childhood friend of mine, Julia Beauchamp. The land here belongs to her father.'

'So you're a local?' Elise was surprised. 'You don't have an accent.'

'I was educated down south,' he said. 'But I'm as local as you can get, believe me. How about you?'

'Well, I'm not local,' Elise admitted.

'I guessed that,' he said, solemnly. They had moved out of sight of the yard and were standing near a dark, open door. Elise could smell the scent of polished leather. His eyes moved to her hair. It was piled loosely and pinned but, as always, its weight was beginning to cause it to unwind. 'I'd remember anyone with red hair like yours.' His voice had dropped in tone. He was watching her intently.

'There are plenty of people with hair like mine,' she said.

His eyes moved from her face down her body and back again. It was casual enough to be friendly, but his faint, approving smile proved that he was not just admiring her shirt and jeans. 'Not round here,' he said.

I am not going to feel flattered, Elise thought. It's probably a chat-up line he's used dozens of times before. And not a very original one, either.

'There are dozens like me in London,' she said, brightly. She was tempted to say 'and prettier, too' but realised that that would just give him an excuse to push the compliments further. Instead she moved back towards the dark doorway and the smell of leather. 'What's in here? Saddles and things?'

'Tack,' he agreed. 'It's a private tack room.' He reached past her head and flicked a light switch on. 'Mine and Julia's.'

She turned to see the saddles resting on their stands and bridles hanging on double hooks. The walls were covered with rosettes and photographs. A pictorial record of dozens of shows and competitions showed Blair Devlin clearing jumps or being presented with rosettes and cups, and a pleasant-looking girl engaging in similar activities. Elise assumed this was Julia Beauchamp.

Devlin was standing behind her, and he was making her feel uncomfortable. He was much too attractive. And, unlike Max Lannsen, she was certain he was available. I don't need this, she thought. But another little voice at the back of her mind tempted: why not? She turned, and found herself closer to him than she expected. He was smiling slightly, the smile of a man who was confident of his own sexual power. Elise wondered how many women had refused Blair Devlin. Not many, she guessed. She felt the wall of the tack room against her back. 'Obviously you've been riding a long time,' she observed, brightly.

'Since I was five,' he said.

His eyes wandered over her again, slower this time, lingering deliberately on the pockets of her shirt, where her nipples were pushing discreetly against the silk. She felt suddenly aroused at the thought of his hands touching her. Lightly? Possessively? Roughly? A tremor ran through her. She saw something like triumph in his eyes and knew that he was aware of her feelings. I don't need this, she thought. I came up here to get away from emotional entanglements, and what happens? I've already started a rich fantasy life involving my employer. Now I'm lusting after the local riding instructor as well.

Suddenly, surprising her, Devlin stepped back. 'Talk to Penny,' he said. 'Book yourself an introductory lesson.' His grey eyes held hers. 'You'll enjoy it,' he said softly. 'I promise.'

'Of course you realise that Mr Devlin is the local stud?' Lorna said, as they drove back to Shilden. 'Maybe I should have warned you.'

'So why didn't you?' Elise asked.

'I thought you were besotted with Max,' Lorna grinned. 'To the exclusion of all else.'

'Max Lannsen seems to be about as unattainable as Pierce Brosnan,' Elise said. 'And Blair Devlin is very . . . attractive.'

Lorna gave a snort of laughter: 'That man has the sexiest bum I've ever seen – allowing that I haven't had the chance to really inspect Max's – and when he walks around in those tight riding breeches I just want to grab hold of him and unzip!'

'And have you?' Elise asked.

'Actually, no,' Lorna admitted.

'Really no?' Elise was sceptical.

'The thing is,' Lorna said, 'I've become quite friendly with Julia Beauchamp. She went to school down south, and she knows some of my friends. She fancies Dev awfully, but they were like brother and sister when they were younger, and that still seems to be how he sees her. It's very frustrating for her. But, silly as it sounds, knowing how she feels I just wouldn't feel right about having a fling with him.'

'Very ethical of you,' Elise murmured. They drove for a while in silence. 'What's the *real* reason?'

Lorna grinned. 'That really is part of the real reason. But also, to be perfectly honest, Dev has never made any kind of pass at me.'

'For a stud, he seems to be missing a lot of opportunities,' Elise commented.

'He chatted you up fast enough,' Lorna said. 'And if you believe Penny, he's had most of the girl grooms. She says he's absolutely hot in bed. But a bit kinky.'

'In what way?' Elise asked.

'Well,' Lorna said carefully, 'haven't you guessed? Penny says he's got this big brass bed and he tied her face down and used that whip of his on her bottom. Nothing seriously painful, I might add. In fact she said it was a turn on – for both of them.'

'Do you believe her?'

Lorna shrugged. 'You heard him yourself. He was more or less hinting it, wasn't he? Penny does like to try and be outrageous, but this time I rather think she was telling the truth.' Elise believed it too. There had been a definite sexual innuendo in Devlin's remarks, and the way he handled the riding crop. 'And then,' Lorna added, casually, 'he got her to do it to him.'

'Whip him?' Elise found that difficult to visualise.

'On that gorgeous bum,' Lorna confirmed. 'Apparently he loved it.'

'But he looks so . . . macho.'

'He is,' Lorna said. 'He goes hunting, and eventing, and even if I was six foot tall and built like Arnie Schwarzenegger, I wouldn't pick a fight with him. He did some martial arts thing when he was at college, so I've been told, and won some trophies too. But in bed it's just fantasy, isn't it. You just have fun. If he wants to

76

change roles occasionally and have a beautiful woman to dominate him, that doesn't make him any less of a man. I'd do it like a shot if I thought it turned him on. And I'd let him spank me, too. I'd enjoy it!'

Would I enjoy it? Elise wondered, later that evening, as she made herself a cup of coffee. What would it be like to be spreadeagled on Devlin's brass bed, naked, with her wrists tied to the bedposts? Or half-naked, with her skirt pushed up, her blouse unbuttoned? What would it be like to feel his hands sliding under her, feeling for her breasts, catching her nipples between his fingers? What would it be like to feel him pulling her panties slowly down to her knees? She imagined his grey eyes admiring her rounded, unprotected behind. She imagined his smile of anticipation. What's come over me? she thought. I never even considered this kind of thing before. I wanted Ralph to be more masterful in bed, but I never imagined him using the flat of his hand on me, let alone a whip! And yet she had to admit that she found the idea physically exciting.

She was less sure about playing the dominant role. But if her partner really wanted it, could she behave like Jemma Harrisford obviously behaved with Ralph? She had a feeling that Ralph's needs were more extreme than Blair Devlin's. But if Devlin wanted her to whip him as a part of their love-making, would she do it? Would it turn me on? she wondered. And then her thoughts wandered. Would I whip Max Lannsen? Somehow she could not imagine that!

But Devlin was obviously attracted to her. His suggestion that she book a riding lesson had implied that the riding he had in mind did not necessarily involve a horse! Was she going to encourage him? Why not, she thought. He's available, and Max Lannsen isn't. And let's be honest – I fancy him! So much for Jannine's warning that anyone with any sex appeal in the north would have already moved to London. So much for her comment about nerds with cloth caps and funny accents. If any of the other locals looked like Blair Devlin she could see Jannine packing her bags and moving north permanently.

If she had read his signals correctly – and she was sure that she had – she would at least enter a relationship with Blair Devlin with her eyes open. It would be a purely physical partnership, with no expectations of permanency on either side. She could be certain that Devlin's interest in her had no ulterior motive. She had nothing he could possibly want. They could enjoy each other's company, and they could enjoy some sexy fun, and no hearts would be broken when it was over. Yes, she thought. I'll book an introductory riding lesson, Mr Devlin. And we'll see where *that* leads.

'We need a horse,' Petra Altham said. 'A big padded horse, with footholds and hand holds.' She held a sheaf of papers and leafed through them. Finding one, she pushed it towards Elise. 'Like that.'

The drawing showed what appeared to be a vaulting horse, but with foot rests projecting from its sides and a top that was curved rather than straight. 'I know just the right supplier,' Petra added. She thought about it. 'Maybe we should order two.' She made a note on her pad.

'One for women and one for men.'

'Is there a difference?' Elise asked, curiously.

'Of course,' Petra said. 'The men's horse has an opening for his balls so that when he's astride, two women can work on him at once. One of them could use a vibrator or a whip or whatever, and the other can get inside the horse and play around with whatever bits she can get hold of. The women's model has the holes in different places, and two for her boobs. I'm not shocking you, am I?'

'No,' Elise said.

Startling me a little, though, she admitted to herself. She had always considered herself fairly open-minded and imaginative where sex was concerned, but unusual equipment had never figured in any of her previous affairs. She thought Ralph would have enjoyed that kind of treatment. She imagined him naked, with two women dressed like Jemma Harrisford in severe, dark suits, black seamed stockings and stiletto heels, one of them with a vibrator (she knew Ralph liked vibrators) and the other kneeling inside the horse, exciting him with her mouth. But the scene was only faintly arousing because of its novelty. Ralph no longer excites me, she thought, with something like relief. I've exorcised him. At last.

But if it was Blair Devlin she could certainly visualise him naked. He would be tautly muscular from all that riding and martial arts training, or whatever it was. She imagined his long legs astride the horse, stretched out, tied to the foot rests so he could not escape. His wrists would be fastened to the hand holds on the top, his sexual equipment fitting snugly in the opening provided; available to her if she wanted to kneel beneath the horse. She could torment or tantalise him, bring him close to orgasm, and then leave him unfulfilled while she moved on to some other part of his body. A prisoner of the horse, there would be nothing he could do about it, except perhaps beg her for relief.

She imagined his neat buttocks unprotected and waiting for whatever treatment she decided to inflict on him. A whip? Her hand? Would he enjoy a session with a vibrator? The idea of having him helpless was surprisingly appealing. And so was the thought that whatever she did to him, he would no doubt pay back in kind!

Could she imagine Max Lannsen tied to the horse? Somehow this was less easy. For a start it was difficult to imagine him stripped. Blair Devlin's lithe body had been discreetly displayed by his tight riding breeches and the open-necked shirt. She had only ever seen

79

Lannsen in a suit which, although beautifully tailored, hinted much less obviously at the body underneath. She knew from the easy elegance of his movements that he would be fit, and probably as lean and muscular as Devlin. And with a natural all-over tan to complement his dark looks, she thought. A hard brown body. A neat bottom. Strong, slim thighs. He would look good in brief swimming trunks. But she could not visualise him naked. She could not visualise him bent over the horse, either, although she could imagine him putting her in that position!

'I said you'll have to redesign the room.' Petra Altham's irritable voice jolted Elise back to reality. 'Wood panelled walls, I think; hooks to hang bridles and whips on, and some fancy brushes. It's amazing what you can do with a nice brush. And get rid of the bed. We'll have bales of straw instead.'

'I thought you approved of this room,' Elise said.

'Well, it was fine as an equestrian themed bedroom,' Petra said, 'but the guests who come in here will be more interested in equestrian themed *games*. And incorporate a mirror, too. I've never yet met a man who doesn't like watching himself in action.'

'You've obviously had more experience with what men like than I have,' Elise said, more sharply than she intended.

'Obviously,' Petra said. 'That's why I'm being paid.'

'You want this to look like a tack room?' Elise asked.

'A classy tack room,' Petra agreed. 'Not one of those tatty rooms you get at a third rate stables, please.'

'Maybe we should put some pictures on the walls,' Elise suggested. 'Photographs, you know, and rosettes?'

She had meant it as sarcasm but, surprisingly, Petra seemed to like the idea. 'Yes. They love that don't they, those horsey types? Pics of themselves jumping over gates and getting bits of cardboard and ribbon pinned on their bridles. It's the sort of thing that Lorna Chorley hyphen Smythe would like. I can arrange some photographs, but they'll be a damned sight more interesting than *that*.'

'And real harness to hang on the walls?' Elise asked.

'No, no,' Petra said. 'Waste of money. If guests want any special restraint gear they'll bring their own. They usually have it custom made; each strap and buckle has got to be just right. Half the fun is getting themselves, or a girl, trussed up, and they don't like using anyone else's leathers.' She stared at Elise. 'You don't look too happy with all this. If you've got a problem, tell me now.'

'It's just that I could have designed this room differently if I'd been given the right instructions to start with,' Elise said. 'As it is, I've wasted a lot of my time.'

'Well, you're being paid,' Petra said sharply. 'And Max did tell you to expect some changes.'

'This is a complete make-over,' Elise said.

'Some of the other rooms will be make-overs too, darling,' Petra said. 'Max has done his bit by employing you, but this is why our mutual bosses are paying *me*. You provide the ground plan, I add the professional details.' She smiled her bright, insincere smile. 'Some of your rooms hardly need any additions. I just love the Victorian bathroom, and that space-age room with the reflective walls is rather nice, too, although I'll have to think up something more exotic than a few moving lights.'

'No doubt you will,' Elise said. 'You seem to have an exotic imagination.'

Petra gave her a sharp look. 'One of us needs to have. The success of this project means a lot to Max. And to me. We have to satisfy our bosses. And you have to satisfy *us*. Just remember that.'

'I'm going to end up punching Miss Petra Altham in the mouth,' Elise predicted. 'Do you think it'll get me the sack?'

81

'Just think about your wage packet,' Lorna soothed. 'And don't take it so personally. I have to liaise with her, and she absolutely loathes me.' The smooth sound of a car engine purred outside. 'That's Max,' Lorna said, brightening up. 'Back from Alnwick.'

Elise followed Lorna to the window. Max Lannsen's dark green Mercedes swung round the forecourt and came to a halt. As Elise watched, Lannsen got out of the driver's seat, walked around the car, and opened the front passenger door. Petra Altham, immaculate in a figure-hugging suit, and with a froth of white lace making a deep white vee at her neck, slid out of the seat, smoothed down her skirt and checked the seams of her stockings.

Elise felt a stab of anger. 'He's been out with the Altham woman!'

'It was a business trip,' Lorna said.

'So why is *Miss* Altham all dressed up?'

'She's always dressed up,' Lorna said.

'They seem to go around a lot together.' Elise wasn't certain if it was really anger she was feeling – or jealousy. 'You don't think they're . . . well – a couple?'

'Is he fucking her, you mean?' Lorna asked. 'I've no idea. If he is, I don't think much of his taste. But let's face it, if the locals are as po-faced to Max as they are to us, he doesn't have a lot of options. He's obviously not interested in us. That only leaves Mrs Stokes or darling Petra. Which would you choose?'

Despite herself, Elise giggled: 'I think Mrs Stokes would be preferable to Petra.'

'But she won't call him master,' Lorna said, in her perfect imitation of the cook's voice and accent. And added in her own voice: 'Perhaps Miss Petra does.'

'I doubt it,' Elise said. 'She doesn't seem like the submissive type.'

'Perhaps Petra does as she's told with gorgeous Max,' Lorna suggested. 'Bossy bitches often like to be dominated in the bedroom. Maybe Max is into corporal punishment, too? Can't you just imagine Petra up-ended over his lap, with that nice designer dress pushed up round her waist? I wonder if she wears any knickers. And have you noticed those seamed stockings? What does she keep them up with? Sexy suspenders bought from one of those mail order people who advertise in dubious Sunday newspapers. Maybe that's what turns Max on. He's into sexy underwear. That's how she's managed to hook him!'

'I just can't imagine Max liking that sort of thing,' Elise said. 'Maybe Blair Devlin would, but not Max.'

Lorna laughed. 'They all like it, believe me. Maybe not crotchless panties and peep-hole bras, but suspenders and stocking tops, and those super basques that you can get with tight lacing down the front. Show me a man who says that sexy underwear doesn't turn him on and I'll show you an outright liar!'

But it didn't seem to turn Ralph on, Elise remembered, as she prepared for bed that night. Not that she had ever overdone the frills and lace. She had never bothered much about really sexy underwear. Some of it looked too uncomfortable. Her special items were silk: classy cami-knickers and short camisoles, tailored for her by a student friend who hoped for a career in lingerie design. And Ralph had never seemed interested either in watching her walking around in it, or removing it. In fact, with hindsight, Elise realised Ralph was probably not turned on by the way she dressed. She liked comfortable, flowing clothes. Kaftans, tunic tops, jeans or loose trousers. Ralph would have undoubtedly preferred her to strut about in her dark tailored Sellick's suit and stilettos.

What would Max Lannsen like? She found it difficult to imagine his personal preferences. She could put him in a fantasy, but that was different. What was he like in real life? Would he be turned on by a sexy basque, stocking tops and suspenders? High heels? A black lace bra? Was Lorna right when she said that all men found this kind of thing exciting? She thought of Max Lannsen's sombre darkness? Would he enjoy seeing her dressed like a stripper? Would he enjoy seeing her strip?

Blair Devlin would, she thought. He had already stripped her with his eyes. She was sure he would enjoy watching her perform to music. Could she do it? Of course I could, she thought. She was wearing her bathrobe and, on an impulse, she moved to her wardrobe, opened the door and struck a pose. She let the robe slip down off her shoulders, then to the floor, and surveyed herself critically. Not a bad figure, she thought, even if I say so myself. My boobs are OK, and my waist is small, and my legs are good. Well, maybe I'd like slimmer thighs, and maybe I'd like bigger boobs. Or maybe I wouldn't. At least I can walk about without a bra and not feel uncomfortable. One of her early boyfriends had said he enjoyed watching bra-less women. It sets the imagination working, he claimed, watching their breasts jiggle about, hoping that you'd see an erect nipple, or even manage to brush your hand over one – accidentally of course. She had told him that his remarks were sexist, and he had agreed. They were watching a film, she remembered – but they hadn't watched much more of it after that!

Her room was warm and she felt comfortable without her clothes. She switched off the main light, left the bedside lamp on, and moved to a shelf containing her CDs. Choosing one, she slipped it into the player and waited for the music's insistent beat. Then she began to dance. At first there was no particular pattern to her movements, but gradually she imagined herself into a stripper's outfit: a basque, silk stockings, high-heeled shoes. And she imagined Blair Devlin watching her. He would be standing just as she remembered him from their first meeting, his legs apart, wearing an open-neck shirt with rolled-up sleeves, knee-high riding boots and tight breeches that clung to his thighs and bulged at the front in a way that hinted that he would look very impressive when they – and any underwear he had on – were removed.

She kept this picture in her mind as she danced. Danced and mimed the removal of her clothes, taking her time. Slipping the imaginary bra straps over her shoulders, flaunting herself provocatively as she twirled round on the carpet. Would Devlin just stand there and watch? she wondered. Or would he join in? It would be much more fun to feel his hands struggling with the flimsy straps, then slip under her arms and peel the lace bra cups slowly down until her breasts were exposed. She would dance against him, aware of his erection pressing into her buttocks. His fingers would brush her nipples, gently at first, teasing them, then pinching harder, rolling the erect peaks between his finger and thumb while she writhed in delight and pushed against him, getting him ready for what was to come.

And then she found her imagination changing direction. Another man stood in front of her, tugging at the laces of her basque. She stood still, startled at this unbidden picture. A man in a suit as dark as his hair, as dark as the shadows that half obscured his face. His eyes watched her intently from under slanting eyebrows; watched the fingers that still massaged her breasts. She knew that it was exciting him to see her handled this way by someone else.

She felt the basque open, freeing her from its restricting embrace. She felt his hands move to her stocking tops and circle her thighs. He unclipped the suspenders, rolling one stocking down, following its silky descent, his palms sliding over her skin, pressing behind her knee, forcing her leg to bend outwards. She lifted her foot and put it over his shoulder, pulling him closer.

The man behind her massaged her breasts harder now, making her groan. He was looking down, turned on by what he knew he was about to see.

She felt the kneeling man's mouth slide along her inner thigh; felt him tug her G-string and break the ribbon ties, pulling the triangle of satiny cloth away. His shoulder pushed her knee even further out so that she was opened and exposed. He stopped then, and looked at her. His fingers stroked her swelling clitoris briefly, sending tremors of pleasure shuddering through her body. The thought was so intense that she could no longer stand, swaying to the music. Stepping back, she all but collapsed on the bed.

In her imagination the warmth of his mouth claimed her. The tantalising movements of his tongue worked on her clitoris. In reality her own hands took over. One mimicked the man who stood behind her, massaging her left breast with its aching nipple. The other worked between her legs, pleasuring herself as expertly as she had always wished a man would do. Using just the right speed and pressure. Building the sensations until they exploded in a jolting erotic shock, and her body shook with spasms of delight.

She lay with her heart pounding. She had never had a fantasy involving two men that she actually knew before. But then, she thought, I've never fancied two men so strongly at the same time before either. Would Max Lannsen really behave like that? Would Blair Devlin? From what Lorna had said, maybe Devlin would. But Lannsen? It was impossible to imagine what he would do. He was still an enigma. Was he having an affair with Petra Altham? Was that how she got her job at Shilden? Despite the fact that Elise did not like Petra, she had to admit that the woman's hard-edged beauty would appeal to some men. If Max Lannsen is turned on by women like Petra Altham, she thought, he's certainly not going to notice me. And yet she remembered their brief physical closeness in the cellar. Had it only been a bit of cynical, sexist baiting? If she had responded, would he really have made love to her – and forgotten it immediately afterwards? She knew that many men would, but somehow she could not believe that Lannsen was one of them. Or was it simply that she did not want to believe it? Was she turning Lannsen into the kind of man she secretly wanted him to be? Would she get a shock if she ever found out the kind of man he was? And what about Blair Devlin? she wondered. What kind of man is he? She had a feeling that when she went for her first riding lesson she was going to find out!

'You'll love it,' Lorna said.

'I feel silly already,' Elise fretted. She had allowed Lorna to talk her into buying some breeches and boots and a hard hat, but somehow she felt that she did not look as confidently efficient as Lorna did in the same outfit. 'A beginner shouldn't dress up like this. I look like a poser. Admit it.'

'You look fine,' Lorna said. 'What's wrong with wearing the right clothes? It's sensible.'

'I'm going to make a fool of myself. I know it.'

'The horse won't laugh. He won't even notice. Riding school horses have seen it all before.'

'I wasn't thinking of the horse,' Elise muttered.

'Penny won't laugh either,' Lorna said. 'She's seen it all before, too.'

'What's Penny got to do with it?'

'She'll be teaching you?'

'But I thought . . .' Elise began.

Lorna grinned. 'So that's why you're getting all temperamental! Relax. Dev doesn't usually teach beginners, even the ones he fancies. Not for the first few lessons, anyway. He's coming out on a hack with us.'

Penny came into the office. 'Elise,' she said, 'you've got Brandysnap.'

'He's a dear,' Lorna said. 'What about me?'

'Solomon.'

'Oh, my God,' Lorna said. 'He's absolutely *not* a dear. Why do you do this to me, Penny?'

'You're one of the few people we get who can handle him,' Penny said. 'Apart from Dev.'

'Who's Dev riding?' Lorna asked.

'Adorable Hobbit,' Penny said, rather wistfully. 'I'm just passionate about that horse. He does everything you want. and so beautifully. Whenever I ride him I feel like I could make the Olympic team.'

'And I get Solomon?' Lorna complained, good naturedly. 'Does someone here really hate me?'

'It's called learning,' Penny corrected. 'You don't have to work with Hobbit. It's just sheer joy.'

They walked out into the yard. Three horses stood waiting, held by two young schoolgirls. Elise learnt later that they worked part time in the stables in exchange for riding lessons. Two of the horses were large, powerful looking and alert, their ears constantly moving. The third was smaller. Elise thought it looked bored.

Lorna swung into the saddle effortlessly. Penny explained to Elise how to mount, but with one foot in the stirrup Elise found it difficult to push herself off the ground. Brandysnap suddenly seemed huge. When she finally landed in the saddle all she could think of was how far away the ground looked.

'Comfortable?' Penny asked cheerfully.

'Yes,' Elise lied.

'Just relax,' Penny said. 'When Brandysnap moves, let your body go with him. He's your partner. You work together. We'll go down to the school and I'll explain about the correct seat.'

'You won't,' a voice said. 'I will.'

Blair Devlin came round the corner into the yard. He

was wearing his riding breeches and boots, but no hat or jacket. His open-necked white shirt had the sleeves characteristically rolled up to his elbows. He carried a riding crop. All three horses pricked up their ears and snickered in welcome. The two young girls smiled.

'You will?' Penny repeated in surprise. 'I thought you were going with Lorna.'

'I was,' Devlin said. 'But I've ricked my ankle.' He walked a few steps with a pronounced limp.

'Oh, dear,' Penny murmured, with a marked lack of sympathy. The two schoolgirls, however, looked worried.

'Are you all right, Dev?' one asked.

Devlin treated her to a charming smile. 'I'm in agony,' he said. 'But I'll survive.' He glanced at his watch. 'Isn't it about time you two went home?'

'We'll stay and help you give the lesson if you like,' the same girl suggested, hopefully.

'I've already been told off about keeping you here when you should be doing homework,' Devlin said. 'On your bikes, both of you.' He moved forward and took Brandysnap's reins. His grey eyes looked up at Elise. 'I think I can just about manage one pupil.' Turning to Penny he added: 'What're you standing around for? Don't you want to take Hobbit out?'

Penny grinned. 'What a question.' She mounted the horse quickly.

'Go round the old track way,' Devlin suggested. 'You'll get a good gallop out there.' He stood by Brandysnap until Penny and Lorna had disappeared from view and the two schoolgirls had reluctantly taken their mountain bikes and pedalled off down the road. When Devlin looked at Elise again his expression was both speculative and amused. 'I think we'll use the small indoor school. It's more cosy.'

'I thought you didn't teach beginners?' Elise said.

'Who told you that?' Brandysnap moved as Devlin

walked forward and Elise, startled by the unfamiliar movement, grabbed the front of the saddle. 'Relax,' Devlin said.

The smaller indoor school had high walls with a narrow opening along the top to let in light and air. Once the door was closed it was impossible to see in from the outside. Devlin let Brandysnap go. The horse wandered gently forward for a few steps while Elise rocked uncomfortably, then stopped and made a noise remarkably like a sigh. Devlin watched in amusement.

'I'd be happier if you'd keep hold of the reins,' Elise said.

'Brandy isn't going to take off at a gallop,' Devlin soothed.

'This is the first time I've ever been on a horse,' Elise reminded him.

'I know,' Devlin said. He walked round her slowly, inspecting her. 'It shows,' he added.

'You've forgotten your rather theatrical limp,' Elise observed acidly.

Devlin laughed. 'I heal quickly.' His grey eyes captured hers again, then moved down her body, but this time there was no sexual challenge in them. 'Now, let's try and make a horsewoman out of you.'

For the next half an hour Elise tried to remember, and put into practice, all of Devlin's instructions. When he ordered her to trot she had difficulty getting Brandysnap to liven up. He handed her the riding crop.

'Brandy knows you're a beginner,' he said. 'Wake him up with this.'

Elise tapped Brandysnap gently, afraid of hurting him. Brandysnap ignored her.

'For God's sake, woman,' Devlin said, irritated. 'Don't stroke him. Use that whip properly.'

A harder whack caused Brandysnap to whinny crossly, but at least encouraged him to amble forward at a faster pace. When he did break into a trot Elise felt as if she was being jolted from head to foot.

'Ride round the school,' Devlin instructed. 'Just sit. Let your body move with the horse. And don't cut corners.'

Elise soon realised that this was easier said than done. Brandysnap knew that she did not really have any idea how to control him. He trotted in increasingly smaller circles until he ended up in the middle of the school. Then he snorted, and stood still. As Elise tried unsuccessfully to make him move, Devlin walked over to her.

'You do understand English?' he enquired, smoothly polite.

'*I* do,' Elise said, breathless and angry. 'This horse doesn't.'

'You've got to let him know you're in control,' Devlin said. 'Trot round the school.' Elise tried to urge Brandysnap forward. Brandysnap refused to move, having obviously decided that he had done enough work for one day. 'He understands the aids,' Devlin insisted. 'Use your legs!'

'He doesn't understand anything!' Elise retaliated, her temper slipping. She thumped her heels against Brandysnap's sides, and even walloped him harder than she intended with the whip. Brandysnap simply turned his head slowly to look at her, and snickered. 'You see?' Elise said, in frustration. 'Why do you give beginners horses that want to sleep through the lesson?'

'Get off,' Devlin said, abruptly.

'Off?' Elise repeated.

'Off,' he confirmed. 'Dismount.' Elise managed to slide to the ground. 'There's nothing wrong with this horse.' Devlin took hold of Brandysnap's reins and mounted swiftly. 'He's sluggish, that's all. And that's an advantage for a beginner. If we gave you a horse like Solomon you'd soon take a fast trip between his ears.' Brandysnap had already perked up. His ears twitched.

Devlin crossed the stirrups over the saddle in front of him. 'You must take control,' he said. 'Watch.'

Brandysnap took a moment to realise that he had a different rider, then he huffed a few times and set off round the school at a lively trot, curving into each corner. After making one circuit, Devlin urged the horse into a canter. With his head up and his tail swishing in excitement Brandysnap looked like a different horse. And Devlin, she thought, looked effortlessly relaxed. She wondered if she would ever achieve even a small degree of the same skill.

Suddenly Devlin changed direction, cut diagonally across the school and stopped in front of her. He dismounted in one fluid movement, and grinned. 'You see? Brandy can do it – if you make him.'

'If I'd been riding since I was five, maybe I'd be able to make him,' Elise retorted.

Devlin laughed. 'That's no excuse. I was no boy wonder. I've had to work at it, and you'll have to do the same. Get back on.' He stood back and watched her as she struggled. 'Hurry up.'

'If you could just help me,' she said crossly. 'It isn't as easy as it looks.'

'You're just totally unfit,' he said. He moved up behind her and she felt his hand under her bottom. It lingered there for just longer than strictly necessary and then suddenly propelled her upward. Taken completely by surprise she pitched forward and ended up face downwards across the saddle. She felt Devlin's hand resting on her thighs.

'That's not quite right,' he said softly. His hand began to move, smoothly and firmly, stroking her leg and moving up to the curve of her bottom. 'But stay there.' One hand rested on the small of her back, holding her, the other slipped between her thighs, probing and pinching gently. He massaged her buttocks with the tips of his fingers and, despite herself, she gasped and wriggled.

'Is this part of the lesson?' she asked, breathlessly.

'No,' he said. 'But it's fun, isn't it?' His fingers searched between her legs. She was protected by the taut cloth of her breeches but she knew that she was already moist with pleasure, and for a moment she wished the breeches could be peeled off. Then she remembered exactly what she must look like. She tried to straighten up.

'What's the matter?' Devlin asked softly.

'Someone might see – ' she began.

'There's no one here,' he said. 'Penny and Lorna won't be back for some time. I sent Penny on the longest route, and she knows why. The two babies should be doing their homework by now, although I'd guess they're probably watching videos of the Horse of the Year show, or something equally educational.' He stopped fondling her, and swung her leg back over the saddle, turning her so that she faced Brandysnap's head. In a few moments, breathless and red faced, she was sitting upright again. 'We're all alone, Miss St John.' The whip tapped the side of his boot. 'Do you want the lesson to continue?'

She looked at him. 'Yes,' she said.

'Right,' he smiled. 'Take your hat off.' She hesitated, surprised. 'Take it off,' he repeated. She obeyed. He took the hat and tossed it to the side of the school. 'Untie your hair,' he said. Again she hesitated. 'You've got beautiful hair,' he said. 'I want to see it.' She reached up and pulled off the net that Lorna had given her. Her hair fell loosely around her shoulders. 'You should wear it like that more often,' he said.

'It gets in my way,' she said.

'When you go out with me,' he said, 'I want it loose.'

'And what makes you think I'm going out with you?' she challenged.

'You are,' he said.

'And suppose I said I wasn't?'

'I wouldn't believe you,' he said. 'Take your blouse off.' She stared, this time certain she had not heard him correctly. He was standing close to her and she looked down and met his expectant grey eyes. He took hold of Brandysnap's reins. 'Take it off,' he repeated. As if in a dream, she undid the buttons, opened the blouse, and let it slide off her shoulders. Underneath she was wearing a white stretch sports bra. He took the blouse from her. 'And that unflattering bra,' he added.

She suddenly realised what she must look like, sitting half-naked on a horse. 'I will not,' she said.

'You will,' he said, smiling. He put one hand on her thigh and moved it upward until he reached the waist band of her breeches. His fingers touched her flesh lightly and she shivered. 'Come on,' he said softly. 'I want to see if your breasts look as good as I think they do.'

She peeled off the bra slowly, pulling it over her head, shaking her hair free again. Devlin watched her. Once free of the bra's restriction she felt unexpectedly sexy. 'Do you like what you see?'

'Very nice,' he said. She waited for him to give her blouse back. 'Now trot,' he said. 'A sitting trot. Round the edge of the school.' When she hesitated, he added: 'If Lady Godiva can do it, you certainly can.'

'Her hair was longer than mine,' Elise said.

'Which will make your ride far more interesting,' he said. But she still looked round at the high walls of the school, briefly nervous. He noticed the look. 'We're alone here,' he repeated. 'This'll be a private performance. Just for me.' He took hold of Brandysnap's reins and led the horse to the edge of the school. Then he ran, forcing Brandysnap into a gentle trot. Letting go of the reins again he stood back. 'That's right,' he said. 'Keep going.'

Rather to Elise's surprise, Brandysnap did keep moving. She felt her breasts bouncing as she jogged round the school. She knew Devlin was watching them. The thought made her nipples harden.

'Very nice,' Devlin approved, when she had made one circuit of the school. 'One of these days you might make it as a rider.' He walked towards her and Brandysnap, seeing him, slowed to a halt. 'I could go on watching you,' he said. 'And you'd look even better if you stripped off the breeches.' She glanced at him, nervous now. 'Don't worry,' he grinned. 'Not in public. What kind of a man do you think I am?'

'I'm not sure,' she said. 'Can I have my blouse back now?'

'Sure,' he said, handing it to her. 'But don't put that terrible bra back on. It looks like a medical support. I like to see a woman's breasts moving about.' He grinned. 'It beats watching television any day.'

'I suppose you're a connoisseur?' She pulled the blouse on.

'I certainly am.' His grey eyes met hers. 'Of all the rounded parts of the female anatomy.'

'I'm glad I meet up to your standards,' she said lightly.

'Don't be too confident,' he said. 'I haven't inspected all of you – yet. Or tested you.' He went to fetch her hard hat and stopped a short distance behind her. 'Your bottom certainly looks interesting,' he said. 'But I'll reserve final judgement until I see it minus the breeches.'

'What makes you think you're going to?' she challenged.

He laughed. 'Stop playing hard to get. It isn't very convincing.' He took hold of Brandysnap's reins. 'Come on. I'll show you how to take Brandy's tack off.'

Back in the yard Devlin was the efficient instructor again. Then he led Elise to the general tack room and showed her where to store Brandysnap's saddle and bridle.

'You'll probably have Brandy next time you come,' he said. 'We like to keep beginners on the same horse for a while, unless they've got any objections.' He was standing very close to her now, a head taller than she was. She felt the wall against her back. 'Have you any objections?' he asked softly.

'To the horse?' Her voice was equally soft.

'Or the lesson?' He put his hands on her shoulders and slid them down until his fingers touched her inner arms. He stroked her lightly, concentrating on the soft skin in the crook of her elbows. 'We could arrange a refund,' he said, his mouth close to hers, 'if you weren't fully satisfied.'

'I haven't been fully satisfied yet,' she murmured.

'That can be arranged too,' he said.

His lips brushed hers, lightly at first. Then she felt the tip of his tongue gently probing. His hands moved to her waist, under her loose blouse, and upward. His mouth still on hers, he cupped her breasts gently, supporting their weight but deliberately avoiding her nipples, which were now taut with need. She felt her body begin to tremble. Her head was pressed back against the wall. Their long kiss became more violent, his tongue searching deeper. She felt him opening her blouse, and then his hands resumed their caresses, but still tantalising rather than satisfying, making her ache for a more demanding touch. She reached for his wrists and forced his fingers higher.

'No,' he said. 'I've got a better idea.'

He bent down and covered one nipple with his mouth. His tongue worked on her, his lips sucking gently. She made little gasping noises of pleasure. His hands slid down to her waist. then round to cup her bottom and pull her closer. She felt his trapped erection throbbing against her. His fingers dug into her flesh, harder now, but she relished the discomfort. She wanted him to rip open the zip on her riding breeches, drag them down, move his hands between her legs, arouse her just a little more, and then unzip himself and thrust into her. Right now, she thought. Standing up. Here. Now.

There was a noise outside. The clattering of hooves on the concrete yard. Devlin looked up. 'Damn,' he said, softly. 'They're back already. I'll give Penny the sack.' He pulled away from her and then glanced down at himself. 'How can I go outside like this? It'll make the horses jealous.'

Despite her feeling of frustration, Elise smiled. 'I'm sure Penny won't be shocked. Hasn't she seen it all before?'

'In her dreams, maybe,' he said, grinning. 'And your friend Lorna would like to.'

Elise buttoned her blouse hastily. 'You have a high opinion of your own charm, Mr Devlin.'

'I know when someone fancies me,' he said.

'And take advantage of it, too,' she said. 'So I've heard.'

He smoothed the front of his breeches. 'I have to admit that I'm not a virgin.' He reached out and fastened the last button of her blouse for her, his fingers brushing her nipples. 'And neither are you.'

'How do you know?' she retaliated.

'Experience,' he said. 'How many men have you had?'

'Mind your own business!' she retorted.

'Not too many,' he guessed. 'And no one like me.'

'What's so special about you?'

'I'm good looking,' he said. 'Virile. Imaginative . . .'

'And modest?' she interrupted.

'That too,' he agreed. 'And psychic.'

'Psychic?' she repeated, in surprise.

'I can predict the future,' he said. 'In a couple of days you'll receive a phone call asking you out to dinner. You'll accept.' His voice lowered. 'And after a splendid meal I'll take you home and show you exactly what you missed out on today.'

'Maybe,' she said. 'If I'm not busy.'

The door opened and Lorna came in with a saddle over her arm and a bridle in her hand.

'And see Penny about your next lesson,' Devlin said, smoothly. He walked towards the door. 'Good ride, Lorna?'

'Super,' Lorna said. She dumped her saddle on its stand and watched Devlin stride across the yard. She turned to Elise: 'Good lesson?'

'Interesting,' Elise said.

'And how were the extracurricula activities?'

'The what?' Elise repeated,

'You fucked, didn't you?' Lorna said bluntly.

'No, we didn't,' Elise said, primly. 'Mr Devlin was a perfect gentleman.'

'*Mr* Devlin?' Lorna repeated in amusement. 'Please! I'm your friend, remember? And I know *Mr* Devlin's reputation. Are you trying to tell me that he didn't even touch you up?' Elise opened her mouth to reply and Lorna added quickly. 'Before you perjure yourself, just take a look at your blouse.'

Elise glanced down and realised that her buttons were in the wrong holes. She blushed. Lorna laughed. 'Don't be embarrassed. Penny and I knew what was going to happen when Dev made that absolutely daft excuse so that he could stay behind and give you a lesson. Ricked his ankle, has he?' She glanced out of the door. 'It's healed pretty quickly. I don't see him limping now. Come on, be fair. We kept out of your way for nearly two hours. You're not going to tell me that Dev spent all that time talking about horses. What happened?'

'Nothing,' Elise repeated. 'Well, nothing much. You came back too soon. And there were no kinky suggestions.'

'I didn't think there would be,' Lorna said. She walked

out into the yard and Elise followed her. 'Not yet. He'll lead up to it gradually. A nice meal, some candlelight preliminaries, and then, later on, maybe a suggestion that you'd enjoy trying something sexy but a little different.'

'Is that what Penny told you?' Elise asked.

'Something like that.'

'Well, according to Dev, Penny's sexy fling is just wishful thinking,' Elise said.

'You didn't expect him to admit it, did you?' Lorna slid into the driving seat of her red Mini. 'He never admits to anything. He wouldn't admit that he's had his hands all over your chest, but I know he jolly well has and, judging from the smug expression on your face when I saw you in the tack room, he's explored a few other places as well!'

During the drive back to Shilden, Lorna tried to pry more details of Elise's riding lesson from her, but Elise refused to satisfy her curiosity. They finally cruised up the long drive to the castle and pulled into the forecourt.

'Look at that,' Lorna said, softly, her attention diverted from Elise at last. Ahead of them Max Lannsen was getting out of his Mercedes, a slim dark figure. 'What is it he's got that turns me on?'

'He's unavailable,' Elise guessed.

'It's a bit more than that,' Lorna said. 'The gardeners here are unavailable, but they don't do a thing for my sex drive.'

Lannsen stood still for a moment and looked up at the castle. Then he ran his hand over his hair and massaged the back of his neck before going inside. If he had noticed Lorna's car and its passengers he gave no sign of it.

'The Master of Shilden,' Lorna said, 'surveying his domain.'

'He always gave me the impression that he didn't really want any of this,' Elise said.

'Oh, really!' Lorna laughed. 'How could anyone *not* want this? You saw that awful house he lived in, in London. Come to think of it, how can he not want me? Here I am, all ready, willing and able, and happy to do anything he fancies and make a few suggestions of my own, too, and what do I get? Ignored!'

'Me too,' Elise said.

'It doesn't matter to you,' Lorna said. 'You've hooked Mr Devlin.'

Maybe I have, Elise thought. I certainly wanted him, back there at White Gates. And I'll accept his invitation if he does phone me. He's attractive and sexy and intelligent. So why does the sight of Max Lannsen still affect me so much? He's probably having an affair with that bossy Petra Altham. He certainly couldn't care less about me. Could he?

Chapter Four

*T*he phone call came when she least expected it. She was in the middle of a morning consultation with Petra Altham.

'Sorry if I've woken you up,' Blair Devlin's voice sounded cheerfully in her ear.

'Woken me up?' she repeated. 'What a cheek. I've been up for ages.'

He sounded amused. 'I thought you artistic types partied all night and got up at midday.'

'So when do you suppose we get our work done?' Elise asked, sweetly.

Petra looked at her suspiciously: 'Who is that? Not Max, surely?'

'A friend,' Elise said, unhelpfully. She was going to explain further, but stopped herself. Her private life was none of Petra Altham's business.

'Remember my promise?' Devlin asked.

'Of course,' she said.

'Want to take me up on it?'

'Yes.'

'I thought you would.'

She guessed that he was smiling. 'Well, you're psychic, aren't you?' She reminded him.

'Among other things,' he agreed. There was a pause. 'How about tomorrow night? The only problem is that I can't come and pick you up. I have a late lesson. Can you drive out here to White Gates? About half eight?'

'Of course.' Elise wondered if he intended to cook her a meal himself. That would make a change, she thought. She had never had a boyfriend who could cook. In order to test her theory she asked casually: 'Where are we going? Do you want me to dress up?'

'Never mind where we're going. You can wear anything you like on the outside. Smart but casual.' His voice changed. 'But if you really want to impress me, I'd like something black and sexy underneath.'

'And what if I haven't got anything like that?' she asked.

Petra was beginning to tap her fingers crossly.

'All women have got something like that,' Devlin said. 'All attractive women, anyway.' His voice lowered in tone. 'A black bra,' he said. 'Black lace, maybe. One of those bras that push your breasts up, with your nipples showing through.'

'I think I can manage that,' Elise said. She knew that Petra was getting more impatient by the minute. 'Anything else?' she asked.

'Black stockings,' he said. 'With seams. Nice thin lines running down the back of your legs, and those wide dark tops like garters. Am I asking too much?'

'No,' she said. 'I'm full of surprises.'

'I hope so.' She guessed he was smiling. 'It's the contrast I like. The black and the pale skin. How about stiletto heels?'

'Yes,' she said. 'Those too.'

'You're a sexy lady, aren't you?'

'Of course.'

In fact, the stockings and shoes had been part of a hastily-put-together costume she had worn to a college 'vicars and tarts' fancy dress party. But she had no intention of telling Blair Devlin that.

There was another pause. 'You don't have one of those corsets, do you? You know – a basque?'

'No,' Elise said. 'Sorry. Too uncomfortable.'

'Well, you wouldn't have to wear it for long,' he said. 'I just thought I'd enjoy undoing those hooks and finding out what's underneath.'

'You know that already,' she reminded him.

'I'm still not certain if you're a natural redhead,' he explained. 'I'm looking forward to finding out.'

Petra tapped her pen sharply on the desk top. 'We have work to do, you know.'

'I've got to go,' Elise said. 'Duty calls.'

'Not Lannsen?' Devlin's voice changed. 'Is he hassling you?'

'He's not even here.' She was surprised at the obvious anger in his voice.

'Don't let him get to you. I've heard he's a bastard to work for.'

'I hardly ever see him,' she said.

'Perhaps that's just as well.' Devlin's voice became warmer again. 'See you tomorrow.' He paused. 'Sorry I can't come for you, but duty calls for me too.'

'If you've quite finished chatting to your ... friend,' Petra said irritably, when Elise put down the phone, 'can we get back to the plans for the dungeon now? It's going to be something of a selling point, so it's got to be good.' She tapped her note pad. 'You know the kind of thing these S&M people like?'

'No,' Elise said. 'I don't.'

'Theatrical stuff,' Petra explained. 'This is a fantasy area, but it's got to look good. Our kind of people will expect that. We're talking class here. We don't want any red light bulbs and tacky wallpaper. Authentic looking, but all good taste.'

'A tasteful torture chamber,' Elise agreed, straight faced.

Petra gave her a sharp look. 'You *are* taking this seriously, I hope?'

'Yes,' Elise said. 'It's just that I find it difficult to associate dungeons with sex.'

'Not your kind of thing?' Petra looked at her calculatingly.

'Not really.'

'So what is?' Petra asked. It sounded casual but Elise had a curious feeling that there was more than just feminine curiosity behind the question.

'Well,' she hedged, 'I'm rather ordinary, I suppose. I just like ... well ... sex with someone I really fancy. Or someone I'm in love with.'

'But if someone you loved wanted something unusual,' Petra persisted, 'you'd experiment, wouldn't you?'

'Maybe,' Elise said, hoping Petra would change the subject.

But Petra seemed unwilling to oblige. 'Haven't you ever wondered what it would be like to try something different? Surely you have fantasies?'

'Of course.'

'You've never wanted to put them into practice?'

'Not really,' Elise lied.

'Oh, come on!' Petra smiled. 'I don't believe you. You might not want to be tied up and whipped, or chained up in a dungeon, even in fun, but there must be *something* that really turns you on?'

'Just being with someone I love?' Elise repeated. The last thing she wanted to do was discuss her sexual preferences and daydreams with Petra Altham.

'The missionary position, and no extras?' Petra laughed unkindly. 'Darling, you're never going to hold a man if you insist on that.'

Because she suspected that Petra was deliberately trying to bait her, Elise was able to keep her temper.

'At the moment, holding a man is the last thing I'm interested in,' she said coolly. 'I want to earn money and then travel the world.' It wasn't strictly true, but she hoped it would stop Petra's questions. 'That's why we're all here, isn't it?' she added. 'For the money?'

Petra stared at her, but obviously sensed that Elise was not going to be forced into any personal admissions.

'Of course,' she agreed, and turned back to her list, the efficient businesswoman again 'Right. We'll have a whipping post, and some form of stand-up stocks. And a rack.' She looked up at Elise. 'Are you making a note of all this?'

'I can remember it,' Elise said. The mention of the rack brought back memories of her previous fantasy. She had been enjoying it, she remembered, until she felt that Max Lannsen was watching her. Would she have gone on enjoying it if he had stepped forward and taken part? She rather thought she would. Maybe she wasn't completely out of sympathy with this form of sexual play.

'And plenty of hooks and chains,' Petra added. 'On the walls and the ceiling. We'll get some builders in to fix some strengthened beams.' Elise smiled and Petra added sharply: 'Is that amusing? Let me in on the joke?'

'I was just wondering what the local builders will think,' Elise said.

'They won't,' Petra said shortly. 'We'll get men from London. The locals gossip enough as it is. They seem to think they own Shilden. But it belongs to Max. And he can do what he likes with it.'

But is this what he likes, Elise wondered? A theme hotel obviously intended to cater for people with somewhat bizarre sexual tastes? He had already told her he needed to make Shilden financially viable. Was this the only idea he could come up with? She had to admit that it would probably be successful. A lot of money was being put into the project. Max Lannsen's backers must have been sure they would get their money back – with profits.

'We need some sketches for the carpenters,' Petra said. 'And I'll want to see your design proposals. But don't make them too dark and gloomy. Remember, people will be coming to this dungeon to have fun.'

'She was quizzing me,' Elise said to Lorna. 'It was almost as if she thought I might be interested in performing in her classy dungeon.'

'Would you?' Lorna asked casually.

'No, of course not.'

'The pay would be good.'

Elise stared at her. 'Exactly what is going to happen here? I assumed businessmen could bring their girl friends up for a fun weekend. But you're suggesting providing women for sex, aren't you? And paying them?'

'Maybe,' Lorna agreed. 'Why not? You'd expect to pay more conventional entertainers, wouldn't you? Singers, dancers, whatever? If women come up here to party as friends of the guests, that's fine. If they're asked to act out some kind of fantasy scenario, what's wrong with that? You've worked in the theatre. Don't actors get paid?'

'Oh, come on!' Elise retorted, with a touch of anger. 'Let's take off the rose-coloured spectacles, for heaven's sake!'

'Selling sex isn't illegal, actually,' Lorna said.

'Living off the proceeds is,' Elise countered.

'No one will be living off the proceeds,' Lorna said. 'Shilden is going to be a viable business concern. If the guests make private arrangements or hand out gifts, that's their business.' She grinned. 'What's bothering you? The morality thing – or are you worried that gorgeous Max will end up in jail?'

'I just like to know where I stand,' Elise said.

'You're an employee,' Lorna said. 'Bona fide, and all that. Just like me. All we've got to do is collect our nice fat wage packets. Any other arrangements we make are our business.' She grinned suddenly. 'And don't play innocent with me, either. You didn't really think you're being paid here just to design pretty rooms for honeymoon couples, did you?'

No, Elise thought, as she showered and changed. I knew that Jannine's assessment was probably right. I guessed it from the first interview, and my first visit to Shilden confirmed it. And Lorna's right. Why should I censor what other people do, as long as no one's forced, and they enjoy it? Why does it bother me? Because, she realised, Max Lannsen is involved. And I suppose I wish he wasn't. I'm not comfortable with the idea of someone living off immoral earnings, or whatever the law calls it, even if the women concerned are happy with the situation. And I'd hate anyone who treated women like merchandise, or as sex objects.

So why did I enjoy making Max Lannsen a white slave trader in my fantasy? she wondered. Because it was precisely that, she thought – make believe. And unlike a real life situation, he was in a position of power over her because she put him there. She was in control. It was like acting. Drama students had often told her how they enjoyed playing parts that were quite alien to their normal character. It was a release. And, she suspected, it was also fun. And this is fun, too, she thought, as she searched through her clothes for the black bra and silk stockings. I'll be tarty for Mr Devlin, if that's what he wants.

She found the bra and stockings bundled up with an old white shirt. The shirt had the face of a once-favourite actor printed on the back. An art college friend had produced it for her as part of a project. She realised that she could look at the picture now without any reaction at all. It was just a good-looking young man, smiling at her. And yet, not so long ago, she would have undressed for him if he had so much as crooked his finger in her direction. Am I fickle, or what? she wondered. No, she told herself, you've simply grown up!

She unrolled the bra and stockings, remembering the 'vicars and tarts' party. It had amazed her that the more reserved looking students had been the ones to flaunt themselves most brazenly. Several girls had worn see-through blouses. One had worn a basque that pushed her naked breasts upward, and had rouged her nipples to emphasise the display. Another, in a short school gymslip, had dispensed with her knickers – and had bent down frequently in order to prove it. A girl who had always dressed in dowdy, unisex-style clothes turned up in an extraordinary rubber corset – and attracted quite a crowd of admiring 'vicars'. And she had surprised herself too, wearing a sexily tight and uncomfortable costume, but secretly enjoying the feeling of erotic restriction that her clothes gave her. She remembered the way the bra had forced her breasts upward and together, giving her an impressive cleavage and making her look a size larger than she actually was. All in all, it had been an enlightening party.

On impulse, she slipped off her silky tunic and put the bra on. It still felt tight and not very comfortable, but it definitely made her feel sexy. More searching unearthed the black stilettos, a black suspender belt, and black panties. She sat on the bed and rolled one stocking carefully over her knee. Stretching out her leg she admired the dark silky sheen it gave her flesh. With both stockings on, pulled taut by the suspenders, she slipped on the stilettos, stood up and went to the full-length mirror attached to her wardrobe door.

She stood with her legs astride. Then turned and straightened the stocking seams. She remembered reading somewhere that men liked seamed stockings because they could imagine the thin black line showing beneath a skirt hem pointing the way to some interesting hidden places. She remembered Blair Devlin's hands exploring her as she lay across Brandysnap's saddle. She imagined his fingers lightly following the seam at the back of her legs. The thought was actually making her wet. He was certainly attractive, no doubt about that. And if he really was the local stud, as Lorna claimed, it might even be a bonus. He would be looking for a no-strings affair. No commitment, just fun. And that's exactly what I want, she told herself.

Bunching her hair, she then twisted it into a loose knot on top of her head, teased out several long curly strands to frame her face, and smiled. Did she really look something like a redheaded version of the young Brigitte Bardot? Maybe I do, she thought, if you sort of half close your eyes and use a bit of imagination. Would this image please Blair Devlin? She rather thought it would.

And what about Max Lannsen? What would he think of this blatantly sexy redhead in black underwear? She imagined his dark-suited figure, his shadowed face, then looked back at her own reflection. Not his style, she decided. But what was? Something more subtle? Or something more outrageous? Maybe he liked his women encased in rubber? Or trussed up in bizarre leather and chains? Why should I care, anyway, she thought crossly. Despite that one brief moment in the cellar, I don't think Max Lannsen has ever really thought of me as a woman.

The following evening Elise decided to take Devlin at his word, and wear something 'smart but casual'. The obvious choice was one of her Sellick's suits but, instead of a primly businesslike white blouse, she chose a pale silk knit top. It was the first time she had worn the scoop necked, sleeveless top with an under-wired bra, and she was slightly startled at the provocative shape it gave her. Even under the loosely tailored jacket her swelling cleavage was quite obvious. Combined with the black stiletto heels the effect was surprisingly sexy.

As she drove towards White Gates, Elise wondered idly why Devlin has asked her to meet him at his home. Even if he had to give a lesson, he could simply have picked her up at a later time. She wondered if he was trying to avoid being seen at Shilden. But by whom? Certainly not Lorna. Mrs Stokes? That was equally ridiculous. Petra Altham? The idea was ludicrous, she had only just arrived at the castle. Max Lannsen? She could not think of any reason for Devlin to avoid Lannsen – even if he disliked him, as most locals seemed to. Perhaps she was just being suspicious. White Gates was nearer to Alnwick than Shilden. It was sensible to go straight from there into town. She drove through the wide white gates that gave the riding school its name and parked in her usual place. The only other car was a black Subaru estate. As she got out of her Mini she saw a door open and Blair Devlin appeared.

He did not look like a man who had just given a riding lesson. He was smartly but casually dressed in pale trousers and a beautifully tailored hacking jacket over a cream coloured polo shirt. She hesitated for a moment, expecting him to walk towards her, but he simply lifted his hand in greeting and smiled. She walked towards him, hoping the thin stiletto heels would not turn on a loose stone. As she approached him she could see his eyes exploring her. She stopped in front of him. His eyes lingered very obviously on her scoop neckline for a few seconds longer, then moved to her face. He grinned.

'Very nice,' he said. 'I love seeing women walk in high-heeled shoes.'

'You've just come from giving a riding lesson, have you?' she countered.

'Well, to be honest,' he said, 'the riding lesson was cancelled at the last minute. Not that I minded. It means we can go and have something to eat right now.' He paused. 'And then come back here.'

'You're nothing if not direct,' she said.

'I'm just planning to keep my promise,' he said.

Rather to her surprise he did not turn the Subaru towards Alnwick, but headed back to Shilden village, going by a route that avoided the castle. The car stereo played soft music, and Devlin skilfully managed to get her to talk about herself. So skilfully, in fact, that when he finally stopped outside the village pub, she realised that she still knew virtually nothing about him although she had told him quite a bit about her own ambitions. She also realised that this was the pub where Lorna had received a less than friendly welcome. Inside it looked cosy enough: genuine beams, horse brasses. darts trophies and one or two locals leaning against the bar. And the middle-aged publican's smile was equally welcoming.

'Hello, Mr Devlin. Nice to see you.' The man's accent was obviously local. His smile switched to Elise; an appreciative smile. 'And your friend.'

'This is Elise, George,' Devlin said. 'She works at Shilden Castle.' George's smile wavered for a moment. He glanced at Devlin. 'Elise is from London,' Devlin said smoothly. 'She's decorating the place for Lannsen. That's all.'

George seemed to relax. He picked up a glass and began to polish it. 'The usual for you, Mr Devlin?' When Devlin nodded, George poured a measure of whisky. His smile was welcoming again. 'And for your lady?'

'A glass of white wine, please,' Elise said.

George poured it for her. 'How do you like Northumberland?' he asked.

'It's beautiful,' Elise said, with genuine enthusiasm.

'Well, I reckon so, too,' George said. 'But then I'm a local.'

'When can we eat?' Devlin asked.

'About half an hour,' George said. 'Margaret's sorting the food out now.'

Devlin led Elise to a corner seat. 'I hope you're not on a diet,' he said. 'Margaret never deals out small portions.'

As they sat and talked more people came into the pub. Elise recognised at least one man from the Shilden work force – a gardener who had never acknowledged her attempts at friendly conversation. He made no effort to mask his surprise when he saw Elise.

Devlin lifted a hand in greeting: 'Bill. How's your hip?'

The gardener seemed to dither for a moment, then walked towards them. 'It's fine, Mr Devlin,' he said, in his lilting Northumberland accent. For a moment his eyes flickered from Devlin to Elise and back again. Devlin smiled.

'Bill had a plastic hip joint fitted,' he explained to Elise. 'It took his wife years to persuade him. He was afraid of going into hospital.'

'Don't trust 'em,' Bill agreed. 'Walk in, come out feet first.'

Devlin laughed. 'You hobbled in, and now look at you.'

'There's always exceptions,' Bill said darkly. 'I was lucky, that's all.' He nodded amicably to them both, then ambled back to the bar.

'I've been trying to get that man to talk to me for weeks,' Elise said. 'He always ignored me.'

'That was when he thought you were part of Lannsen's staff,' Devlin said. 'Now you're with me.'

'And that makes a difference?'

'Of course.'

112

'Why?'

Devlin smiled. 'Because I'm a local,' he said.

But she knew there was more to it than that. Blair Devlin was obviously well liked by this community, but they treated him with unusual respect. George and Bill were much older than Devlin, but they both called him 'mister'? George had called all his other customers, regardless of age, by their first names. When George's wife, Margaret, brought their meal – an excellent traditional roast – the pattern was repeated. She gave Elise a friendly smile of welcome, but Elise knew she was accepted only because she was Devlin's companion. It was a strange feeling, rather like being with royalty.

She wondered what Blair Devlin had done to deserve this treatment. He was obviously rich. White Gates proved that. Even if he shared the costs with a partner you needed money to run a riding school. Perhaps he had other financial interests that provided the locals with jobs? That would undoubtedly make him popular. Would everyone have been so respectful if they had known what *Mr* Devlin was planning to do with the rest of his evening, she wondered?

She glanced across the table at him. Blair Devlin was probably about the same age as Max Lannsen, she thought but, although his lean, tanned face showed strength and determination, it lacked the edge of danger that Lannsen projected. She could not imagine him as a ruthless businessman. She admitted to herself that originally she had not been able to see Lannsen in this role either but, now she knew exactly what he had planned for Shilden Castle, she was beginning to change her mind.

After the meal, Devlin seemed in no hurry to leave. By the time he finally suggested she might like a brief tour of the countryside she felt that nearly all the residents of Shilden village had seen her. Maybe that was what he had intended, she thought, as they walked towards the car. Maybe he wanted her to be seen, knowing that it would ensure that she was accepted.

'Have you been to Just Man's Hill?' he asked, as she snapped her seat belt on.

'No.' she said. 'I've been very busy. I haven't really had time to explore the countryside.'

'Slave driver, is he?' Devlin started the engine.

'Max Lannsen?' She knew very well that was who he meant. 'I don't see that much of him. I work with a woman called Petra Altham at the moment.'

'But you both take orders from Lannsen?'

'We both get a wage packet from him, too,' she countered.

But, as she said it, she wondered if it was strictly true. Lorna had already said there were many other investors involved in the castle's transformation. Devlin drove in silence for a while.

'So Max Lannsen really is the money behind all that's going on at Shilden?' he said at last, turning the car into a narrow side road.

'I don't know,' Elise admitted. 'He owns Shilden. I think there are other people involved in his plans. Why are you so interested?'

'It's a local thing,' Devlin said, lightly. 'Shilden has always been part of our lives. We're a bit concerned about what's happening to it.'

'Nothing's happening to it,' Elise said. 'If anything, you might say Max Lannsen has improved the place. A lot of money's been spent on renovations.'

Devlin parked the car and switched off the engine. 'That's one way of looking at it, I suppose,' he said, in a neutral voice. Then his voice changed. 'Come on, I'll show you one of the local beauty sites.'

Elise looked out of the car and saw a steep path winding upward through trees. 'You don't expect me to walk, do you?' she asked.

'Why not?' he grinned. 'You're a healthy young woman.'

'You seem to have forgotten that my shoes aren't exactly designed for hiking.'

'I hadn't forgotten,' he said. 'Take them off. There's a pair of trainers in the boot. I'll get them.'

When he came back with the shoes she had already swung her legs out of the car. 'Prepared for everything, aren't you?' she teased.

'Five years in the Boy Scouts,' he explained gravely. 'It leaves its mark.' His gaze shifted from her face to her knees. 'And take those stockings off. They're too nice to get laddered.'

She pulled her skirt up until it reached her black suspenders. 'Don't look,' she chided.

'I intend to do more than look,' he said. 'Later on.'

She rolled one stocking down slowly, aware of his eyes. As she lifted her knee Devlin shifted his position, but before he could move in front of her and take advantage of the view under her skirt, she pulled the stocking off and tossed it over her shoulder. He stayed where he was, waiting for her to repeat the action. She took her time, rather enjoying this chaste striptease. Again she stretched out her leg, and bent it – she knew she had good legs, and she certainly did not mind displaying them – but this time she kept her thighs as close as possible, spoiling the view he was obviously hoping for. She pulled the trainers on and stood up, smoothing down her skirt.

'Spoilsport,' he said.

'I won a badge for it,' she explained, sweetly. 'In the Girl Guides.'

She followed him up the winding path to the top of the hill. The trees thinned, revealing an unexpected, sweeping panorama of fields. With the sun beginning to set and the shadows lengthening, it had a peaceful beauty of a simple watercolour.

'It's lovely,' Elise said, and meant it.

'Typical Northumberland country,' Devlin said. There was obvious pride in his voice.

'Is there any reason why this is called Just Man's Hill?' she asked.

'It's supposed to have been the site where the villagers settled any local disputes,' Devlin said. 'They came up here and sorted things out, one way or another. The Just Man was the name given to the arbiter, or judge.'

'Who was it? The Master of Shilden?'

Devlin lifted an eyebrow. 'You've heard all about that?'

'I've heard a little,' she said. 'The owner is Shilden Castle automatically becomes the master, isn't that right?'

'Not exactly,' Devlin said. 'Until now the castle has always passed to a direct descendant of the acting master, or to a family member he named. This time it didn't happen. The old master died unexpectedly, and no one found a will. Inheriting Shilden makes Lannsen the legal owner, but the villagers will never accept him as master, even if his schemes are providing a bit of local work.'

'I don't think he really wants the title, anyway,' she said.

'It wouldn't make any difference if he did,' Devlin said shortly.

A cold wind blew suddenly and the sun disappeared behind some night clouds. Elise shivered.

'Back to the car,' Devlin said. 'You'll feel warmer with your stockings on.'

The went into the trees again. As they walked, Devlin reached out and snapped off a thin branch. He bent it between his hands, then slapped it lightly against the side of his leg.

'Missing your whip?' Elise asked, innocently.

He grinned. 'I can always improvise.' He tapped her

gently under the chin. She stood still. 'That's something else I learnt in the Boy Scouts.' The tip of the branch traced a line down her neck. It felt like a rough finger touching her skin. Travelling along the edge of her neckline, it began to explore the round swell of her breasts. It probed her cleavage, then searched for her nipples, but it was such a light touch she could hardly feel it through the lace cups of the underwired bra. It was tantalising because it promised, and did not deliver.

Devlin stepped closer. Holding the branch in both hands he rested it under her breasts, then pushed upwards, lifting them. His thumbs moved to her nipples, and he rubbed gently until he felt them harden under his touch. Still fondling her, he bent forward and kissed her, lightly. She responded by opening her mouth and meeting his exploring tongue with her own. As the kiss grew deeper she could feel him trying to tug down the scoop neck of her silky top and free her breasts. The top gave way easily enough, but the underwired bra was too tight for him to move.

'Unfasten this damn thing,' he muttered.

'You wanted me to wear a black bra,' she murmured back, her lips teasing his ear.

'This isn't a bra,' he growled. 'It's armour.'

She laughed softly and reached behind her back to undo the hook. As he felt the straps loosen, Devlin pushed her jacket back over her shoulders with one hand and used the other to ease her breasts upward, out of the bra.

'That's better.' He moved back to look at her. The tip of the branch touched each nipple in turn. She shuddered with need as he played with her. 'I hope it won't be as difficult to get the rest of your clothes off.' Leaning forward he explored her exposed skin with his mouth and tongue, until he reached the hard bud of her nipple and nipped it gently between his teeth, tugging just hard enough to be exciting.

'Ouch!' she said. 'They didn't teach you that in the Boy Scouts!'

He looked up and grinned lazily. 'They were sadly lacking in some educational departments,' he agreed. His eyes admired her again. 'But we were taught to keep our word – and I said I'd take you back to the car. Come on.'

Once inside the Subaru, Devlin reached for the silk stockings. 'Stretch out your legs,' he ordered. When she did so he eased a stocking over her foot and unfurled it slowly to her knee. 'Lift your skirt.' She obeyed. He continued to slide the stocking up to her thigh. He surprised her by fastening the suspenders without difficulty.

'You've done that before,' she said.

'Every chance I get,' he agreed. 'Which isn't often enough.'

He put on the second stocking with equal skill but, this time, his hand lingered on her thigh. His fingers reached up until they found the edge of her panties. She felt him searching, and knew that the moist warmth between her legs would tell him what he wanted to know. She was right. He slid his hand round underneath her bottom, and pulled her up towards him. His lips touched her ear.

'Enjoying yourself?' he murmured.

'Yes, thank you, sir,' she replied.

'I'd like to take your knickers off and tongue you right now,' he said. 'But it's damned uncomfortable in a car. Let's go home.'

She reached between his legs and closed her fingers round the bulge of his erection 'Think you'll last out?' She massaged him, gently increasing the pressure.

'Not if you do that,' he admitted.

She withdrew her hand. 'All right. Concentrate on the road.'

It was dark when they arrived back at White Gates. A

horse snickered softly. Elise thought she heard an owl hoot. Inside the house Devlin switched on the hall light.

'You live here on your own?' Elise asked.

'Through choice,' he said.

'You mean you could have dozen female companions if you wanted to?'

'I mean, I'm not the marrying kind,' he said. He moved closer to her. 'But you knew that, didn't you?'

'I suspected it,' she admitted, lightly.

'And it doesn't bother you?'

'I'm glad,' she said. 'Right now, I'm not the marrying kind either.'

'Sensible lady,' he said, softly. 'We'll have the fun without the heartache. Agreed?'

'Sounds good,' she said.

She followed him into his living room. It was furnished with old-fashioned easy chairs and a settee. There were several small tables, one of them stacked with riding magazines. Hanging over the large fireplace was a painting of a woman urging a massive horse over a jump. There were photographs of horses on shelves, and on the tables, and several pictures of Devlin accepting rosettes and trophies. Elise could not help contrasting the room's comfortable, lived-in feeling with the sterile perfection of Ralph's flat.

Devlin her poured her a drink. He's sexy and he's honest, she thought. And he can't possibly have any ulterior motive about starting an affair with me. What could I possibly have that he wants? He's certainly not interested in a modelling contract. But he would look great on the glossy pages of a men's magazine, she thought. Better than Ralph, in fact. More masculine. Ralph thought he looked good with his carefully built muscles, but Blair Devlin had the casual, rangey hardness that came from his outdoor lifestyle. Although she disliked blood sports she imagined him in hunting clothes: pale breeches, glossy boots, and a black jacket topped by the neatly tied stock. He would wear the clothes with the natural ease of familiarity. Ralph could pose by a stable gate, in an elegant riding outfit, next to a horse, but he would always look like a model, playing let's pretend.

And what would Max Lannsen look like, dressed for the hunt? Dark and slim, with that dangerous element of the unknown about him. The image came to her unexpectedly, and made her suddenly angry. Why am I thinking about Lannsen? she thought. He sure as hell isn't thinking about me. And neither is Ralph. He's too busy having his bottom smacked by his bossy dominatrix mistress! She grinned suddenly at the thought.

'What's funny?' Devlin handed her a glass of wine.

'Just remembering my former boyfriend,' she said, truthfully.

'He was amusing?'

'He was a bastard. I was thinking about him with his girlfriend.'

'The one after you?'

'The one he had at the same time as me,' she said.

'He had both of you?' Devlin sounded surprised. And interested. 'Together, or one at a time?'

'Separately,' she said. 'Only I didn't know it.' She briefly explained what had happened, but pretended she had found the affair amusing rather than hurtful. 'So that was the end of that little fling,' she finished.

'Is that why you came to Shilden?' Devlin asked. 'Too many memories in London?'

'I wanted a change of scenery,' she said lightly.

'London's loss is my gain.' He smiled and looked at her speculatively over his whisky glass.

'Would you ever consider a threesome?'

'Me – and two men?' she parried. 'Well, I might.'

'I meant me – and two women,' he said, grinning.

'You think you could satisfy two of us?'

'I know damn well I could.'

'You've done it before?'

He laughed. 'No, I haven't. But I'd like to try.' He paused. 'Would you like to test me?'

She put her wine glass down. 'I'd like to see how well you perform with one woman first,' she said.

He finished his whisky, walked towards her and held out his hands. 'Then stand up,' he said. She let him pull her to her feet. 'And walk,' he ordered. He moved behind her and sat in her chair. 'Walk round the room. And take off that jacket.' She walked slowly, unbuttoned the jacket and dropped it on the floor. 'Untidy,' he said, 'but I don't mind. Now the skirt.' She unzipped it and it fell to her ankles. 'I'm impressed,' he said, appreciatively. 'You've got a great arse, you know that? And great legs. And you move well. Now get that top off.' She stood still and began to pull the silky top up over her head. 'But keep walking,' he added. 'Keep moving.' Pulling the top over her head loosened her hair. She encouraged it to fall by shaking her head. Then she reached for the straps of her bra. Slipping them over her shoulders she peeled the lace cups down, unfastened the back hook, and tossed the garment over her shoulder. Smiling, she pirouetted in front of him, her hands covering her nipples.

'Come here,' he said.

'You want to inspect the merchandise?' she teased. 'How much are you offering for a quick peek?'

'I've seen your nipples, remember?' he said. 'And tasted them. I want to see if you're a natural redhead. Stand in front of me.' She obeyed. 'Closer,' he said. She stood with her own knees almost touching his. 'Spread your legs,' he ordered. 'Stop playing the bashful virgin.'

She straddled his thighs. He reached out and pulled the edge of her lacy black panties aside, revealing her curly, red-gold pubic hair.

'Satisfied?' she asked lightly.

'Not yet,' he said.

121

One finger searched between her legs. His thumb found her erect clitoris. He rubbed it for a few minutes, until her breathing quickened and her hips began to thrust and wriggle. Then he pushed one exploratory finger inside her. Although his hand was restricted by the tight panties he managed to keep his thumb in a position that continued to give her pleasure. She moaned softly, and writhed against him. He thrust harder, his thumb still rubbing, and she moaned again. Her legs bent and suddenly she was sitting astride his lap, her nipples close to his mouth. He brushed them with his lips, tickled the hardening buds with the tip of his tongue, then leant back to watch as they contracted into even tighter peaks.

'Beautiful,' he said. 'I love to see a woman get excited.' He licked her again. 'What does it feel like when I do this?'

'Nice,' she groaned.

'Nice?' he repeated. His tongue traced a path round each nipple in turn, gently. Then he closed his lips, caught her with his teeth, and sucked hard. It was so unexpected that she gave a little squeal of surprise. He withdrew his finger from her vagina but, before she could protest, he reinserted two fingers, pushing them higher than before, moving them more rapidly, and resuming his expert fondling of her clitoris. 'Just nice? Come on, now. You can do better than that. Which excites you more? This?' He pushed with his hand. 'Or this?' His thumb circled and rubbed.

'Both,' she gasped.

'No preference?'

'No.' Her body was beginning to shake with need.

'How about this?' His mouth fondled her again, and she felt his tongue working.

'It's good.'

'You want me to stay up here?' he persisted. 'Or move down a little?'

'Move,' she said. She was not really concentrating on his questions – or her answers. Whatever he did was fine by her. As long as he did not stop!

'Down?' he said. His thumb pushed against her. 'Down here? How quickly will you come if I tongue you? Let's test your self-control.' He withdrew his hand suddenly and grasped the sides of her panties. 'Move back,' he said.

She stepped backwards and, in a moment, her panties were round her knees, then on the floor. He stood up and turned her round, resting his hands briefly on her bottom. Then he pushed her down in the armchair where he had been sitting a moment before. Before she realised it he had knelt between her legs. She was already swollen and wet. The warmth of his mouth and the probing excitement of his tongue brought her to a climax almost at once. Her hips thrust upwards and she cried out as her body shuddered and jerked. With her heart pounding, she lay back. Through half-closed eyes she could see Devlin watching her.

'Not a lot of self-control,' he said. 'But you looked good. You looked great.' He gave her a few minutes to recover, then tugged her to her feet again, and reversed their positions. 'I'll show you self-control,' he said. 'Use your mouth. Mouth and hands. If you can make me come, I'll give you free riding lessons for a year.'

She unzipped his trousers and freed his impressive erection. His cock was so stiff she felt certain it would be easy to tease it into orgasm. She tried all the tricks she knew, licking and nibbling, sucking and biting, working on him gently and roughly, trying to discover which treatment he liked the best but, although he groaned and writhed in the chair, especially when she cupped his balls in her hands, massaging him with insistent fingers and with strong movements of her tongue, he retained his erection despite all her efforts.

'You'll have to go on paying for your lessons, won't you?' he said finally.

She looked up at him: 'Another minute?'

'No way.' At least his voice sounded strained, she thought. 'Time's up.'

'I didn't know there was a time limit,' she protested.

He reached for her, positioning her astride his knees. His hands slid up to her bottom. He pulled her closer and entered her smoothly. 'Make me come now,' he said huskily. 'Do it for me.'

She sat still. 'Another minute and I'd have won,' she accused.

'Move your arse, woman,' he groaned. 'Work!'

She smiled, and tightened her vaginal muscles, gripping him, pulling him deeper.

'That's right,' he murmured. 'Keep doing it.'

'What about my free riding lessons?' she insisted, sitting still again.

He groaned. 'You've got them!'

She held him as he thrust into her, then rocked backwards and forwards, enjoying the sensation of his cock deep inside her, enjoying the slow build-up of her own sensations. He moved rhythmically, his eyes closed. At first his movements were controlled, but soon she felt his body begin to shake as the orgasmic spasms gripped him. Hoping to climax with him she thrust harder against him. She felt his fingers digging into her flesh, but relished the slight pain it caused her because the expression on his face, and the violence of his movements, proved the intensity of his pleasure. He climaxed suddenly, writhing so violently she thought they would both be deposited on the floor. After a few moments his body calmed and he sighed deeply. Her own orgasm was less powerful this time, but she was happy enough to know that she had pleased him.

'Jesus,' he said, 'that was good.'

They lay close together for a while then Devlin said:

'If you'd like to tidy yourself up I'll make us both a coffee. Or would you like something stronger?'

'Coffee would be fine,' she said.

He directed her to the bathroom. She had a quick shower, but stuffed her underwired bra in her bag rather than put it back on. Then she powdered herself with some of Devlin's pleasantly masculine talc. There was no evidence that any female used this bathroom, which was panelled with dark wood and had Victorian-style brass taps. Back in the living room she smelt fresh coffee and almost immediately after she sat down Devlin arrived with a tray. The coffee was excellent, and she told him so.

'Another of my many talents,' he said modestly. 'I'm not a bad cook, either. I'll prove it to you sometime.'

'Is there anything you can't do well?' she teased.

'I can't think of anything at the moment,' he admitted, grinning. 'Teaching, cooking, making coffee, making love. I'm good at all of them.'

'Well, I'll have plenty of chances to test the teaching,' she said. 'Don't forget you owe me free riding lessons for a year.'

'I haven't forgotten.' He grinned. 'You can ride me every day for a year, and it won't cost you a penny. How's that?'

'That wasn't quite what I had in mind,' she said.

'But you're not objecting?' He leant back lazily and watched her through half-closed eyes. 'If you think I'd be too much for you, I'll arrange for another woman to join us. With my control I could ride both of you in turn and make you both come, then choose which of you could do the honours for me.'

She put her coffee cup down. 'And supposing we rebelled? Two to one – you wouldn't stand a chance.'

'I'm more than a match for two women.'

'Don't be too sure. We could drug your coffee. You'd fall asleep and wake up tied and helpless.'

He leant forward and slipped his arm round her waist, pulling her towards him. His other hand slipped under the hem of her silk top, and reached up to cup her breast. 'And then what?' he asked softly.

'We'd exhaust you,' she said.

'It'll take more than two women to exhaust me.' He thumbed her nipple gently.

'We'd use a vibrator on you,' she threatened. 'I'd like to see how long your self-control lasted then.'

'I might just enjoy that,' he said. 'But later on I'd have to remind you who was the real boss in our relationship.'

'Violence?' She pretended to sound shocked. 'And I thought you were a gentleman.'

'I am,' he said. 'And a gentleman knows how to keep his women in order.' His fingers pinched her nipple suddenly and unexpectedly; just hard enough to make her give a startled yelp. 'A little bit of erotic punishment,' he said. 'It works wonders, I guarantee it.'

'You've used it on women before?'

He smiled lazily. 'Let's just say that I've experimented.' He paused. 'Does that bother you?'

She remembered her slave fantasies. 'No,' she said.

'Did your boyfriend ever tie you up? Whip you, maybe?'

'No. He was only interested in being on the receiving end.'

'But you wouldn't have minded reversing the roles?' He began to massage her breasts, more roughly than before. His urgency aroused her, and she felt her body respond. 'You'd enjoy it, wouldn't you?' he murmured. 'You'd enjoy it if I stripped you, and upended you, and spanked you. Just hard enough to sting. Just hard enough to make you struggle. To make you yell.'

'Like you did to Penny?' she challenged.

He laughed. 'Penny's a nice girl. A *very* nice girl. But I've never had an affair with her. She's not my type. I like my women with rounded curves. Penny's built like a boy.'

'Apparently she said you whipped her,' Elise said. 'Not that she was complaining. And then she whipped you.'

He grinned. 'What an imagination. Mind you, it could be fun – with the right woman.' He stood up suddenly, lifting Elise up with him. His hands went round her waist and slid downwards. 'With someone like you.' He pulled her close and kissed her. His fingers worked on her skirt, easing it up until her bottom was exposed. His hands slipped under the elastic of her panties and cupped her full cheeks, massaging them. 'If I spank a woman I like to feel my palm land on something like this. Something like your bottom. And I've a feeling you might like it too.'

'Maybe I would,' she murmured huskily in his ear.

She could feel the warmth of his body, and the movement of his penis as it swelled and hardened. She reached down. Her fingers traced the length of his cock, trapped against his stomach.

'Why don't we try it?' he muttered huskily. 'You're half-naked now. You left your bra off, and these knickers will be round your ankles in a minute. You want fucking. Admit it?'

'I thought you were suggesting a spanking?' She unzipped his trousers and slid her hand inside. She felt him bulging against the thin stretch cloth of his briefs. 'You were going to strip me and up-end me.' She lifted his cock and balls, deftly freeing them from the restricting briefs, and heard him groan. 'That was what you promised me, wasn't it?' She continued to massage him and felt him grow even larger under her caresses. 'You'd hold me down, and spank me. I bet you'd enjoy hearing your palm land on my bottom. And you'd enjoy hearing me yell. Or maybe you'd use that riding crop of yours.'

She slid down suddenly on her knees and took him in her mouth.

'No,' he protested hoarsely. 'Wait . . .'

But she used her lips and her tongue to bring him to a sudden climax. He cried out once, and she held him in her mouth until the tremors that shook his body had subsided. He caught her head and ran his fingers through her hair, lifting her face up to him as she knelt.

She smiled: 'What happened to your famous self-control?'

'You're a witch,' he said. 'You did that on purpose. You had no intention of letting me spank you. You were just trying to turn me on.'

'Trying?' she laughed. 'I did! The score's even now, and I'll look forward to being punished for my wickedness later.'

'That's a date,' he said. 'I won't forget.'

She kissed him lightly on the lips. 'I won't let you forget,' she promised.

Later, as she drove back to Shilden, Elise thought: I could get fond of him. I could get *very* fond of him. She turned into the drive and the dark square shape of the castle loomed in front of her. And at least he thinks of me as a red-blooded woman, she thought, parking the car.

There was a yellow light glowing in the west tower. She knew this was Max Lannsen's office. He was working late. She tried to picture him sitting at his desk. All work and no play, she thought. Did he ever play? How did he relax? How would he entertain a woman? Was he into spanking and sexy games? How many times could he make love in one evening? Oh, for God's sake, she reproved herself as she locked the car and walked towards the castle, you're getting as bad as Lorna! You've got a fun relationship starting. Be thankful for that. Max Lannsen is not interested in you.

* * *

But the next few days seemed determined to prove her wrong. The phone rang early in the morning and she picked it up expecting it to be Petra Altham. Instead she heard Max Lannsen's voice.

'Please meet me in the east wing, Miss St John. Bring your notepad. You might have to take some measurements.'

Despite the coolness of his tone she felt a little thrill of excitement. She wished she was wearing her slim Sellick's skirt and seamed stockings, instead of her usual loose kaftan and silky trousers. Don't be an idiot, she told herself. What difference does it make? You might as well be wearing tassels on your nipples and a G-string for all the notice Max Lannsen will take of you.

On the way to the east wing she passed one of the local women who cleaned the staff quarters. The cleaning staff usually ignored Elise, but this time the woman gave her a nod and a sunny smile. Surprised, Elise smiled back. Why the sudden change of attitude? she wondered. Surely it hasn't got anything to do with Blair Devlin? How would this woman know about her date, anyway? The answer came to her almost immediately: her husband was probably in the pub when Devlin took her for their meal. If this was really the case she did not know whether to feel pleased or angry. She would have preferred to have been accepted for herself, rather than as Blair Devlin's girlfriend.

She unlocked the east wing door and went up the stairs. Max Lannsen was standing at the end of the corridor and, for a moment, Elise did not recognise him. He was wearing faded jeans, a white shirt with rolled-up sleeves, and canvas deck shoes. His thick black hair glinted in the sunlight. He looked slim and fit and relaxed. He watched her approach, but did not smile.

'I want you to come to the top floor with me,' he said. 'We may need you redecorate the rooms.'

'The mysterious top floor?' she said lightly. 'I've been looking forward to seeing it.'

'There's nothing mysterious about it,' he said abruptly. He turned away from her and started walking, obviously expecting her to follow.

'What about Petra Altham?' she asked.

He stopped, and turned. 'What about her?' He sounded irritated.

'Wouldn't it be better if she was consulted about any design plans right from the start?' Elise suggested. 'That would save her pulling all my ideas to pieces afterwards, wouldn't it?'

She thought she noticed his mouth quirk slightly, but if he had intended to smile he suppressed it. 'She hasn't pulled all of your ideas to pieces,' he said. 'And this has nothing to do with Miss Altham. It will be a private suite of rooms for our investors to use if they want to stay at Shilden.'

At the top of the last flight of stairs, there was a door fastened with a padlock. Lannsen unlocked it and walked in. Elise followed. The first thing that surprised her was that there was carpet on the floor, and framed photographs on the walls. She looked at one as she passed. A group of men in caps and white cricket pullovers stared solemnly at her. The caption said: Shilden Cricket Team, 1932. Lannsen was already half-way down the corridor. She ran to catch him up.

'Does someone still live up here,' she asked.

'Not any more,' he said abruptly. He pushed open a door. She followed him into a room that was full of old-fashioned, dusty furniture. There was a leather-covered settee, scuffed and worn, but covered with fat cushions. A glass-fronted bookcase. An old-fashioned record player. A fireplace with a set of brass fire irons in the grate. A small table held a deep ashtray and a pipe stand. Despite the age of the furniture and the fading wallpaper, the room had a comfortable, lived-in atmosphere. Elise would not have been surprised if an untidy, but welcoming, old man had come shuffling in and offered them a cup of tea.

'This is where Bennett used to live,' Lannsen said.

'Bennett?' she questioned.

'The previous owner,' Lannsen said. 'The one they used to call Master of Shilden.' He walked over to the window. 'I wasn't going to touch this floor, but as I've been told to convert it to an executive suite.' He swung round and gazed out of the window. 'No doubt it'll give the locals another reason to dislike me.'

'Oh, I'm sure they don't really dislike you,' she lied.

'Don't patronise me, Miss St John,' he said coldly. 'They hate me. This place was a crumbling ruin when I took over. Bennett hadn't spent any money on it in years. You'd think the locals would be grateful to me for getting some repairs done. And for giving some of them a few months' work.'

'Perhaps that's the answer,' Elise said brightly. 'It's only temporary work. Maybe you could employ more local people later on.'

He gave her a bleak smile that did not reach his eyes. 'What as, exactly?' he asked.

'Well,' she hesitated. 'Maybe as hotel staff?'

The smile stayed. That was a start, she thought – even if it did not contain much humour. 'Miss St John, can you really see the locals working with the kind of people we expect to stay here?' He stared at her. 'You're not that naïve, are you?'

'No,' she admitted. 'Will all your staff come from outside the area?'

'Probably,' he shrugged. 'It's not my problem.' He turned away from her and stuck his hands in his pockets. The gesture made him look unexpectedly boyish and, she thought guiltily, it also pulled the faded blue denim tightly and attractively over his extremely neat behind. 'What do you think of this view?' he asked.

The question took her by surprise His voice sounded almost friendly. She walked over and stood beside him, looking out at the rolling Northumberland countryside. 'It's beautiful.' she said.

'You don't miss London?'

'I don't miss it at all,' she said. For a moment she thought he was going to carry on with the conversation. Then he turned away. Afraid of losing the moment she added: 'Did you like London, or do you prefer it here?'

'I liked London,' he said. He paused. 'Once.'

She took this as an encouragement. 'But something unhappy happened to you there?' she prompted.

Another pause. 'Yes,' he said shortly.

It sounded final, but as this was the nearest she had ever got to a personal statement, she wanted him to carry on.

'I had an unhappy experience in London, too,' she said. 'That's why I wanted to come here, away from everything. But I'm glad I came. I love Shilden.'

He turned to her then, and she saw both pain and anger in his eyes. 'I could love it,' he said. 'If I was allowed to.'

She knew she had to keep this conversation going. Some kind of rapport was just beginning to link them, and she did not want to lose it. 'The locals don't like change,' she said. 'Country people are often like that. But I'm sure they'll accept things, given time.' He did not respond, and shifted his gaze to the window again. She continued: 'If you won't – can't – employ the villagers at Shilden, why not try and encourage the guests to use the local amenities? That will bring an income into the area.'

He paused for such a long time that she began to think he had not been listening to her. 'I had considered it.' he said at last. 'But there doesn't seem to be much here.'

His attitude encouraged her. She thought suddenly

that if Blair Devlin could learn to accept Lannsen, at least as a benefactor to the area, the villagers would accept him too. And a business deal that would benefit both men would be an ideal way of bringing them together.

'What about riding?' she suggested.

He turned to her: 'You ride, Miss St John?'

'I've just started lessons,' she said brightly. 'At White Gates. It's a very good stables, and – '

She saw his expression change. His face darkened with anger, and his body tensed. 'I don't want anything to do with White Gates,' he said abruptly. 'Or with Mr Blair Devlin.' He smiled, but this time there was no warmth in it. Or in his voice. 'You've met the charming Mr Devlin, of course?'

'Well, yes,' she admitted.

'No doubt he told you exactly what he thought about the outsiders who've taken over Shilden?'

'Look,' she said, beginning to get angry. 'I know you two don't like each other very much. I don't really understand why, but surely – '

'There's nothing to understand,' Lannsen interrupted coldly. 'Mr Devlin knows that I own Shilden. And he knows that has no legal rights where Shilden is concerned. I have no wish to have any dealings whatsoever with him, and I'm sure he feels exactly the same way about me.'

'But I thought . . .' she began.

'Don't think,' Lannsen said, turning away from her and striding towards the door. 'Just do your job. And if you intend to offer yourself to Mr Devlin in payment for riding lessons, please do it on his premises and not mine. If you bring him to the staff quarters, I shall sack you on the spot.'

Chapter Five

'Well, Max has obviously heard the rumours about you and Dev,' Lorna said. 'Doesn't juicy news travel fast? Offer yourself in payment, indeed. What a nerve.' She added: 'Mind you, I suppose you did, in a way.'

'I did *not*,' Elise said crossly. 'I paid for my lesson. And I'll pay for all the others too.'

'More fool you,' Lorna said, lightly. 'I don't think Dev'll take your money, though. I've been told that he's pretty generous when it comes to his women.'

'You make me sound like one of a harem,' Elise said.

'Are you complaining?' Lorna grinned. 'Give me a man with experience any day. I hate fumbling virgins who don't know where your clitoris is, let alone what it's for, or those boring thoughtful types who keep whingeing about whether they're hurting you, and asking you if you're really sure you want it. I always feel like asking them if I'd have my hand round their balls, or whatever, if I didn't want to fuck.' She put a mug of coffee in front of Elise. 'And talking of whingeing, have you seen dear Petra this morning?'

'No, but I will later,' Elise said. 'What's she been whingeing about?'

'Oh, this and that,' Lorna said vaguely.

'About me?' Elise persisted. 'You can tell me, you know. In fact, I'd rather know.'

'Not about you,' Lorna said. 'About me, actually.'

'You haven't been spreading stories about her and Max?'

'God, no,' Lorna said. 'Who'd listen, anyway? You're the only one I can talk to, and you've heard all my gossip. I'll be glad when some of my friends come up from London.'

'Your friends are coming up as staff?' Elise said.

Lorna looked uncomfortable. 'Well . . . yes. Sort of.'

'As entertainers?' Elise hinted.

'Escorts,' Lorna said, firmly. 'They do it in London, too. A businessman wants a nice intelligent companion for the evening, or maybe for the weekend, someone who won't show him up in restaurants or bore him to tears talking about soap operas. I've got lots of friends who need the money. You can't pay the rent with A levels, or a degree.'

Elise suddenly remembered Lorna's comment about being employed because of her contacts. 'You're a madam,' she teased.

'I'm just being a good friend,' Lorna corrected. 'Lending a helping hand, you might say. Helping my chums pay their bills. But Miss Altham isn't very happy with the situation.'

'She sees you as competition?' Elise guessed.

'Absolutely,' Lorna confirmed. 'And she's right. I'll put her out of business if I can.'

When her phone rang Elise made a bet with herself that it would be either Max Lannsen or Blair Devlin; her money was on Devlin. She was right.

'When am I going to see you again?' He paused. 'Preferably without your clothes on?'

'Wow,' she said, admiringly. 'You certainly don't beat about the bush, do you?'

'What's the point?' he answered cheerfully. 'You know what I want, and I know what you want. And we both want the same thing. So how about tonight, about half eight? I'll take you into town for a meal.'

'Are you coming here to pick me up?' she asked.

He paused. 'If I said I had a late lesson, would you believe me?'

'No,' she said.

Another pause. 'Will you come out to White Gates? I know it's ungallant of me, but there is a reason.'

'It is ungallant of you,' she agreed. 'And I'm sure there's a reason. What is it?'

Devlin's voice was suddenly cold. 'I came to Shilden once while Lannsen was there. We had ... words.'

'You had a row?' she translated.

'A disagreement,' Devlin said.

'What about?'

'Nothing much,' Devlin said. 'Lannsen ordered me off the premises. Not very politely, I might add.' He paused. 'I did consider decking him, especially when he more or less challenged me to try it, but I resisted the temptation.'

Elise had a brief mental picture of the two of them squaring up to each other. They were both tall and slim, and both looked wiry and strong. She remembered Lorna telling her that Devlin had won some martial arts trophies. But what about Max Lannsen? There was something about him that made her feel he was well able to take care of himself.

'You were arguing about "nothing much" and it nearly led to a fist fight?' She was sceptical. 'It sounds like quite an important "nothing much" to me.'

'Well, it seemed important at the time,' Devlin said.

'You're not going to tell me?'

'Not over the phone.' He paused. 'It's a long story. I'll tell you tonight. That's a promise.'

Petra Altham came into the room just as Elise put the phone down. 'Max has just told you the news?' she guessed.

Elise shook her head. 'I haven't been talking to Mr Lannsen.'

Petra found a chair and arranged herself elegantly in it. 'Well, I suppose Max tells me things and forgets he hasn't told you as well,' she smirked. 'We're opening at the weekend.'

'But the east wing isn't finished,' Elise protested.

'Darling, the bookings are coming in. The rooms that aren't finished will have to be locked up for now. We can't turn business away.' Petra opened the black folder she was carrying. 'The Victorian rooms are ready, and so is the dungeon. The photographer's studio only needs some more cameras. The leather room's fine, and so is the shoe shop. There's some special equipment coming for the gym. It should be here by the end of the week, or someone is going to get a rocket from me. Most of the period theme rooms only want a few finishing touches. If you could just think up something interesting as entertainment in the space-age hotel room, we could open that as well.'

'I'm just the designer,' Elise said sweetly. 'Entertainment is your field, isn't it?'

Petra gave her a sharp look. 'Entertainment is important, darling. The guests aren't coming up here to look at the wallpaper. Mind you,' she lounged back, recrossed her legs and treated Elise to her wide insincere smile, 'you've done a very good job. Max is quite pleased with your work.'

'So why hasn't he told me so?' Elise asked

'Oh, well, he wouldn't, would he?' Petra's voice turned husky. 'Poor Max. He does find it difficult to . . . unwind. But once he does, he's *very* good company. Very good company indeed.'

* * *

No Miss Petra Altham isn't having an affair with Max Lannsen, Elise thought furiously, as she showered and dressed that evening. She's just one of those women who likes everyone to think all men find her irresistible. What would Max Lannsen see in her, anyway? She's too immaculate. Too glossy. Too hard.

But maybe he would like that. Maybe he would find it exciting to ruffle Petra Altham's polished exterior. To see her change expression. To see her lose control as he opened the tiny buttons on her expensive designer blouse and searched inside. What underwear would she have on? Nothing from a chain store, Elise thought sourly. Cream satin and lace, maybe. Hand made. Something of impeccably good taste.

She imagined Max Lannsen's long fingers easing the narrow silk straps over Petra Altham's shoulders; him looking at her eyes, judging her reactions, then letting his gaze slide downwards as he slowly uncovered her breasts. Why am I thinking about this? she wondered. Why am I remembering Lannsen's hands, for God's sake? Because they were quite beautiful, she reminded herself. She closed her eyes. And I'd like to know what it feels like to have them slowly undressing me. To feel his thumbs brushing the tips of my nipples. To see him smile as he felt them tighten under his touch. Her body was beginning to respond. She opened her eyes again, quickly.

The black underwired bra lay on the bed. She picked it up. Would an uplift bra appeal to Max Lannsen? It doesn't matter what appeals to him, she told herself angrily. Stop thinking about him. Tonight you're going to see Blair Devlin, and it's what appeals to him that counts. So what would it be? She tossed the wired bra aside. Something looser, she thought. Something more personal. Last time I dressed for Devlin. This time I'll dress for myself.

She chose a dark green silky bra that gave her a

natural shape, matching cami-knickers with a narrow lace border, and sheer black stockings with support tops. She had to admit that there was something about dark stockings that made one's legs look sexy. She decided on a plain, silky black dress with a long, hidden back zip and narrow shoulder straps that were purely decorative. It fitted her without clinging, and was one of her favourites. Instead of the stiletto heels she had worn previously she selected a pair of medium heeled evening shoes with a narrow strap across the instep. She posed in front of the full-length mirror. Sexy, but still with a hint of decorum, she decided. She lifted her hair experimentally, and then decided to leave it loose; a cascade of red to contrast with the simple darkness of the dress.

Blair Devlin was waiting for her in his car. When he saw her he got out and opened the passenger door. He was wearing a dark suit, and for a moment he reminded her of Max Lannsen. She walked towards him. There were sounds of activity coming from the indoor school. She heard a horse whinny, and a girl's voice shouting instructions. She thought it sounded like Penny.

'Very nice,' said Blair Devlin as he gave her a slow inspection. 'You look as if you've forgotten to put your dress on.'

'This outfit cost me a lot of money,' she said, in mock anger.

'I'm sure it did,' he agreed. 'But it still looks like you're wearing underwear. I approve.'

There was a clatter of hooves and a horse and rider came round the corner, towards the car. The horse looked powerful and alert. The rider was a girl of about Elise's age, wearing breeches and boots and a sweatshirt with 'I Support the PDSA' on it. Even under the severe riding cap Elise could see that she had the kind of fresh natural beauty that looked good without make-up.

'Going to the school?' Devlin asked.

'I like Penny's classes,' the girl said. She smiled at

Elise. 'Watch yourself with this man. He has a terrible reputation.'

'Elise knows all about my reputation,' Devlin said. 'That's why she's agreed to go out with me.'

'Elise? You're the one who works at Shilden with Lorna?' When Elise nodded the girl added: 'I'm Julia Beauchamp. Dev's business partner. Maybe Lorna's mentioned me?'

'Yes, she did,' Elise said. And she also mentioned that you fancied Blair Devlin, she thought. Suddenly she felt uncomfortable, almost guilty. How did Julia feel seeing Devlin about to take out another woman? She must have guessed how the evening was going to end!

But from her expression Julia did not seem to be experiencing any pangs of jealousy. Her smile was sunny and warm. 'Have a lovely evening,' she said to Elise. 'See you tomorrow, Dev.'

'She's a nice kid,' Devlin said, starting the car.

'Kid?' Elise repeated. 'She's probably the same age as me.'

'To me she's like a kid sister,' Devlin admitted. 'We more or less grew up together; until she went to school in some foreign county down south. Sussex, I think.'

'Be careful,' she warned. 'I come from the south.'

He grinned. 'Don't apologise. If you stay here long enough we'll civilise you.'

The restaurant he had chosen was small and intimate with low lights and a simple but delicious menu. Devlin was an amusing companion, entertaining Elise with stories and skilfully encouraging her to reveal her own ideas and interests. It was only when they returned to White Gates that Elise realised she had once again talked a lot about herself, but had learnt very little about Blair Devlin in return.

'Did you enjoy the meal?' He shut the car doors and walked beside her.

'Very much,' she said. She preceded him through the front door.

'Good food,' he agreed. 'But fattening.' He stood behind her and rested his hands on her shoulders. 'I would estimate you've gained more pounds than you'd like to admit.' His hands slid down her arms to her waist. 'Here.' They moved to her bottom. 'And definitely here.'

'Rubbish,' she said lightly.

He shifted his hands to her hips and spun her round. 'I can feel rolls of fat,' he said.

'You can feel bones,' she corrected.

His mouth was closing on hers. 'I'll have to do something – ' he said, then kissed her once, deeply. When their lips parted again he finished, ' – about it.'

'Instant slimming?' she teased. 'You'd make a fortune.'

'With the kind of treatment I'm thinking of,' he agreed, 'I probably would. Like to try it?' She allowed him to guide her through a door that led onto a narrow passage. Another door opened into a pitch black room. It smelt of oil, steel and leather. For a moment she hesitated. Devlin propelled her gently forward. 'Welcome to my den,' he said.

The light clicked on. There was a complicated piece of equipment standing in the middle of the room on the floor and, because Elise was not certain what she was expecting to see, it took her a moment to realise that it was a multi-gym. Then she noticed the rowing machine, the running treadmill, a floor-to-ceiling punch ball, and a padded bench. Variously sized free weights rested on racks. She moved forward and saw herself reflected in the mirrored wall opposite. Devlin stood behind her.

'You're a fitness fanatic?' she challenged, lightly.

'I just like to keep healthy,' he said.

'I thought riding would do that,' she said.

'It does,' he agreed. She felt the shoulders of her dress

141

slipping and realised that he had unzipped her. 'But it doesn't cater for the whole body.' She made a half-hearted attempt to stop the dress slithering to her waist. He caught her wrists and held them. 'There are other parts of the male physique that need exercising,' he said softly. His hands moved to her stomach, pulling her back against his body. She felt the swell of his erection against her buttocks. He caressed her hips and then spun her round. Her dress fell to her feet. His hands moved down to the back of her thighs, sliding over the dark green silk cami-knickers, exploring under the loose lace-trimmed hem. 'Definitely too much fat,' he murmured. He cupped her buttocks, fingers probing the crevice between her cheeks. 'But don't worry. I have the remedy.'

'And what's that?' She leant back, enjoying the sensation of his body against hers, feeling his warmth and strength. She was wondering what it would be like to make love on the floor of this room. She was sure that was what he had in mind.

'Exercise,' he said brightly, twisting her away from him, and making her face the middle of the room. 'I have the equipment. You're going to use it.'

'You're joking,' she protested.

'I'm not,' he said. He stood back and looked at her. 'You're even dressed for it. Those silky shorts are very becoming.' His eyes travelled down her legs. 'The stockings are OK, too. But you'll have to take the shoes off.' He assessed her again. 'And the bra,' he added.

'You don't expect me to work out with weights?' She kicked off her shoes.

'Not this time,' he said. 'Although I'm sure you'd look great doing it. You're going to run.' He pointed to the treadmill machine. 'On there.'

'Well, if I'm going to run,' she said, lightly, 'I'm keeping my bra on!'

'Off,' he corrected. He reached towards her and his

fingers played with the narrow straps, pulling them over her shoulders. She tried, playfully, to stop him, backing away, but he followed her until he had trapped her up against the wall.

'No,' she protested. 'It's uncomfortable running without a bra.'

'But it looks great,' he said. 'I want you half-naked. You looked great riding Brandysnap, remember? You'll look even better on the running machine.'

'Mr Devlin,' she said, in mock reproof, 'you're kinky.'

'I'm normal,' he corrected. 'I don't get turned on by statues. I like to see a woman's body moving about. Most men do.' He lifted her breasts, thumbs sliding over the green silk. 'I want to see these bouncing about.' His hands went behind her back, searching for the bra clasp. 'So do as you're told, and strip.'

He tugged at the bra and she struggled with him, laughing. Suddenly she felt his grip strengthen. He caught her wrists in one hand and held them behind her back.

'Playtime's over,' he said. With his free hand he unfastened the bra and the next moment she was naked to the waist. 'That's better.' His hand began to roam over her stomach and then moved upwards. His finger traced the curve of her breast, then carried on until it found the hard bud of her nipple. He played with her, gently at first, then tugging and pinching more roughly until she gasped.

'Like it?' His mouth was close to her ear.

'I like it,' she murmured.

'Fingers or tongue, you like them both, don't you?' He was pushing her towards the treadmill. 'Now give me a little of what I like. Let me see you running.'

She was on the treadmill before she realised it. It had a handrail on both sides. Suddenly she felt the wide belt beneath her feet begin to move. She was forced into a gentle jog. Once she accustomed herself to the movement she realised that it was quite pleasant. She looked up and saw herself in the mirrored wall: a half-naked girl with wild red hair and black stockings, wearing what certainly did look like a sexy pair of green satin running shorts. Blair Devlin stood and watched her. After a few minutes she realised that she was running faster. Devlin had increased the belt speed.

'Hey,' she gasped. 'Stop this thing. I want a breather.'

'Think of the calories you're burning,' he said cheerfully.

'Sod the calories!' she protested. 'I'm puffed.'

She tried to back off the machine, but he prevented her. 'Keep going,' he said. 'You haven't even worked up a sweat.'

Now she was racing, and her heart began to pound. Grabbing the handrail she jumped off the moving belt and balanced with her legs astride, her feet on the narrow edge of the treadmill base.

'Enough!' she said.

He grinned, and climbed up behind her, the toes of his polished shoes touching her heels. She felt the buttons of his jacket against her back. His hand slipped between her outstretched legs, under the hem of her silky cami-knickers.

'We haven't even started yet,' he murmured.

She felt his fingers exploring. When they slid over her clitoris she gasped as much with surprise as need. She had not realised how aroused she had become. He teased her expertly, and she responded with instinctive movements of her hips, pushing herself against him as he stood behind her. She wanted to reach back and unzip him, free the bulging erection she could feel pressing against her bottom, but she was leaning too far forward. If she let go of the handrails she knew she would lose her balance. If she stepped back on the treadmill she would have to start running again. Then his hand withdrew. She felt him bunch the loose leg of

144

her cami-knickers to one side and heard his zip opening. Both hands slipped between her thighs, forcing her legs to bend and open wider. He switched off the treadmill.

'This isn't how I planned it,' he muttered, 'but I've got to have you – right now.'

He entered her so suddenly that she gasped. His hands clasped her waist and he held her securely in position while he began to thrust with increasing speed. She felt his strength like an iron embrace.

'Slower,' she entreated. 'Make it last.'

But this time he seemed intent on his own pleasure. He ignored her request. Then his body begin to tremble. He groaned softly, in time with the rhythm of his thrusting. His passion excited her and she no longer cared whether she climaxed with him or not, or even if she climaxed at all. She wanted him to be satisfied. It was enough to know that she could excite him into losing control. The violence of his final release jolted his body against hers. She felt his fingers dig into her flesh as he grasped her. He stayed inside her until he finally stopped shaking.

'Good?' she asked softly.

He pulled away from her then, in control again. 'Good,' he confirmed. 'And for you?'

'Good for me, because it was good for you,' she said.

'That's diplomatic of you.' He smiled. 'I didn't plan that. I was going to put you through a full work-out. The multi-gym, free weights, even a session on the punchbag. I was going to enjoy watching you – and giving you the benefit of my expert instruction, of course.' He ran his hands lightly over her body, and let them rest on the curve of her bottom. 'Maybe encourage you a little if I thought you needed it. The treadmill was just to warm you up.'

'Well, it did that all right,' she agreed. 'And not only me!'

'You've no idea how sexy you looked,' he said softly.

'Standing there with your legs spread, panting as if you'd just been making love. There's something about women's bodies when they're active that really turns me on.'

'I was panting because I was out of breath,' she said.

'Be careful,' he said. 'I might decide you can do a full work-out after all. You're not used to doing sport, are you?'

'Agreed,' she said cheerfully. 'I like all the wrong things. But right now I'd like a shower and a drink.'

Back in the living room, refreshed from her shower, Elise sat opposite Blair Devlin, a glass of white wine in her hand. Devlin had shed his coat, unbuttoned his immaculate white shirt and rolled his sleeves up to his elbows. He looked relaxed and extremely attractive. She imagined him as a schoolboy. He probably spent his free time galloping around the countryside, a daredevil on a horse. And as a teenager, lean and athletic, with that charming smile, he was probably aware of his ability to attract the opposite sex, but laid back enough not to use it too obviously. No wonder Julia Beauchamp had fallen for him. Why didn't Devlin return her interest? Even if he had grown up thinking of Julia as a sister, they were both adults now. Plenty of couples who had grown up together started relationships without feeling any guilt. Julia was a beauty. And a sports-woman, too. Elise could not believe that Blair Devlin did not find her attractive. Why was he holding back?

'What are you thinking about?' he asked. 'You were miles away.'

'I was wondering why you were arguing with Max Lannsen,' Elise improvised, quickly. Devlin stared at her over the rim of his whisky glass. 'And why you won't come to Shilden any more. You promised to explain, remember?'

'I did, didn't I,' he agreed. He paused. 'Lannsen and I had a disagreement about his plans for the castle. He told me to get off his land and not come back. I admit his attitude infuriated me. I told him that the next time I came to Shilden through the front gates it would be because I had regained my rightful status. A bit theatrical, but I couldn't resist it. It rather limits my methods of entry, but I made the promise, and I'm sticking to it.'

'Rightful status?' Elise questioned. 'Don't hold out on me, Dev. I skill don't know what you're talking about.'

'My rightful status as Master of Shilden,' Blair Devlin said.

'You?' She stared at him incredulously. 'But I thought ... .'

'Tradition says the owner of Shilden is the master?' Devlin explained. 'Well, legally Max Lannsen is the owner, but the locals will never accept him.' He leant back in his chair, stretching his legs, surveying her with half closed eyes. There was a touch of arrogance on his face now. 'They accept me, whatever the law says. And they always will.'

Elise believed him. She remembered the respect he had received in the pub. It made sense now. 'But if what you say is true, why didn't you inherit Shilden?' she asked.

He smiled briefly. 'My grandfather misbehaved, so my family line comes from what they used to call "the wrong side of the blanket". I'm not a legitimate descendant, but I have far more Bennett blood in me than Max Lannsen. And the Old Man accepted me. We got on really well. He was like a second father to me. He wanted me to have Shilden. I know that, and the village knows it.' His voice hardened. 'But the law said the castle belonged to Max Lannsen. And he took it.'

'I would have thought you could have come to some kind of agreement,' Elise suggested. 'I always had the impression that Max Lannsen was not too happy about his inheritance.'

'I didn't get that impression at all,' Devlin said, coolly.

'He came up here fast enough when he realised he could use Shilden to make a profit. He stands to make money hand over fist, and none of it is going back into the local community.'

'Well, I did suggest he worked something out with you,' Elise said. 'Maybe arranged for guests to ride at White Gates.'

Devlin laughed unkindly. 'I bet he just loved that idea. Not that I'd have any of his damned guests anywhere near my horses.'

'Then you're being as awkward as he is,' Elise accused.

Devlin stared at her gravely. 'This isn't just a personality clash,' he said. 'It goes deeper than that. Shilden means a lot to me. I believe I have a right to it. It would alter my life in more ways that you could imagine if the law would only back me up. But it won't. So I have to watch Max Lannsen ruining what should be mine – and there's nothing I can do about it.'

'Well, I just hope they know what they're doing!' Elise heard Petra's voice coming from inside Lorna's office and hesitated.

'Of course they do,' Lorna sounded angry. 'They've all done this kind of work before, you know.'

The door opened and Petra came sweeping out. 'I do hate working with amateurs.' She saw Elise and smiled. 'Oh, good. I was just coming for you. We have simply masses of work to do.' Elise had been about to ask Lorna if she wanted a cup of coffee. She just had time to glance back at her friend and shrug. 'You've got to do some alterations in the Victorian bathroom,' Petra said, striding down the corridor. 'A redesign job. And fast.'

'I'm working on plans for the executive suite,' Elise began.

'Oh, you can shelve that for the time being,' Petra said irritably. 'Those tatty rooms will take forever to renovate, and they're just a perk for the investors, anyway. This damrn place needs to start making money.'

'Mr Lannsen wants me to work on the suite,' Elise said.

'Tough!' Petra snapped. '*I* want you to work on the Victorian bathroom.' She gave Elise an icy look, and Elise realised for the first time that Petra would make an unpleasant enemy.

'And what I say goes. Understand?'

Elise had finished her new plans for the bathroom. Petra Altham wanted the shower moved, although Elise could not understand why. She took a last look at the room. It was on the ground floor of the east wing, and had originally been part of an entrance foyer. As she was about to leave, Elise heard voices. Two workmen came into the room. She knew them as part of a contract team brought to Shilden from London, and had seen them several times before. They greeted her cheerfully.

'Finished in here, love? We've got to knock a hole in the wall.'

'Whatever for?' she asked.

'Spyhole,' the second man explained. He looked at a plan, then pointed above the brass taps of the wash basin. 'About there.'

'You mean you've got to make a room behind the wall?' she asked.

'There's one already there,' the first workman told her. 'There's a space between this wall and the next. They're false walls, see? This whole wing has been mucked about with so much it's like a rabbit warren. Handy, though. When we've finished, a bloke can sit there nice and comfy and watch the ladies having a wash. Talk about whatever turns you on.'

So that's why Petra wanted the shower moved, Elise thought. Now it was directly in line with the spy hole.

'You're expecting some funny old customers in this hotel of yours, aren't you?' the workman said, grinning.

How many more double walls were there? Elise wondered, curiously. She had already made her own measurements, but had never bothered to check them with the originals. Out of interest she went over the older layouts. In many instances she realised that the east block rooms were linked by narrow man-made spaces between the old walls and the later Victorian renovations. At one point, building work in the past had left a passage leading to the next wing. I could walk behind Max Lannsen's walls without being seen, she realised. And if there were any cracks or holes – and there probably would be – I could check if he really was spending his free time with Petra Altham. Or with someone else.

The idea of watching Max Lannsen through a spy hole was extremely appealing. She imagined him walking in, dressed in his dark suit, then slipping off his jacket, unbuttoning his shirt cuffs, then the shirt itself. The shirt would come off, leaving him bare chested. That was easy enough to visualise. In her mind's eye she let him wander around for a while, getting a drink, turning on the shower, while she admired his wide shoulders, his narrow waist, the hard flat muscles of his stomach, and the panther-like way he moved.

Then the trousers would come off. And here her imagination faltered. She knew that his buttocks would be tight and neat; she had seen their outline under the denim jeans. She knew that his legs were long and, if they fitted the rest of his physique, would be sleek and lean muscled. But what about the rest of him? Her imagination could provide him with sexual equipment to rival a horse, but his jeans had not been tight enough to give her any hint of his real size. For once she found daydreaming unsatisfactory. She realised that for the first time in her life, she really wanted to see him naked.

The thought stayed with her. She knew it would be easy to get into the passageway behind the walls. She had only to go into one of the unfinished rooms in the east wing and force open a wall panel. But she would have to do it soon, before the work was completed.

The opportunity did not come until the following week. Petra Altham's constant hassling over last-minute changes kept Elise busy during the day, and making notes kept her occupied in the evenings. She rarely saw Lorna, who had to make several trips to London, and she did not see Blair Devlin at all. She was still in the east wing, making notes for the next day when she heard the workmen leaving and realised that it was much later than she thought. The men went down the stairs, laughing and talking. If I want to explore, she thought, now's the time to do it.

It was easy to force an entry by levering one of the wooden wall panels away from its casing, and a lot easier than she thought to make her way between the original wall and the false ones. She edged along, with only her small torch to guide her. Then she heard music: a flowing sound that seemed to consist mainly of subtle changes of rhythm and chords. She knew she must be near Max Lannsen's quarters. What was he doing? Planning a seduction? It certainly didn't sound like the right kind of music for that. She could see slivers of light escaping through cracks in the wall ahead of her. She moved closer and put her eye against one of them.

She was looking into Max Lannsen's living room. It was surprisingly spartan, with a large expanse of uncarpeted floor. A half-empty whisky bottle and a glass stood on a small table, next to an armchair. The only other item of note was a rather old-fashioned hi-fi. It was an impersonal room. It gave nothing away. Rather like its occupant, she thought. Then she noticed the pictures. They were unframed paintings, water colours and drawings, and as far as she could make out they were all of the same woman. It was difficult to see them properly from her hidden position, but the woman looked like a beauty – dark haired and imperious. When Max Lannsen came into the room he walked straight to the table and poured himself a drink. He was wearing a silky, black calf-length kimono. His feet were bare and his hair was tousled as if he had just dragged a shirt or sweater over his head. He stood with the glass in his hand, listening to the soft flow of the music.

Elise was certain he was naked under the kimono. She felt a stab of desire that startled her. She wanted to explore his body, slowly and comprehensively. To feel the hard strength of his muscles under the silk. She wanted to take his nipples in her mouth and force them to harden as she kissed and teased them. To smooth her hands over the flat stomach and search between his legs. She wanted to feel him swell and stiffen as she worked on him, her fingers stroking and cupping his balls, discovering what turned him on. She wanted to use her mouth, licking and nipping, gently and then roughly, sucking him until he groaned and writhed, his control weakening. She would make it last as long as possible, doing the things he liked but inflicting a little erotic torture by holding back just when she knew he wanted more. I'd teach you to ignore me, Mr Max Lannsen, Master of Shilden, she thought, with pleasurable anger. If I could only make love to you once, I guarantee you'd never ignore me again!

Her thoughts were making her wet. She wriggled uncomfortably, and then realised that if she moved too much now he might well hear her. As she watched, he began to pace about the room. He stopped in front of one of the paintings, looked at it for a moment, and then finished his drink in one gulp. Going back to the table he filled his glass again, sat down in the chair and stretched out his legs and sighed. The kimono tumbled in folds between his thighs. He rubbed the palm of one hand over his knee and then let it move upwards, slowly. He finished his drink, put the glass down, and slid further into the chair. She thought she could see a bulge that could have been a partial erection under the silk. Or was it just her imagination? Why didn't he move, and reveal more of his body? If wishful thinking could have stripped him, he would have already been naked. He would have been turned to face her, forced to lay with those lean thighs apart, displaying his assets for her enjoyment. Why didn't the kimono at least fall open, so that she could see if his sexual equipment matched up to her imagination?

He glanced at the whisky bottle, reached for it, then changed his mind. His other hand began to move, sliding over the black silk. He closed his eyes. That's right, she thought, excited. Perform for me. Let me see how you like it. Show me. Teach me. The thought of it was already having its effect on her. She let her hand move downwards, under the band of her briefs, until her fingers found her clitoris, wet and swollen now, aching for relief. If just looking at him makes me like this, she thought, what would happen if he touched me? His hand was still moving. His eyes were closed. Who was he thinking of, she wondered. She touched herself gently, wanting to prolong the sensations, waiting for him to push the silk kimono aside.

The phone rang. She saw Lannsen's eyes open and for a moment he seemed disorientated. Then he stood up. The skirts of his kimono swirled briefly. Too briefly to display the partial erection she hoped to see. He walked to the phone and his voice revealed nothing of his activities a moment before. It was cold and controlled. 'Yes?' A pause. 'Why do you want to discuss it now?' Another pause. This time he sounded distinctly irritated. 'Even if you send an order to the London office, they won't see it until tomorrow.' And then, with a sigh. 'Very well, I'll be with you in a quarter of an hour.'

Damn you, Petra Altham, Elise thought. It had to be Petra. No one else at Shilden would summon Max Lannsen during his free time and get a response. He put the phone down and left the room. She heard the shower running. She waited until he reappeared, formal in his dark suit, before she made her way back to the east wing, replaced the wall panel and returned to her own room. You certainly ruined things, Miss Altham, she thought, as she lay on her bed. But at least I'm now convinced that Max Lannsen isn't having an affair with you. Whatever sexy fantasy he was indulging in, it didn't feature you. Otherwise he would have looked delighted instead of angry when you phoned. Was he thinking of the woman in the paintings, she wondered? Why did he have so many pictures of her? Who was she? An ex-wife?

The thought came unexpectedly. She had never imagined Lannsen being married. If he had a wife, she certainly didn't seem to figure in his life. Maybe she had died. That would explain his sombre attitude. He was still grieving. In fact it would explain a lot of things, including why he had wanted to leave London: too many memories? He must have been very much in love, she thought drowsily, to have commissioned someone to paint so many different pictures. She rather liked the idea of Max Lannsen as a tragic widower.

'You must be crazy,' Lorna said, when she mentioned her theory the next day. 'I don't believe gorgeous Max has a heart to break. And I certainly don't even believe he was ever married. Whatever gave you that idea?'

Elise shrugged. 'I'm just trying to find out what makes Max tick.'

She had no intention of telling Lorna about her spying escapade. She knew Lorna would want to play Peeping Tom, too, and she was already feeling slightly guilty about the whole affair. How would she have reacted if the positions had been reversed? If Max Lannsen had sneaked behind her wall and watched her laying naked on the bed, pleasuring herself. Watched as she caressed her own nipples. Watched as her body shook in orgasmic delight. Maybe I wouldn't have minded, she thought, but that's just because I fancy him so much. Since he undoubtedly doesn't fancy *me*, he probably wouldn't get any kind of pleasure out of knowing that he had me as an audience.

'Men like Max don't get married for love,' Lorna said, positively. 'They might do it for social advancement, or business, or something absolutely practical like that, but the idea of Max going all sloppy over a woman is just too ridiculous. I simply won't believe it. Maybe he's really a closet gay?'

'Rubbish,' Elise said. 'You're just frustrated because he hasn't made a pass at you!'

'Yet,' Lorna grinned. 'But he might, this weekend, when our first guests start to socialise properly, and he realises that I'm not the blushing virgin he probably thought I was.'

'You're not ... entertaining?' Elise was genuinely shocked.

'Yes, I am,' Lorna said cheerfully. 'Why not? I could do with the money. And if my boss wants to sample my talents, then I'll perform. And enjoy it.' She looked at Elise critically.

'The early formal do will be quite stuffy and boring. We'll all stand around being polite to each other. But why don't you get yourself into something tight and revealing and come to the informal party later on? You might end up a few hundred pounds richer.'

'I'd rather stay poor, thank you,' Elise said, primly.

'God,' Lorna laughed, 'I think I've actually shocked you!'

Elise blushed. 'No, you haven't.'

'I have! You think I'm a whore.'

'I don't!'

'I might meet a man at the party,' Lorna said. 'And I might end up fucking him. What's wrong with that? You do it with Dev.'

'That's different.'

'You're not going to try and tell me you're in love?'

'No,' Elise said. 'He's sexy and fun, but I'm not in love with him.'

'Well, thank God for that,' Lorna said. 'Because you can be certain he's not in love with you. The point I'm making is that my friends do what you're doing. No one twists their arms. If they don't like the guy, they say no. The difference is, when they fuck, they get paid. It sounds like common sense to me.'

'And to me,' Elise said. 'But I don't think I could do it.'

'You're not hard up enough,' Lorna said.

Time passed so quickly that Elise could hardly believe the calendar that told her it was Wednesday morning. She had just come out of the shower when the phone rang.

'How about Friday night?' It was Blair Devlin's voice.

'I can't,' she said with genuine regret.

'You've got another date?' She knew he was teasing.

'We're opening this weekend. There's a sort of introductory cocktail party thing on Friday evening. I'm expected to be there.'

There was a pause. 'I see.' Devlin's voice sounded cool.

'It's my job,' she said.

'OK.' He still sounded distant. 'I understand.'

She tried to lighten the conversation. 'I'd like to show you some of the rooms I've designed. I think you'd enjoy the gym.'

'I probably would.' He sounded warmer now. 'Would you give me a guided tour?'

'Any time,' she promised. 'But how would you get in? I wouldn't want to tempt you into breaking your word and coming through the front door.'

'You could tempt me into a lot of things,' he said, 'but not that. Believe me, when I made that promise to Lannsen, I meant it.' He paused. 'But if I could find a way in, would your offer still hold?'

'A tour? You'd really like that?' She thought about it. It would probably be several weeks before the castle was in continual use. 'I daresay I could arrange it,' she said. 'But supposing you were seen?'

'Mr Lannsen would be very angry,' Devlin said. 'He could even try to throw me out – which could prove interesting.'

'I'm not going to be responsible for you two scrapping,' she said quickly. 'But if you think you could get yourself in here without being seen, I'll show you the Shilden Castle Pleasure House.'

'It's a date,' he said.

Elise put the phone down, smiling. It was a nice idea. She would like to show him round. She was sure he would enjoy the gym, although some of the equipment there would never be found in a conventional establishment, particularly the pair of 'horses' designed to secure a man or woman in a variety of positions that made every part of their body easily accessible. She remembered Devlin saying he would have liked a threesome. But would he like to be strapped on the horse, while she crouched beneath him and excited his cock and balls, and another girl straddled him from behind, using a vibrator, forcing it gently but firmly into him? Which would he like the best – her mouth or the electric dildo? Which one would bring him to a climax first? And then what? she thought. When he had recovered, it was only fair that he should be given the chance to turn the tables. Which piece of equipment would he choose for each of them?

There were vibrating belts and massage machines. Chains and pulleys pretending to be weight lifting equipment but in reality designed simply to restrain and hold their victims in interesting positions. There were padded benches and mats, useful bases for erotic push-ups. There were electric 'toning' machines that had clips and probes obviously intended to stimulate parts of the anatomy that traditional designers had never even considered needed attention. There were flat rubber paddles that could be used to increase circulation – or erotic excitement – depending on where they landed!

Would he like the shoe shop, where every kind of footwear was available, plus a catwalk for the model to strut and pose on as she displayed a selection of stiletto heels or buttoned and laced thigh-length boots for her partner to choose from? And then, surrounded by mirrors, allow him to pleasure himself with his choice. Or maybe he would enjoy the photographic studio, equipped with backdrops and props and enough instant cameras to enable any budding photographer to have fun and see immediate results. Perhaps he would enjoy a session in the school room, where he could learn – or be taught – some very adult lessons. Or maybe he would simply prefer making love in one of the theme rooms, where she had re-created various period settings, and where wardrobes were supplied with the appropriate clothes, and underwear, for the guests to wear.

She had a feeling that Blair Devlin would have enjoyed all of these facilities, but she was equally certain that he would never see them. Even if he had not made his theatrical promise to Max Lannsen, she could not see how he could get into the castle without anyone seeing him. In the early days, when most of the staff were local, they would probably have protected him. Now only the gardeners, the cleaners and Mrs Stokes were left. Mrs Stokes still managed the staff kitchen. She constantly threatened to give notice, but never did. Elise felt that, whatever happened, she did not really want to leave Shilden. She had worked at the castle for most of her life. Once the news of Elise's friendship with Blair Devlin had reached her Mrs Stokes had been much more friendly, and had once admitted that she had always hoped to see 'the new master return to Shilden' before she finally retired. But would she, Elise thought. She rather doubted it. She had a feeling that Max Lannsen was there to stay.

Chapter Six

*S*hilden was no longer peaceful. Young men and women with flat southern accents wandered about in the staff quarters, smoking and chattering. They complained about everything: their quarters, the uniforms they were expected to wear, and the lack of entertainment in the village. Elise found them superficial and irritating, and their London gossip no longer interested her. Even Petra was beginning to look harassed as the opening night drew nearer.

In contrast, Lorna seemed delighted at the surge of activity, especially when several leggy beauties who looked as if they had just stepped off a catwalk made their way to her office, greeted her with hugs and kisses, and began to swop stories about mutual friends with improbable nick-names and even more improbable life styles.

'It's great to catch up with the scandal,' Lorna was saying enthusiastically, as Elise entered her office carrying two mugs of coffee.

A stunning black woman got up from her chair and smiled at Elise. 'Hi. You must be Elise? I'm Patricia. Or Tish. Or Tshuna N'Gato, if you believe my professional card.' She had the same county accent as Lorna, and in her high-heeled shoes she was well over six feet tall.

'Lorna's told me all about you. Apparently you've kept her sane. This place is a bit of a morgue, isn't it?'

'Don't say that to Elise,' Lorna warned. 'She's fallen in love with the local desolation. Not to mention the actual locals. Or one of them.'

'You like all this open space?' Tish gave a theatrical shiver. 'I think it's creepy. I like to see brick walls and bright lights.' She gazed at Elise with obvious interest. 'Have you really found an interesting local – apart from the rather delightful Max Lannsen?'

'A riding instructor,' Lorna explained. 'All strong legs, knee-high boots and tight breeches.'

'Sounds like fun,' Tish said. 'Is he coming to this cocktail do?'

'God, no!' Lorna laughed. 'He and Max don't exactly see eye to eye.'

'Pity.' Tish grinned widely at Elise. 'But lucky for you. Otherwise I might have put one of my voodoo spells on him, and stolen him from you.'

'You couldn't concoct a voodoo spell to save your life,' Lorna scoffed. 'You can't even make a decent cup of coffee.'

'I'll have you know I do a damn good voodoo dance,' Tish said. 'Lots of eye-ball rolling and breast shaking. Real primitive stuff. Guaranteed to raise anything you thought might be absolutely dead.' She winked at Elise. 'Very popular with older gentlemen. If your riding instructor has problems, just send him to me.'

'Tish used to be a teacher,' Lorna said, after the statuesque black woman had left. 'She's an Oxford grad. But teaching didn't pay very well, and some of the kids were absolutely appalling. So here she is. Earning a fortune. She'll probably retire by the time she's thirty.' She grinned at Elise. 'You really should get on this bandwagon, you know. With your face and figure you'd make a bomb. Think about it.'

'I don't believe you're really doing this!' Elise said.

Jannine grinned. 'Two hundred quid, plus expenses and anything I make on the side's my own? You'd better believe I'm doing it.' When her friend had knocked on her door and walked in dressed in a beautifully tailored suit, her once dark hair now silver blonde, Elise had not recognised her. *This* was the Jannine Blake who lived in Oxfam sweaters and scruffy jeans? This svelte, glossy, high-heeled beauty? 'The only thing I can't understand,' Jannine added, 'is why you aren't doing it too?'

'For a start, I'm in this – relationship,' Elise said.

'With that riding instructor you told me about?' Jannine shrugged. 'So what? It's not the big 'til death us do part thing, is it? He hasn't bought you a diamond ring. And come clean, baby, he doesn't even *intend* to buy you a diamond ring. It's a fun relationship – and I quote. My memory is perfect. Those were your exact words.'

They had been her words, Elise remembered. *That's how I saw it to start with. And that's undoubtedly how Blair Devlin still sees it. We like each other's company. We enjoy sex. No strings. No heartaches. Except that I think about him a lot. I look forward to hearing him on the phone. He turns me on in a way Ralph never did. Maybe Max Lannsen could do the same, but I'm not likely to ever put that to the test. Am I?*

'You've got that gleam in your eye,' Jannine challenged. 'You're thinking about sex.'

'I'm not,' Elise said.

'Don't lie to Auntie Jannine. I know you too well.'

'If you think I'd sell myself to some stranger, you don't know me at all,' Elise said.

'Who's talking about a stranger?' Jannine grinned. 'You'd have all evening to get acquainted. And if you didn't like him, it's cheerio, buster. But if you did like him – it's hello, money!'

'And you were the one who was always going on about your art,' Elise said.

'I'm practising my art,' Jannine said. 'I'm acting. This,' she twirled round, hitching up her skirt and displaying black suspenders, 'isn't *me*. In real time I'm still your sloppy mate who shops at flea markets and eats baked beans straight out of the tin.' She looked at herself critically in the mirror. 'That's a make-believe woman. She just looks like me. But I'll tell you this much, she's damn well going to get paid more for her performances this weekend than I ever got for doing The Bard or washing dishes. And she's going to make sure she enjoys it, too!'

Elise thought it looked like a scene out of a film. The main hall glowed with the soft gold warmth of candlelight. True, the candles were electric reproductions, but high on the walls and suspended on hoops from the ceiling, they were believable imitations, their mock flames dancing and flickering. Heavy tapestries with medieval scenes hung against the stone walls. Shields filled the spaces between them. It looked good, even if she said so herself.

Guests helped themselves from a table piled high with delicacies, and took drinks from the waiters who moved silently and expertly among them. The women were all beautiful enough to be models or stars – even if some of the men fell a little short of similar perfection. She watched Jannine, in a thigh-skimming dress, charming two middle-aged guests. She noticed Tish, a good head taller than most of the men, sheathed in sedate and unrevealing black, a single stand of glittering stones around her neck. Lorna looked deceptively demure in an ankle-length skirt and silk blouse. Petra Altham wore a short-skirted suit, its jacket cut along masculine lines that somehow managed to emphasise her curves.

Elise had settled for the black dress she had worn when she went out with Blair Devlin, and her hair was knotted loosely, with some free strands framing her face. She realised that, compared with the elegant 'escorts' brought to Shilden by Lorna and Petra, she probably looked young and unsophisticated. At least no one will proposition me, she thought.

She mixed with the guests, swopped polite and meaningless pleasantries, smiled a lot, and tried to watch Max Lannsen. He looked remote and sombre in a black suit, his darkness enlivened only by a crisply pleated white shirt and the white band of his cuffs emphasising his long-fingered hands. She had a strong suspicion that he was not enjoying himself.

'Darling, I've got a proposition for you.' Petra's voice turned Elise round.

'If it's what I think,' Elise said quickly. 'The answer's no.'

'I'm sure it isn't what you think,' Petra said smoothly. 'But it means three hundred pounds in your hand.' She stopped Elise's protest. 'Darling, just listen. See that old boy over there? The bald one?'

Elise shifted her gaze from Lannsen. 'Yes,' she said.

'That's George Farrow,' Petra said.

Elise stared at her blankly. 'Is that supposed to mean something to me?'

'Well, it should. He has more money than he knows what to do with, and some of it is invested in Shilden.'

'The answer's still no.'

'You haven't heard the proposition,' Petra said irritably. 'Don't jump to conclusions. George is one of those men who gets himself off by watching. Remember that little room the workmen fitted up next to the Victorian bathroom? That was George's idea. He likes to be a naughty boy and watch the ladies undress and take a shower. That's all. You give him his little show, and you get three hundred pounds.' Elise stared at her, still not believing it.

'What are you dithering for?' Petra asked crossly. 'Any one of my girls would *jump* at it.'

'Why don't you ask them?'

'Because George wants you,' Petra snapped. The idea obviously annoyed her. 'He likes your red hair. He thinks you look innocent.' She switched on a smile. 'If George is happy, everyone's happy. He's a major shareholder, you know. I told him you weren't one of my girls, but he still wanted me to ask you.' She paused. 'You have my word that he only wants to watch. You won't even see him.'

'No hidden cameras?' Elise asked. 'I wouldn't find out afterwards I'd been performing for a much bigger audience?'

'No, you wouldn't.' Petra said. She added, rather sharply: 'I have professionals working for me, darling! I don't need you. This is just to humour George. And don't take too long thinking about it. George would like his show tomorrow evening. He's heading back home on Sunday.'

'You won't believe this!' Lorna found Elise in her room, swopping gossip with Jannine. 'I don't believe it! I damn well don't want to believe it!'

'We'll believe it,' Jannine said. 'Tell!'

'Gorgeous Max is human,' Lorna said. 'He had Tish in his room for a private session!'

'Tish?' Jannine repeated. 'Well, at least he's got good taste. Or kinky taste. I've heard that our voodoo priestess is pretty versatile!'

'Oh, she's versatile,' Lorna agreed. 'But so am I! Why didn't he pick *me*? I would have done it for free!'

'He paid her?' Elise said.

'Of course he paid her,' Lorna nodded. 'She's a pro.'

'Well, duckie,' Jannine said to Elise. 'Now's your big chance to find out if the object of your desire is any good in the sack. Let's go ask!'

'I couldn't,' Elise said primly.

'Well, I could,' Lorna said. 'And I'm going to!' She went to the door. then turned. 'You mean you don't want to listen?'

They found Tish in her room, and closed in on her like a crowd of starving gossip columnists.

'Come on, Tish,' Lorna said. 'We want details! What was it like fucking Max Lannsen?'

'A public school education hasn't done a thing for your vocabulary,' Tish drawled. 'Or your manners. You don't ask a lady questions like that!'

'We're not asking a lady,' Lornan said. 'We're asking *you*.'

'At least tell us if it was good?' Elise requested.

'Was he well hung?' Jannine added.

'Really, Jannine,' Elise said, primly. 'How crude can you get?'

'You mean you're not interested?' Jannine challenged. 'You're agog, baby! Don't deny it. And so am I. Your Mr Lannsen is quite an interesting-looking guy.'

'Sorry,' Tish said loftily. 'You'll just have to curb your lascivious imaginations.' She grinned. 'In a word – I ain't sneakin'!' She lay back in her chair and stretched her long legs. 'My lips are sealed. It's called professional- ism. And anyway, I promised.'

'He told you not to tell?' Jannine asked.

'Sure did,' Tish nodded.

'Kinky, was it?' Jannine persisted.

'Something I've never done before,' Tish said.

'*That* kinky?' Lorna was amazed. 'I mean, let's be honest – you've done everything!'

'I haven't,' Tish objected. 'There are a lot of things I draw the line at, darling. But I will tell you this, I enjoyed every minute of my time with Max Lannsen, and the finale was stunning. If he asks me for a repeat performance I'll do it again anytime – for free!'

'And this is your costume.' Petra pointed to the bed where a full set of Victorian underwear lay waiting.

'It'll take me ages to get all that off,' Elise said.

'That's the point,' Petra said. 'Let it take ages. George will be having orgasms watching you, and the more the better. Give him his money's worth. Undress slowly. That's what he likes. And wash yourself slowly too, plenty of soapsuds, rub them all over, then turn round and round in the shower washing it off. And don't forget exactly where he's sitting. Don't show him everything. Tease him a little.' She glanced at Elise and added: 'If you get cold feet, just think of the money.'

'I said I'd do it, and I will,' Elise said.

She had allowed herself a night to think about it. At least it helped take her mind of picturing Max Lannsen and Tish. She did not know whether she felt delighted, or sick with jealousy, to learn that Lannsen was good enough to impress such an experienced woman. And what had Tish meant by the 'finale'? It sounded as if they had acted out a fantasy.

She imagined Tish doing her erotic voodoo dance. Did Max Lannsen play the part of the master, ordering her to perform, then taking her suddenly and violently, flinging her on the bed, or the floor, while she struggled to escape – struggles that soon became a willing complement to his sexual thrusting? Or did she take control from the start, teasing him but holding him at arm's length, eventually ordering him to go down on his knees and worship her body with his hands, his tongue, and finally his cock?

She did not want to think about it. It seemed to have placed him even further out of reach. If he could afford a professional like Tish he certainly would not want her! She tried to concentrate on George Farrow and his fairly innocent wishes. She had convinced herself to perform for him without too much trouble. The more she thought about it, the more foolish it seemed to refuse. What was wrong with being looked at? She was not even being asked to do anything overtly erotic, just more or less what she did every morning – strip and wash. Only this time a middle-aged man would be watching her.

What would Dev think of this? she wondered, then realised that he'd probably approve. In fact, she thought, he'd probably be happy to sit with George Farrow and swop comments on my performance. He liked seeing women's bodies on the move, didn't he? He might even ask her to repeat the entertainment for him when they were alone together – only Elise was certain that in such a situation he would not be content to remain a passive onlooker. This thought finally convinced her that she could perform for George Farrow. She would simply pretend it was Blair Devlin hidden behind the wall, getting turned on by her body.

It took her longer to get dressed that she expected. The clothes had obviously been designed more for their erotic effect that their authenticity. Did Victorians really wear such frilly suspenders under knee-length pantaloons? Such pale, silky stockings? Were their corsets boned to push the breasts up quite so provocatively? Didn't they really lace down the back not the front? On the other hand, she thought, as she pulled the corset tight, I could never put them on by myself if they weren't designed like this. Or take them off.

She had been warned that a light would flash when George Farrow was ready for her. When she reached the Victorian bathroom she felt far less nervous than she had expected. The room was very familiar, and she knew exactly where George Farrow would be sitting. Somehow this gave her a feeling of being in control. He would only see what she intended him to see.

She remembered Petra's instructions and took her

time wandering round the room, admiring herself in the mirror, turning slowly. As she posed she realised that if she lifted her arms high enough her nipples would rise above the boned corset top. She exploited this tease, turning toward the spyhole, then turning away, playing with her hair, pinning it up, experimenting, imagining George Farrow watching her. I hope you're sweating, she thought. Or whatever. Perhaps I'll make you come before I've even stepped into the shower.

When she felt that she had tantalised him enough she put her hands on the buttoned corset front and began to undo it, slowly. She pretended Blair Devlin was watching her. Dark eyes? An unsmiling face? She realised that her mind had conjured up Max Lannsen. Damn the man, she thought, with sudden anger. Why can't I get him out of my head? It's got to be because he's so remote and unavailable. Once I'd got him into bed all this silly daydreaming would probably end.

But she could not stop wishing that he was there. She unlaced the corset and imagined him behind the spyhole. Imagined him shifting uncomfortably as he grew hard. She dropped the corset on the floor and pirouetted. It was much easier to perform for Max Lannsen than elderly George Farrow. She slipped the pantaloons down and stepped out of them. Now she was wearing just the silky stockings and her low-heeled, buttoned boots.

She took her time with the boots, balancing one leg on a stool, turning so that her hidden watcher had only a few fleeting glimpses of the curly red hair between her legs. When the boots were off she rolled down the stockings, bending over again so that her bottom was displayed, parting her legs just wide enough to tease. She imagined Max Lannsen squirming in his chair as he grew progressively more uncomfortable. Then she reminded herself that it was middle-aged George

Farrow who was actually watching her, and her mood was spoilt.

Once under the shower she remembered Petra Altham's instructions, and soaped herself as slowly as possible, covering her body with the sweet-scented suds, revealing parts of her anatomy as she turned under the warm spray. How long should I do this? she wondered. Suddenly, she wanted it to be over. Max Lannsen was probably socialising with guests, looking darkly sexy in his evening suit, and Lorna and her friends were undoubtedly eyeing him up as a prospective client, hoping they'd be able to discover if the body under the suit was as athletic and attractive as outward appearances promised. Petra's 'escorts' would probably be doing the same. Would he take one of them up on an offer of sex with no strings? Was that the only kind of sex he could allow himself to enjoy?

The warm water cascaded over her. Stop daydreaming, she told herself. Move about. You're working for money, remember? She writhed sinuously under the shower, sliding her hands over her body, cupping her breasts, delving between her legs. She bent and stretched, turned and twisted. She did everything except actually pleasure herself. That wasn't in my contract, she decided. But when she finally stepped out of the shower and dried herself on the huge white towel, she felt confident that she had given George Farrow good value for his money. That wasn't difficult, she thought. If the silly old fool wants to give me another three hundred pounds, I'll do it again for him sometime!

'Well, he's hardly going to rape you,' Petra said irritably. 'Why don't you just have dinner with him? I know it'll be in his room, but do you really think he'd risk his reputation by doing something ridiculous? He's much too afraid his wife would get to hear about it.'

'I didn't know he was married,' Elise said. Her first

170

reaction had been to reject George Farrow's invitation to meet him for a meal. Petra was trying to persuade her to reconsider.

'Of course he's married. Men like George are always married. He's got two grown-up daughters. Will you just sit down and have a meal with him and talk? He'll probably show you pictures of his grandchildren?'

George Farrow did not show her any photographs. but he did talk about his family. It was difficult to believe that this rotund, bald little man was a millionaire, and had made his money by astute business dealings on the international market. He seemed equally interested in her career, and she found herself telling him far more about her life than she'd intended.

It was only after the meal was over and he had poured her a drink, that George Farrow mentioned their previous arrangement.

'I was thrilled with you,' he said. 'You're so young, so unspoilt. You have such a beautiful body, and such a lovely face.' He gazed at her with genuine feeling. 'You wouldn't ... I couldn't persuade you to ... make me even happier?'

'If you mean sleep with you,' she said, 'no, I couldn't do that.'

'I wouldn't ask for anything unusual,' he promised quickly. 'I'd be very kind to you. And I'd pay you. Very well indeed.'

'No,' she repeated. 'I couldn't.'

'I wish I was a younger man,' he said, mournfully.

He looked so unhappy she felt sorry for him.

'That wouldn't make any difference,' she said. 'It's just that I don't do that kind of thing. I only did the shower performance because Petra Altham told me you were a major shareholder here.'

'She didn't force you?' His voice was suddenly cold. It occurred to her that George Farrow could be a formidable enemy.

171

'No,' she said quickly. 'No one forced me.'

He leant towards her and she realised that he was genuinely anxious. 'You wouldn't be afraid to tell me? I won't permit force, or blackmail, or any of those tricks women like Petra sometimes use.'

'I did it willingly,' she said. 'But I'm in a good relationship with someone, and sleeping with you would be cheating.'

She was glad when he seemed to accept this partial truth.

'You don't think too badly of me do you?' He sounded anxious now. 'I'd like you to see me as a friend. I have contacts in London, you know. In the theatre. When you leave here it's quite likely I can be helpful to you.' His round face beamed enthusiastically. 'You have only to call me. Don't forget.'

Although Elise took George Farrow's offer of help with a generous pinch of salt, she realised that she had actually liked him. It seemed extraordinary that someone who could afford to pay any of the most expensive professionals in the business actually preferred just to watch her undress and take a shower. Looking back it all seemed very innocent, and she almost felt guilty about taking his money. Nevertheless she did not tell Jannine what had happened when her friend (who admitted to being 'much richer now' and 'looking forward to coming back') quizzed her about the weekend before leaving. And she did not tell Blair Devlin about it when she met him the following week, either.

She had just finished a riding lesson with Penny when she saw him coming across the yard. He walked beside her. 'How did the cocktail party go?' he asked.

'Very well,' she said.

One of the schoolgirls ran forward to take Brandy-snap's reins. 'Shall I untack for you, Elise?'

172

'Thanks.' Elise dismounted and the girl led Brandy-snap away.

'Does this mean your job's finished?' Devlin asked.

'Far from it,' she said. 'I've still got to start work on the top floor of the east wing.'

'They're altering the old master's rooms?' He sounded surprised.

'I've got to turn them into an executive suite,' she said.

'Lannsen's going to alter everything, isn't he?' Devlin sounded bitter. 'Those rooms have remained unchanged for as long as I can remember. Now they're going to be pulled apart, just because Lannsen wants to live in a plush executive suite.'

'He's not going to use it,' Elise said. 'It's for visitors.'

'Have you started work yet?'

'No. I've just been measuring up, and playing with ideas.'

'I'd like to see the place again,' Devlin said. 'Just once more, before it disappears for good.'

'Well, I have the key,' she said.

'And you did promise me a guided tour,' he reminded her.

'That's true,' she agreed. 'But can you really get into the castle?'

'No problem,' he grinned. 'I have contacts.'

'It'll be risky,' she said. 'We'll have to do it late at night, when there aren't any guests. And preferably when Max Lannsen is away. He has a key to those rooms as well.'

'So what?' Devlin shrugged. 'He wouldn't be wandering round them in the middle of the night, would he?'

'I suppose not,' Elise agreed. She wanted to let Blair Devlin see the rooms. The castle had been part of his life, and it did not seem fair to destroy them without giving him one last chance to see them again. Especially after what he had told her about the old master's wishes.

She suspected that if Max Lannsen found out, she would be instantly dismissed. Well, I'll just have to make certain he doesn't find out, she thought.

Her chance came the following week, quite by accident. She had been called to Petra's office for what Petra had described as a 'brainstorming meeting about that damned space-age hotel room'.

'We've got to get something going in there,' she said to Elise. 'I don't care what it is. Just come up with an idea – and preferably soon. Do try and give me something I can show Max when he gets back on Thursday.'

Later that evening Elise checked with Lorna and discovered that not only had Max Lannsen gone to London that afternoon, no guests were expected during the week. She phoned Blair Devlin later that evening.

'I'll meet you in the staff kitchen,' he said. 'Mrs Stokes is always pleased to see me.'

'I know you're not going to bang on the main doors,' Elise said. 'But do try and get in without being seen. There are still some London staff about. And Petra's here, too.'

He laughed. 'No one will see me come in,' he said. 'I guarantee it.'

True to his word he was in the kitchen at the pre-arranged time, chatting to Mrs Stokes. He was wearing black jeans, a black polo neck sweater and dark canvas shoes. She had decided on a loose kaftan and jeans.

'You look like a terrorist,' she teased. 'All you need is a balaclava mask.'

'I thought I just looked suitably casual,' he said. 'Like you.' He stood up and stretched. The close-fitting shirt and trousers emphasised his wide shoulders and narrow hips. 'But if anyone wants trouble . . .' He threw a punch, so fast and unexpected that she flinched. '. . . I'm ready. Out of practice, but ready.'

'You don't look out of practice to me,' she said.

174

'Oh, that was slow,' he grinned. 'You should have seen me when I was younger.'

'Please be careful,' Mrs Stokes said to Devlin. 'It'll cause trouble if you're seen.'

'You mean I'll get Elise into trouble,' he said. He put his hand on Elise's shoulder. 'Don't worry. I'll look after her.'

'Once we're in the east wing we'll be all right,' Elise said. 'They'll be no one in there at this time of night. None of the staff have a key.'

'What about that Altham woman?' Mrs Stokes asked.

'There's no reason why she should go into the east wing,' Elise said. 'But I saw her go out in her car earlier on, anyway.'

They went into the corridor. Elise was about to lead the way but realised that Devlin knew exactly where he was going.

'I hate what they've done to this place,' he said. 'I suppose I should be grateful they've left the outside alone. They've certainly ruined it inside.'

'But people seem to have been altering the inside all the time,' she said. 'We found lots of rooms divided up with false walls.'

'That was probably done in Victorian times,' he said. 'You'll find the same thing in the old master's rooms. I know for a fact that he was interested in photography, and had a darkroom and studio built. He used to make the village cricket team pose for portraits.'

'The pictures are still there,' she said.

'Are they?' He sounded interested.

'Actually I was thinking of using some of them in my new designs,' she said.

The reached the door to the east wing. When Elise unlocked it Devlin moved forward confidently, striding along the corridors to the stairs. Elise had brought a small torch with her, but realised that she would not need it. One of the things she found attractive about the northern half of England was the way the summer evenings seemed to stay light for so long.

On the top floor she unlocked the old master's rooms. Devlin walked through the rooms silently, like a man remembering past times or – she thought, with some surprise – a man looking for something. He opened cupboard doors and pulled out drawers.

'They've certainly cleared this place gut,' he said. 'I bet they've burned a lot of stuff. His voice sounded bitter. 'Things that probably looked like rubbish to Lannsen and his solicitors. Things that would have meant a lot to me.'

'I don't think anyone's burned anything,' Elise said. 'I think someone pushed everything into some cases and boxes. I haven't even started to look through them yet. If I find anything interesting I'll save it for you,' she smiled. 'Max Lannsen need never know.'

'I'd like that,' he said. 'Bundles of letters, old photo albums, things like that. Mementos of the past.' He turned towards the door. 'I'm glad you let me look round, but it's depressed me. It's a bit like going back to a place you knew as a child, and finding all the familiar landmarks gone. Show me something that'll cheer me up.'

'I can certainly do that!' she promised. She led the way this time, down the darkening corridors until she reached the gym. 'You'll love this,' she said. Knowing that the windows were effectively blacked out, she switched on the lights. She watched Devlin's expression as he looked round the room and realised that the equipment that looked quite normal at first glance was far from orthodox when inspected properly.

He walked over to the 'horses' and ran his hand over the one designed for women, working the levers and pulleys that could manoeuvre the woman strapped to its padded back into any number of uncomfortable, but erotic, positions.

'Like it?' she asked.

'Love it,' he said. 'I'd like to see you riding this beast. I could give you a really interesting lesson.' He experimented with a lever. 'See how the stirrups down there move outwards?' He moved closer to her and she felt his warm hand on the back of her neck. He massaged her gently, his fingers pushing upwards through her hair. 'If your feet were in those stirrups, and your knees on those pads, I could open your legs as wide as I like.' He moved his mouth close to her ear. 'I could slide underneath you and tongue you. I'd take my time. Just lightly to start with, just the tip of my tongue on you. I'd make you work those lovely hips of yours. It would be much more fun for you than riding Brandysnap. And for me. With all these mirrors around it'd be great watching you. If you asked nicely enough, I might give you an orgasm before you were worn out with doing a rising trot.'

'I'll tell you something,' she said. 'You couldn't wear me out.'

'Like to bet?' She felt his hands move round to her chin and then down the front of her loose kaftan. 'You women like to think you can go on forever, while we poor men have to spend time recuperating. But if I got you on that horse,' he was bunching her kaftan now, pulling it upwards, 'I'd show you what it was like to have multiple orgasms!' Her kaftan was above her breasts now. She felt his fingers on her naked flesh, massaging. 'You're not wearing your lacy armour,' he said softly, his mouth nuzzling her neck. 'You were hoping I'd give you a work over. Admit it.'

'Of course I was,' she said. 'But not here.'

'Why not?' He stroked her nipples with his thumb. 'This place is designed for it. I'd like to try that toning machine, too.'

'I'm sure it would do you the world of good,' she said.

'I meant on you,' he said. His mouth moved down and captured a nipple. He sucked gently, then harder. 'Come on,' he said, after a while. 'Let me experiment.'

'I just couldn't relax,' she said. 'I'd be afraid someone was coming.'

'They would be,' he murmured. 'You!' He had undone her jeans and was easing them down, still working on her with his mouth. She felt her resistance weaken. The idea of being strapped to the toning machine was suddenly exciting. She would never get another chance like this. Why shouldn't she enjoy a little experimenting with a man she found exciting and attractive?

She was about to give way to her feelings when a door slammed. The shock of it froze her for a moment. Devlin was so intent on pushing her jeans further down he did not seem to have heard anything.

'Stop,' she said, trying to pull her jeans up again.

'You don't mean that?' He struggled with her, playfully. 'You know you're interested. Let's try that machine.'

Now she could hear footsteps. 'Someone's coming!' she insisted. She struggled to zip up her jeans. 'It must be Petra. She's the only one with a key. And there's someone with her.'

'Maybe they're not coming in here,' he said.

'We can't take the risk. She's probably just showing someone round, but we've got to hide.'

'Where?' He looked round. The voices were nearer now.

'In the horse,' she said. 'Switch out the light. Quick.'

The 'male' horse was the biggest. The first thing Devlin noticed was the hole cut in the top.

'At least we won't suffocate,' he muttered. 'What's that for, anyway?'

'The man can lay face down on this thing,' she whispered back. 'So use your imagination and guess what it's for!'

They heard the door open, and the light clicked on, filtering through the slatted body of the horse. Then Petra's voice, domineering and strident, ordered: 'OK. Get stripped!' A meek female voice replied 'Yes, madame,' giving the title a French accent. They could both hear someone striding about, high-heeled shoes clicking on the wooden floor. 'Hurry it up!' It was Petra's voice again, clipped and authoritative. 'Do you usually take this long to undress, you lazy bitch? No wonder your master has sent you to me for training. It looks like you need it.' There was a swishing noise, followed by an unmistakable slapping sound and a high-pitched squeal of protest. 'There's more to come, if you don't learn fast enough,' Petra threatened. Again her heels clicked on the floor as she walked around the room. 'Let's see. This machine looks like a good place to start. No!' Her voice was whiplash sharp. 'Leave the stockings on. And the shoes. Your master likes to see you almost naked. Turn around, slowly. Let me inspect you.' A pause. 'Well,' Petra's voice was a purr, 'you're a pretty poor specimen, aren't you? I can't imagine what any man sees in you, let alone someone as distinguished as your master. Come here. Stand in front of me.' Another pause. 'Call these breasts? They're so small you could be mistaken for a boy! Now – see this machine? I've been told that you're lazy and disobedient. When your master honours you by using your body you don't respond fast enough. We're going to alter that. I'm going to teach you how to react. These clips go on your nipples – like this. And this nice little dildo goes up here. Now let's see if I can get a reaction out of you.'

There were muffled sounds of protest, and demands from Petra that her companion 'stand still and stop wriggling'. Gasps and theatrical moans issued from the other woman. Devlin had managed to turn his head so that he could look through one of the gaps in the horse's side. Elise could see nothing. Whatever the two women were doing, she was close enough to Devlin to know that he was finding it very stimulating to watch. She reached down and caught hold of him. Sliding her fingers over his cock, she could feel it swell as it pushed against his tight jeans. He was so intent on the performance outside that he was taken by surprise, and gave an audible gasp. Luckily, Petra and her partner were too intent on their own fun to notice, and the gasp coincided with a flurry of squealing and orgasmic moaning from Petra's companion.

'That's better,' Petra said. 'That's the kind of reaction your master wants when he uses you. You don't just lay there like a dumb sheep. You dance for him. When he touches you here, and pushes his cock in here, you react! You sing! You know the song. Let me hear you singing!'

The woman yelled lustily, promising to be obedient, but there was no doubt in Elise's mind that the yells were phoney. This was a performance and, judging from Devlin's interest, it was exciting him as much as it was presumably pleasing Petra Altham.

'I think you've learnt your lesson for today.' Petra's voice was soothing now. 'Now I'm going to let you thank me. You know how to thank me, don't you? You know what I want?'

'Yes, madame,' the other woman said, sounding meekly submissive.

'If you please me, I'll tell your master you've been an excellent pupil. You'd like that, wouldn't you?' Petra's voice was purring now. 'So I'm going to relax on that padded bench, and you're going to come over and show me just how much you remember from last time.'

Judging from Petra's noisy moans of pleasure it seemed likely that her 'pupil' had certainly remembered how to please her. Elise was beginning to get pins and needles in her legs, and she wished that Petra would stop her constant instructions and overenthusiastic sound effects. She was also annoyed that Devlin seemed to be thoroughly enjoying his experience as a voyeur.

After what seemed to Elise to be an extremely long time the two women concluded their sex play and Petra order her companion to get dressed. This took a lot less time than getting undressed, and soon the light in the gym clicked off and Elise and Devlin were in darkness. They heard the key turn in the lock.

'Do you think they'll be back for another session?' Devlin asked.

'God, I hope not!' Elise said. 'My legs have gone to sleep, and I don't think I could stomach any more episodes of Petra's passion!'

'I could,' Devlin said.

They climbed out of the horse. 'I noticed you were enjoying yourself,' Elise commented, drily.

'Most men would have enjoyed that floor show,' Devlin said. He began to stretch and loosen up.

'Well, I'll have to take your word for it,' she said, pointedly. 'I didn't actually get to see any of it, did I? I just had to listen to the sound effects. But I had no idea that two lesbians doing an S&M scene is your kind of thing. Are you kinky, or what?'

'You don't have to be kinky to enjoy watching two women making out,' he said. 'Ask any man.'

The sight of Devlin stretching, and the obvious bulge of his erection pushing against the zip of his jeans, was turning Elise on.

'But it sounded so phoney,' she said. 'They were obviously acting. Why do you think they were doing it? Is that what Petra enjoys?'

'Who cares?' he shrugged. He moved closer to her. 'It was good to watch. I suppose it's the power thing; the fantasy that one person is controlling another, forcing them to perform. If most men were truthful, they'd admit that's a turn on. And that young girl certainly knew how to use her tongue!'

181

'Better than me?' Elise challenged.

'I wouldn't know,' he said. 'I'd have to check her personally.' He put his hands on her head and pressed downwards. 'But right now I fancy trying you!'

'Not here.' She let him push her to her knees. He unzipped his jeans and she realised that he was not wearing anything underneath.

'Right here,' he murmured, holding her in position. 'Right now. Do it!'

Elise let him pull her head towards his cock. Her need for him overcame her worry that Petra might come back. She pulled his jeans down and took his erection in her mouth, closing her lips over its rounded tip, running her tongue round the ridged cap, then sliding her mouth down the shaft. She felt his body trembling and knew that it would not take very long before he came. She was right. She had hardly begun to work on him when he caught her hands and pulled her to her feet.

'I want to fuck you properly,' he muttered. 'I don't want to waste this.' He dragged down her zip, pushing her back towards one of the padded benches at the same time. 'I want to get right inside you and see your face when you come.'

With her jeans round her knees, and with Devlin trying to push her back at the same time, Elise found it difficult to keep her balance. In the end she gave up the struggle and collapsed, giggling, on the floor. Devlin fell half on top of her.

'Stop laughing, woman!' He managed to pull her jeans off one leg. 'This is goddamned serious!'

She was so wet that he entered her smoothly and quickly. She tightened her muscles and pulled him in even further. He knelt over her, thrusting with a passion that was almost anger, and he came suddenly and violently, his body jerking and shuddering, and his face contorted with orgasmic pleasure. She had not yet reached her own climax, but realised that she did not mind. She felt a warm satisfaction knowing that she had pleased him.

'I'm sorry,' he said, when he finally withdrew from her. 'That was selfish of me.'

'I enjoyed it,' she said.

'Don't be polite,' he said. 'I behaved like a teenager who couldn't control himself. You deserve better.'

'Well then, you'll have to make it up to me,' she teased. 'But first we've got to get out of here. Petra might be coming back for some more fun and games, and I couldn't take another minute inside that horse!'

'Can we go to your room?' he suggested.

'No,' she said. 'I simply can't risk it with Petra here. It's going to be difficult enough getting you out of here without being seen.'

'It isn't,' he said, grinning. 'Come on, we'll go back to the kitchen. I'm sure Mistress Petra won't go there.'

Elise was surprised to find Mrs Stokes still waiting up for them. She looked worried.

'Mr Devlin, that Altham woman has come back, and she's brought another London hussy with her. She looked like one of *those women* to me.'

'Don't worry,' Devlin said. 'I'm leaving.' He smiled at Mrs Stokes. 'You needn't have stayed up, you know. Elise can help me.'

'I stayed to warn you,' Mrs Stokes said grimly. 'I don't trust that Altham woman. She's as bad as the riff-raff she brings here. She'd make trouble for you, given a chance.'

'She won't get a chance,' Devlin said. He turned to Elise. 'Come and watch.'

He turned to a small room adjacent to the kitchen. A tall cupboard had been pulled back and, behind it, Elise saw a dark opening.

'Secret passage,' Devlin grinned. 'All the best castles have them.'

Elise peered through the opening and saw rough steps leading downwards.

'Does it lead to a priest hole?' she asked.

Devlin laughed. 'Nothing so romantic. At one time the laundry was washed and dried in an outbuilding. This passage was built so that the servants could carry things back without getting them wet. The old master had both entrances boarded up to stop me using it when I was younger. He thought it was dangerous, although it's actually very solidly built. I was forbidden to explore.'

'But you did?' Elise guessed.

'He was a disobedient child,' Mrs Stokes remembered affectionately. 'Very strong willed.'

'You can't tell a young boy not to explore a secret passage,' Devlin said. 'And look how useful it's been.' He turned to Elise. 'It takes me into the wooded part of the grounds. From there it's easy to get to the road. No one will see me. Mrs Stokes and the gardeners are the only ones who know it exists.'

'Isn't it on the plans?' Elise asked.

'It's on the originals,' Devlin said. 'But Lannsen doesn't have those. He thinks the originals have been lost. He has copies.'

'And you won't tell him, of course?' Mrs Stokes sounded slightly anxious.

Devlin put his hand briefly on Elise's head. 'Of course she won't,' he said, softly.

After Devlin had gone, Mrs Stokes pushed the tall cupboard back into place and insisted on making Elise a cup of tea.

'I'm very glad you're helping us,' she said. 'Mr Devlin deserves it.'

'I'm very fond of him,' Elise said, slightly mystified.

'He should be the master,' Mrs Stokes said. 'The old master wished it. I heard him say so, many times.' She put a steaming mug of almost black tea in front of Elise.

'Of course he made a will. I never doubted it. It's just that the silly old fool didn't like lawyers.' She nodded at Elise. 'He could be very stubborn, you know. Just like young Mr Devlin.'

Elise sipped the tea, trying to make sense of what Mrs Stokes was saying.

'He wouldn't admit he was getting old,' Mrs Stokes said. 'As if there's any shame in that! He was cranky in many ways, but not stupid. He knew young Mr Devlin would have no rights if there wasn't a will.' She wagged a finger at Elise. 'Lannsen knows it, too. I'm sure of it. He had those lawyers down before the old master was cold in his grave. The rooms were locked up, so no one could search them. But the will's there somewhere, and if there's any justice in the world – which I sometimes doubt – young Mr Devlin will find it.' She looked at Elise and smiled. 'Or maybe you'll find it for him, when you start to work on the old master's rooms.'

Elise felt the hot tea was choking her. Despite Mrs Stokes's offer of another cup, and despite the cook's obvious desire to carry on talking, she felt she had to get away.

She walked back to her room with her mind in turmoil. Why hadn't Devlin told her any of this? Didn't he trust her? Another thought nagged her. Was this why he had started an affair with her? Memories of Ralph Burnes flooded back. Was she being used again?

She thought about it all the following day. Later that evening, after trying unsuccessfully to concentrate on the television, her depression gave way to anger. If Devlin wanted her to hunt for a will, he could tell her so himself. She picked up the phone and dialled his personal number. There was no point in turning things over endlessly in her mind. She would have it out with him. The phone rang four times and then Devlin's voice said: 'Thanks for phoning. I've had an unexpected call to go down south and look at some new horses. I'll probably be gone for a few days. I'll be moving around so I can't give you a number. If you want any information about riding, contact Julia. If you want to leave a message, speak after the tone, and I'll get back to you later.'

The tone beeped in her ear and she was tempted to say something short and very rude, but her pride stopped her. Why hadn't he phoned her before leaving? Surely he had a mobile? Why hadn't he given her his number? Out of sight, out of mind, she thought. It seems I'm just useful when you want someone to search rooms for you, Mr Devlin. Or when you want no-strings sex!

'Have you had any ideas about that space-age room?' Petra sat opposite Elise, her legs crossed, one high-heeled shoe tapping impatiently in the air.

'A striptease,' Elise said.

'Hardly original,' Petra objected.

'This one would put the man in control, not the woman.'

'How does that tie in with a striptease?' Petra sounded unconvinced.

'We use lights,' Elise said. 'The man would have a choice of coloured beams, and the woman would react when they touched her. He could caress her, or even administer a little pain, depending on what colours he used. The woman would have to remember how she was supposed to react. We could stage it quite exotically. I think it could be popular.' She added sweetly: 'I've been told men like the idea of power. This floor show would let them think they were in total control.

'It has possibilities,' Petra conceded. 'Most of the fantasies we arrange use that theme. And women go for it too.' She gazed at Elise. 'That little scene you did for George Farrow. You enjoyed that, didn't you?'

'I enjoyed the money,' Elise said. 'I didn't really feel I was being controlled.'

'But you were,' Petra said. 'You were doing what George wanted. He paid. You performed.' She smiled. 'But it wasn't so bad, was it? And like you say, you can always think about the money.'

'I suppose so,' Elise said cautiously. She suspected that Petra was leading up to something – and she was right.

'So you wouldn't mind doing it again?'

'Another bath scene for George Farrow?' Elise thought about it. 'I wouldn't mind.'

'Well, not George, actually,' Petra said. 'Not this time. George isn't the only man who likes to pretend he's playing Peeping Tom. Listen to the scenario: the maid comes into the bedroom and sees all her mistress's beautiful evening clothes laid out ready for a night on the town. She can't resist stripping off and trying the other stuff on. Can you think of an easier way to earn two hundred pounds?'

'Who would be watching me?'

'Does it matter?' Petra shrugged. 'You won't see him.' She got up to leave. 'Let me know by this weekend, and I'll arrange it.'

Well, why not? Elise thought, later. Being looked at doesn't hurt. And if someone wants to pay me two hundred pounds to see me do what I do every night and morning, why shouldn't I oblige them?

'You'll be in the thirties theme room,' Petra said. She pointed to a wardrobe cupboard. 'You've got the full maid's outfit in there: frilly cap and apron, silk stockings with garters, and old-fashioned knickers. You take off the pair you're wearing and put another pair on. This man is heavily into knickers, so take your time with them. Give him his money's worth.' She opened the door to leave. 'Put your hair up in a bun or something, it doesn't have to be terribly authentic, and wear some make-up. There's a box of it in the drawer.' She smiled. 'You've got about half an hour to get ready. Have fun.'

The maid's costume reminded Elise of the kind of thing supporting players in old-fashioned stage farces wore, although she knew that servants in the twenties and thirties did have to wear a similar kind of uniform. She thought the silk stockings and garters were attractive, and she liked the patent leather shoes with their tiny heels. The knickers were silk, but plain and, she thought, not particularly erotic, although her hidden audience of one presumably found them a turn-on.

She had believed it would be easy to perform to an unknown pair of eyes, but she discovered that made her feel slightly nervous. Was the hidden voyeur young or old? What was he thinking about when he saw her walk into the room and mime surprise at seeing the clothes laid out on the bed? When he saw her hold the dress up against her body and admire herself in the mirror? Pretend to think about trying it on, Elise had told herself. Look round and check if anyone is coming, then start to undress slowly, remembering where he's hidden, teasing him with brief glimpses of your breasts as you unbutton the dress.

She had stripped to the waist, and wore only the knickers, the silk stockings, the garters and the shoes, when the door opened and a man walked in.

He said, abruptly, 'Get your knickers down!'

Elise was so shocked she stared at him dumbly. He was in his late forties, neatly dressed in an expensive suit and, she registered without really thinking, quite distinguished looking.

'You know you shouldn't be playing with your mistress's clothes.' He walked towards her. 'I'm going to teach you to behave.' Elise backed away and the man smiled wolfishly.

'Nervous of me, are you? Well, I don't blame you. You know you're going to be punished, don't you? You know what I'm going to do.' He moved closer. Elise took another step back. 'But I'm willing to be fair with you. Get your knickers down and bend over, and when I've finished with your bottom you can let me fuck you. If I think you've performed well, I'll forget all about your disobedience.'

'There's been a mistake,' Elise said.

'Yes,' he agreed. 'You've been caught in your mistress's bedroom, misbehaving yourself!'

'No,' she said. 'I mean, I was told you would just watch.'

'Watch?' His face turned ugly. 'What the hell's the point of that? You've got a lovely round arse. I want to do more than just watch.' He moved forward and grabbed her arm. 'Don't make me angry, girl. I've paid my money, now you're going to perform.' Elise tried to pull away from him but his grip tightened. 'Getting cold feet?' He taunted. 'Don't think you can take it? Heard about me, have you? I've got the hardest hands in the business.'

He tried to wrestle her down on the bed. Elise bunched her fist and aimed a punch at him. When he dodged she brought up her knee. He dodged that as well, but at least he let her go. She ran for the door. He followed her, caught hold of her, and threw her back across the room. She sprawled on the bed.

'Keep fighting,' he said. 'It makes it more fun.'

He leant over her and grabbed the elastic waist of her knickers. Elise managed to roll away from him, and ran for the door again. She wrenched it open, and cannoned into someone who was coming in. Panicking, she lashed out. Two strong hands caught her wrists.

'What the hell's going on here?'

For a confused moment she hardly recognised Max Lannsen, tall and elegant in his black city suit

'I might ask you the same thing,' the other man moved forward. 'We're both just enjoying a bit of fun.'

Lannsen's dark eyes moved quickly over Elise's half-naked body and her distraught face.

'Both?' he repeated coldly. 'I don't think so.'

'Look,' the man protested, 'the girl's just acting the part. She's supposed to be frightened. It's in the script.'

Lannsen looked at Elise. There was no recognition in his sombre, expressionless eyes. 'Is that correct?'

'No,' she said, feeling the hot flush of embarrassment colour her face. 'I didn't agree to this.'

Lannsen stood back and surveyed her dispassionately as she stood there in her silk stockings and old-fashioned knickers, her hair dishevelled. She wished the ground would open up and swallow her. 'You mean you were dragged here against your will?' The sarcasm in his voice was obvious.

'No,' she said, in a small voice.

'Then what exactly do you mean?' he persisted.

'I was told someone would watch me,' she said. 'Just watch.'

Lannsen turned to the other man. 'Is that true?'

The man shrugged, and smiled lopsidedly. 'Does it matter what we agreed? She's a pro, isn't she? Why shouldn't I use her? We could have negotiated a new price afterwards.'

'If you make an agreement, you keep to it,' Lannsen said. 'And you've just terminated yours.' He turned to Elise. 'Put your dress on,' he said.

The man moved forward aggressively. 'You can't do that,' he challenged.

'I can,' Lannsen said. 'We have strict rules here, and you've just broken several of them.'

'Think a lot of your whores, don't you?' the man jeered.

'I just don't like people who break agreements,' Lannsen said. 'Next time you arrange a session, spell out exactly what you want.'

'There won't be a next time,' the man said, walking

190

towards the door. 'Not in this place, anyway!' He turned to Elise, his face ugly. 'You should pay me, you bitch,' he said. 'For wasting my time!'

As she struggled into the maid's dress, Elise realised that her hands were trembling. She hoped Lannsen would not notice. If the worldly-wise Tish was his kind of woman he would think she was an idiot for getting upset over an incident like this.

Lannsen watched her. 'Perhaps you'd like to give me your version of this affair, Miss St John?' he suggested, with cold politeness.

She felt suddenly small and foolish. 'I don't have a version,' she said.

'Who arranged this charade?' he asked.

'Petra,' she admitted. 'But I didn't expect – I didn't understand – what could happen,' she added miserably. 'I'm sorry. I've probably made you lose a lot of money.'

'Don't be so damned stupid!' he snapped, with an unexpected show of emotion. 'Do you think I care about that? Miss Altham had no right to involve you.'

'No one forced me into this,' Elise said. Her voice caught in her throat. She realised that the affair had upset her more than she realised. 'I just thought it was an easy way to earn some extra money. You can't blame Petra.'

'I'll blame who the hell I like,' he said irritably. 'And stop sniffling. You're much too old to cry.'

'I'm not crying,' she mumbled. 'I feel . . . silly.'

'Well, you've been silly,' he agreed, uncompromisingly. 'You're lucky I came back from London earlier than I intended. I saw the lights on. There was no booking recorded for the east wing and I thought – ' He checked himself suddenly. 'I thought I should investigate,' he finished. 'Luckily for you.' He looked at her more closely. 'You're shaking,' he said, in surprise. 'I think you need a drink. Come with me. I'll get you a whisky.'

She followed him without thinking and without checking where they were going. It was almost a surprise to find herself in his room, in a large armchair, with a glass of whisky in her hand. She had never liked spirits, but she sipped the fiery liquid gratefully. He stood watching her. She managed to swallow a couple of mouthfuls then put the glass down. He looked at her critically. 'This really has upset you, hasn't it?' His voice was surprisingly gentle. 'Stay here until you feel better. Then I'll take you back to your room.'

The unaccustomed warmth of the whisky, and the realisation that she had really had a narrow escape from what could have been a very nasty incident, suddenly overwhelmed Elise. She felt tears welling up in her eyes, and then she was crying, uncontrollably. She did not know whether it was from relief, or from anger at having been made to look stupid in front of Max Lannsen. Or a combination of the two.

'For heaven's sake, woman.' Lannsen stepped forward and put his hands lightly on her shoulders. 'It's over. No one's going to hurt you now.'

'I know,' she gulped. 'I'm being stupid. I'll go. Thank you for the whisky.'

She stood up, expecting him to move back. But he stayed where he was. He stood in front of her, close enough to kiss, and all she could think of was how awful she must look, with her tear-stained face and her mascara probably running.

'It won't ever happen again, will it?' he asked. 'You wouldn't agree to do that sort of thing again?'

She drew a deep, shuddering breath, and realised that the whisky had made her slightly light-headed. 'No,' she said.

He reached out and touched the coiled hair at the nape of her neck, lightly, but with enough pressure to draw her towards him until her head was resting on his chest. She felt the smooth cloth of his jacket against her face; smelt the freshness of his crisply laundered shirt, and the more evasive sharpness of his aftershave. And, when he tipped her face upwards, she smelt the scent of his skin and then, still hardly registering what was happening, she felt the warmth of his mouth on hers.

It was a long kiss, gently passionate, his tongue barely caressing hers, its touch sending tremors of pleasure through her body. When it ended she stood with her eyes closed, waiting. The second kiss was more self-assured. He held her face in position. His mouth explored hers, moved to her jaw, to the side of her neck, and then back to her lips. Finally he pulled away from her.

'Well,' he said, with the trace of a smile. 'At least you've stopped crying.'

'Yes,' she said.

She felt him undoing the buttons on her dress. 'Say stop,' he said. 'And I'll stop. I'll take you back to your room. We'll never mention this again.'

'Don't stop,' she said. She did not even try to understand why this was happening. 'Please don't stop.'

His hands slipped inside the half-opened dress. His fingers explored, and found her nipples. They were hard, and as he touched them they contracted even more. She gasped. He pushed her backwards and she went with him. As she moved he continued to open the dress, pulling it off her shoulders. He captured one breast and closed his mouth over the tight bud of her nipple, then slid one hand down to cup her bottom. Her whole body was tingling. The dress fell on the floor and she realised that he was guiding her towards the bed.

She let him push her on to her back, delighting in the closeness of his body; the sensation of his hands moving over her skin; the touch of his mouth as it travelled from her breasts to her lips, then down over her stomach to the bush of red hair between her thighs. She opened her legs slightly, enjoying the sensation of his searching

193

tongue. He moved back then, looking at her for a moment with an intensity that she found almost as exciting as being touched. Then he reached out and parted her legs still further, his fingers sliding over the warm, wet proof of her total arousal. When he started to tongue her properly she felt her control quickly slipping. But she wanted to come with him inside her.

'No,' she said. She reached for him and pulled him up. For a moment she felt resistance, as if he was unwilling to let her take over. Then he seemed to relax. She unzipped him and felt him huge and hard in her hands. She had dreamt about inspecting him, discovering if he met up with her flattering imagination, but now it did not seem important. What mattered was to have him enter her, to feel him inside her, to know that they were joined and they were both pleasuring each other.

'Now,' she said. 'Please . . . now.'

He entered her smoothly. She was wet and totally relaxed. His first thrusts were slow, as if he was teasing her, and she groaned, pushing her hips against him, demanding more action. He laughed softly, his mouth buried in her dishevelled hair, then pushed harder. The sensations he was giving her swamped her with delightful, frustrating intensity. Her fingers dug into the crisp cotton shirt and felt the hard muscles of his back and shoulders. Her body began to shake. He thrust harder, and faster.

'Don't stop,' she gasped. 'Please, don't stop.'

Now his body was shaking as passionately as her own. His hands gripped her and held her. She felt the violence of his thrusting increase and expected him to climax. She wanted it, and yet he seemed to be holding back. Suddenly it seemed incredibly important to give him this release. It did not matter if she came with him, or after him, or not at all. She contracted her inner muscles and pulled him even deeper. His movements became faster and she heard him groan.

'Let me . . .' she murmured. 'Let me give you – this. Let me . . .'

He came suddenly, with a cry that seemed like one of relief. And his orgasmic spasms brought her to a climax too. Less violent, but no less satisfying. When he withdrew from her he rolled away, tided himself up and lay on his back. She looked at his profile, at the thick black hair stranded over his damp forehead, and the strong line of his jaw. Just looking at him made her feel like making love all over again.

Suddenly he said: 'I didn't think it would ever be like that again.' He sounded almost angry. 'I told myself it never would be. I wanted sex to be a quick relief. Nothing more. I didn't want to be trapped again.' He turned to her and she could see both pain and a trace of humour in his eye. 'Damn it, why did you have to cry?'

'I cried because I was relieved,' she said. 'You saved me from a nasty situation. It certainly wasn't my intention to trap you.'

He surprised her by laughing with genuine amusement. 'That's how you did it. The way you talk. The way you look. The way you bristle when I annoy you. That's really why I came to the east wing this evening. I thought you were working late. I wanted to talk to you.' He reached out and touched her face. A quick, gentle caress. 'Don't change,' he said. 'Don't disappoint me. I don't think I could take that again.'

'You'll have to write me out a set of rules,' she suggested, light heartedly.

He smiled suddenly, a smile that transformed his normally sombre face. 'Don't look so worried. I'm not that hard to please. Just be honest with me. I'm sure you've had affairs before me. Just promise me that you won't have any while you're with me. And no more performances for paying customers.'

'I promise,' she said.

It was an easy promise to make. When she looked at him she could not imagine wanting anyone else. Blair Devlin had been fun, and she had to admit that the sex had been marvellous, but neither of them had intended the relationship to be serious. She knew she could have become far too fond of him, but his behaviour had ruined that. That affair was over. For good.

Chapter Seven

'*S*he's going!' Lorna was delighted. 'Sacked. Your services are no longer required, Miss Altham. It's the best news I've had in simply ages.'

'I didn't even know about it,' Elise said. 'I don't need to see much of Petra now. Thank goodness.'

'You might not know about it,' Lorna said, putting a mug of coffee in front of Elise, 'but you're partly responsible, and maybe that should worry you a little. Apparently that show Petra arranged was unofficial, and she was planning to pocket the profits. Definitely not the thing to do, especially as she's getting an absolutely marvellous wage, the greedy cow. Max gave her a positively devastating dressing down, and he must have mentioned it to George Farrow. George has quite a lot of say about what goes on round here. He probably told Max to give Petra her marching orders. But Petra blames you, you know? You've made an enemy – and maybe a bad one. Miss Altham can be a first-class bitch.'

'Well, she's leaving, so it doesn't really matter,' Elise shrugged. 'Although the sack seems rather drastic. I mean, I did agree to do the scene, although it wasn't the one her client had in mind.'

'Well, actually I think Petra's been rubbing people up the wrong way for some time,' Lorna drawled. 'And George has taken quite a shine to you.' She grinned wickedly. 'Must be something you did for him, do you think?' She leant back in her chair. 'Come to think of it, he's not your only admirer, is he? For someone who's supposed to be indifferent to women, gorgeous Max certainly galloped to your defence.' She leant forward: 'Come on now. Tell all. Have you, or haven't you?'

Elise knew there was no point in trying to keep anything from Lorna. Before long her new relationship would be common knowledge. 'Yes,' she said.

'And was it marvellous?'

'Yes.'

'Well, for God's sake,' Lorna protested, 'I want something better than that. Did the earth move? Was he kinky? How did he compare with Dev, on a scale of ten?'

'I'm sorry, I can't talk about it like that,' Elise said, 'It was . . . just lovely.'

'Oh my goodness, Miss St John,' Lorna grinned. 'I think you're sort of half in love.'

'I think I'm sort of wholly in love,' Elise said.

'Well, good luck to you. I'm madly jealous, of course. But do be careful not to get hurt.'

'Nothing can hurt me now,' Elise said, confidently.

'I hope you're right,' Lorna said. 'But believe me, if Petra could find a way to do it – she will.'

But Petra Altham was the least of Elise's worries. The main problem on her mind was Blair Devlin. Their brief time together had been good. Despite her initial anger over what she believed to be his deceit, she did not want to hurt him.

It worried her, but when she went to Max Lannsen's rooms in the evening, and curled up in one of his large armchairs with a glass of wine on the table next to her, all her worries faded. He sat opposite her, in jeans and a pale blue shirt with rolled-up sleeves. He was so relaxed that she could hardly believe he was the same remote, barely polite, dark figure she had first seen in London. He often did not seem to want to talk. He simply looked at her as if he was trying to store every detail of her face and body in his mind.

'I know so little about you,' she said. 'And I want to know everything.'

'There's nothing to tell,' he said. 'I'm the man who inherited this castle, came up here – and found you.' He got up then and walked over to her, took her hands and encouraged her to stand. Pulling her close he kissed her. A long, lingering kiss. An exploratory kiss. A lover's kiss. After a few minutes he added: 'I got lucky. It was about time.' He started to kiss her again but she pushed him gently back.

'Not in here,' she said.

'Why not?'

'I don't like being watched,' she said.

For a moment he looked startled. Then he saw that she was looking at the nearest portrait on the wall: a huge original oil of the raven-haired woman who featured in all of the other pictures in the room. 'Oh,' he said blankly. 'You mean Jeanette.'

'That's her name, is it?' she asked. He nodded, but did not volunteer any further information. 'You must like her a lot?' she hinted.

He stood back and suddenly his face looked dark again. 'I loved her,' he said. 'She was my wife. And before you ask any more questions, we're divorced.' His hands tightened on her shoulders. 'It's over,' he said. 'It's been over a long time.' He turned her round suddenly. 'If you don't like the pictures, get into the bedroom. There aren't any in there.' He pushed her almost roughly through the door. His bedroom was as spartan as his living room. 'Forget the pictures,' he said.

He guided her to the bed. 'That's the past. This is the present.'

She felt his hands loosen her hair from its casual knot. She wanted to know why he still kept so many portraits of his wife on his wall if his marriage was really over, but his mouth closed over hers before she could ask him anything else, and his hand began to wander lightly down her spine, tracing a line to the cleft between her buttocks, circling there until she arched her back and pressed against him in an effort to relieve the intensely erotic sensations.

'On the bed,' he said, softly.

He turned her round, still caressing her, and lowered her gently, positioning himself above her, astride her. His hands moved round to the front of her kaftan. He opened the buttons and parted the silky cloth, so that she lay half-naked. His long legs held her prisoner. He bent over her and his mouth began to trace a path over the curve of her neck, into the hollow of her shoulders, along her inner arms, his teeth nipping her gently through the silk. She closed her eyes and made little sounds of pleasure.

His tongue found her nipple, hard with excitement. He sucked and bit gently. His hand took her other breast and covered it with his outstretched fingers. He massaged her slowly, then faster, and then his thumb rubbed the hard pink bud, causing it to contract with a need that was almost painful. As she writhed in a pleasurable agony of anticipation his caresses grew more impassioned, and more demanding. He tugged on the drawstring of her loose trousers and she felt the silky cloth sliding over her legs as he pulled them off. His hands searched for her briefs – and then discovered that she was not wearing any.

She heard him laugh softly, and then felt his palms on her inner thighs, parting them. She resisted, just for the pleasure of feeling his strength as he forced her into a position where he could get a good view of the swollen tip of her clitoris peeping through the red curls of her pubic hair. He stopped for a moment to look at her. His fingers played with her demandingly, opening her still more. And then the warmth of his mouth closed over her, and his tongue continued the action of his fingers. She closed her eyes. His tongue worked faster, exciting her with short insistent strokes. He held her legs apart so that she was his willing prisoner. When her climax came it startled her with its intensity. Her body jolted upwards to a sitting position and she gave a wild, involuntary cry before falling back on the bed, as exhausted as if she had been running.

He smiled. She could see the bulge of his erection and she reached out for him. He helped her, tugging down the zip of his jeans. Her hands explored, cupping his heavy balls. She felt the strength of his cock straining in her hand.

'Yes,' she said, pulling him closer. 'Yes, please. Now.'

She did not expect another orgasm so soon after the last one, but the closeness of his body as he entered her and began to thrust with obvious excitement, and the sight of his face above hers, his black hair dishevelled and damp with sweat now, turned her on more intensely then she had ever experienced before. My God, she thought wildly, I could have an orgasm, just *looking* at this man.

He came with a cry that was almost a shout. She held him as the violent spasms subsided. He gently withdrew from her, and then lay beside her, on his back. His hand found hers and he grasped it tightly.

'I'd almost forgotten how good it can be,' he said. 'With the right woman.'

Elise was working in her office. Outside, the sky was overcast but her memories of the night before made it seem as golden as sunlight. She remembered Max Lannsen's cry of delight; remembered the sensation of closeness when he entered her. Then the phone rang.

'I'm back.' It was Blair Devlin's voice. 'When can I see you? Tonight.'

'No,' she said.

Even that single word seemed to alert him that something was wrong. 'Tomorrow?' He sounded cautious.

'No,' she repeated.

He paused. 'All right. Is it because I left without saying good-bye? I had to go in a hurry. I know I didn't leave any phone number, but it was only for a week.'

'It's got nothing to do with that,' she said. 'It's just that . . . it's over.'

There was a much longer pause this time. When he spoke again his voice was cold. 'May I ask why?'

'Look,' she said. 'We agreed it was a no-strings affair. A fun thing. We didn't make any promises.'

'It wasn't necessary to make promises,' he said. 'I just assumed that we enjoyed each other's company, and it was going to last a while, that's all. And I assumed that when it ended, we'd both more or less agree on it. Obviously you had a different agenda.'

He was making her feel guilty. She responded with anger. 'Talking of agendas, what about yours? What about the will you hoped I'd find for you in the old master's rooms?'

Another pause. This time his voice was as angry as hers: 'So you've heard that ridiculous story?'

'Is it ridiculous?' she challenged. 'Mrs Stokes believes it.'

'She's the only one who does,' he said abruptly. 'There is no will. Whatever the old master wanted for me, it won't happen. I've accepted that.

'I'm sorry,' Elise said. 'Maybe that's true. But it doesn't make any difference.'

'I don't really think this has anything to do with a

fairy story about a lost will.' His voice was cold. 'It's about the way you see your future. You've been reassessing your physical assets since you came to Shilden, haven't you?'

The bitterness in his voice startled her. 'Just what's that supposed to mean?' she asked.

'I heard about your little striptease,' he said. 'Your friend Lorna just loves to gossip, and so does Penny. I'm a fairly broad-minded man, but it seems it hasn't taken you long to get seduced by the big money.' He paused. 'Well, I don't blame you, sweetheart. Why do it for free, when you can do it for cash?'

'That,' she said, 'is a disgusting thing to say.'

'Is it?' He laughed unkindly. 'It might be, but it's true, isn't it? Well, thanks for ditching me. I wouldn't want to share you with a crowd of paying customers, anyway. Your evenings are going to be pretty busy from now on, aren't they? Good luck to you, if that's what you want! And good-bye!'

The phone slammed down.

Should I have told Blair Devlin the truth? Elise wondered. He was going to find out soon enough anyway, if Lorna was prone to gossiping to Penny. This isn't how I wanted things to happen, she thought, but nothing has happened the way I expected. Did I ever dream I'd be sitting here waiting for Max Lannsen to pour me a drink, waiting for him to sit opposite me and look at me with that strange, almost impersonal gaze. Then waiting for his look to change. Waiting for him to start to make love to me . . .

She stared at Max Lannsen's broad-shouldered back, at his long, slightly parted legs, and his tautly attractive denim-covered bottom. I liked looking at Ralph, she remembered. I liked looking at Blair Devlin. But neither of them made me feel as instantly sexy as this intensely private man that I've made love to but hardly know anything about. Except that he was married, to a beautiful woman, and it's over. Or so he says.

Her eyes strayed round the walls. Bold oil paintings, self-assured pencil sketches, a delicate water colour. Two charcoal nudes. Even allowing that they were the work of a talented artist and beautiful pictures in their own right, she could not help wondering why he kept so many reminders of his ex-wife in his room. She looked up suddenly. Lannsen's dark eyes were watching her.

'You were miles away,' he said. He handed her a glass of wine. 'What were you thinking about?'

'That I'd like to do whatever it was you did with Tish,' she improvised quickly – and not wholly untruthfully.

He looked at her with the trace of a smile. 'Are you sure? I was going to suggest that when you finished your wine I undressed you very slowly and tried to discover which parts of your body you really liked me to touch, and how you liked it done, and then maybe check if my tongue could arouse your nipples faster than my fingers, and then – '

'Just do what you did to Tish?' she said firmly.

'You might not enjoy it.'

'I will,' Elise said. 'She did. She loved it. She said so. In fact she said she'd do it again, for free.'

'How flattering,' he murmured. 'Perhaps I'll ask her.'

'You won't!' Elise said quickly. 'You don't need to. Whatever it was, I'll do it.'

This time he grinned openly, walked to the door, then stopped and turned. 'Are you sure you're up to it? I don't want you backing out after we've started. That would really annoy me.'

'Anything Tish can do, I can do,' Elise said, hoping it was true.

He stopped smiling. 'Then get your clothes off,' he said coldly. 'I'll go and get my equipment.'

She stood in the middle of the room and stripped, suddenly wondering if she had made a mistake. What equipment was he fetching? Maybe Tish had some really bizarre sexual tastes? Maybe that was why she had enjoyed her session? When Max Lannsen came back, all he seemed to be carrying was a large, flat folder. She stood in the middle of the room, feeling vulnerable and nervous. He looked at her critically, and she felt that it was not a purely sexual assessment.

'Sit on the floor,' he said. He went into the bedroom and returned with a straight-backed chair. She was still standing up. 'For heaven's sake,' he said, irritably. 'Sit down.'

She sat down, and he walked round her. 'Pull one leg up,' he instructed. 'Put your arms round it. That's right. Now lay your head on your knee. Comfortable?'

'Not very,' she admitted.

'Too bad,' he said. He sat down on the chair and opened the folder. Taking a pencil out of his pocket he began to draw. She moved her head to look at him. 'Stop fidgeting,' he said. 'Keep still.'

'How long for?' she asked. She could feel her nose itching.

'For as long as it takes.' His hand was moving swiftly. 'You wanted to do this, remember?'

'*This* is what you did with Tish?' She could hardly believe it.

'Yes,' he said. 'And she was very good. A marvellous body, beautiful lines, and she didn't move a muscle.' He looked up at Elise as she wriggled uncomfortably. 'Unlike you.'

'But she said she enjoyed it!'

'Why shouldn't she enjoy it?' he asked. 'She was very pleased with the result. She flattered me shamelessly, so I gave it to her.'

Elise said suddenly: 'These portraits – you did them?'

'Yes,' he said shortly.

'But they're beautiful. You're very talented.'

'Well, don't sound so damned surprised,' he said.

'I had no idea you were an artist,' she said. 'Did you sell a lot of work?'

'I didn't have much to sell,' he said. 'My father hated the idea of me being a painter. He didn't think it was masculine enough. So I went in the army and learnt how to kill people. I was quite good at it. I stuck with it until I met Jeanette. She didn't want to be an army wife, but she didn't want be married to a struggling painter either, so I became a businessman. I was good at that, too. I made a lot of money. And Jeanette spent it.' He paused. 'On her various boyfriends.' Another pause. 'Everyone knew, except me. I was too much in love.'

'And so you divorced?'

'Eventually.'

'But you still kept her portraits?' Elise said. 'Didn't she want them?'

'I thought I was entitled to keep my own work,' he said.

'I would have thought you were entitled to more than that,' she said.

'I let Jeanette divorce me,' he said. 'I gave her everything she wanted. I actually thought if I agreed to all her demands I might get her back. And she took everything.' He stood up suddenly and put his drawing pad down. Turning abruptly he walked to the window. She was reminded of the first time she had seen him, a dark silhouette. 'Everything,' he said. 'Including my faith in women.'

'And has it come back yet?' she asked softly.

He turned back to her again, and smiled. 'Partly,' he said. He walked towards her. 'Because of you.' She knelt in front of him. He put his hands on her head. 'I didn't believe I could ever feel anything for another woman. Or trust one. I built a wall round myself. If a woman showed interest, I'd usually ignore her. Sometimes I'd use her and ditch her. Either way, I hoped it hurt. I'd been hurt, so I wanted to hurt back.' The pressure on her head pulled her towards him. 'Until I met you.'

'Love at first sight?' she smiled up at him.

'No,' he said. 'But I was attracted. Especially after you rejected me when I first showed you round the castle. Do you remember that?'

'Yes,' she said.

'What did you think of me then?' he asked.

'I almost wished I'd let you have me,' she said.

He laughed. 'I kept thinking about you. I fantasised.'

'What was I doing?'

'In one of my favourites you were kneeling in front of me,' he said. 'Naked. You were a slave I was thinking of buying. I'd stripped you, and inspected you, and approved of you. That was the first part. The second was to try you out. So I stood there and gave you orders.'

She could see his erection pushing against the zip of his jeans. 'Like what?' she asked softly.

'Like ... let me see how good you are with your mouth,' he said.

She unzipped him and cupped her hands under his balls, nuzzling against him, nipping him with her teeth, feeling him swell, knowing that when she freed his cock it would spring out, ready for her. He helped her, pushing his briefs down. She closed her lips round him and let them slide along the length of his penis, moistening it with her tongue. She felt his body shake, and knew that it would not take long to give him the ultimate sensation. She tried to make it last, but he came almost at once, his body rocking as she held him. She heard him groan once, a deep sound that ended in something like a sigh.

'Have I passed the test?' She looked up at him and smiled. 'Will you purchase me?'

He ran his fingers through her hair with possessive

strength. 'Not yet.' he said. 'I'm a hard taskmaster. There are lots of other skills I'll have to test you on first.'

'Max has gone to London,' Lorna said. She looked surprised. 'I thought you knew.'

Elise stared at her. 'But he didn't say anything to me. When did he go?'

'About an hour ago.' Lorna looked distinctly uncomfortable. 'Actually, I thought he looked angry. Well, to be honest, I thought you'd had a row.'

Elise had spent the previous day finishing her designs for the space-age striptease, and the afternoon working in the old master's rooms, planning their conversion. She was happy in the sunny, comfortable, slightly dusty apartment. Life's great, she thought. I can spend my days up here, with no Petra Altham nagging me, and my evenings and nights with Max, talking about art and drama, listening to music, making love.

'Didn't he say *anything*?' she persisted. 'Haven't you got any idea what all this is about?'

Lorna fidgeted. 'I'm as much in the dark as you. All I can tell you is that Max seemed fine when we discussed your striptease ideas this morning. Then the post came, and he got a small parcel. He went off with it and I didn't see him again. I just got a very abrupt phone call saying he was leaving. And the next thing I knew, his car had gone.'

After three days Elise was in despair. All her attempts to contact Max Lannsen had ended in failure. She had no idea where he was staying. Lorna's colleagues in London were unhelpful. Mr Lannsen's only official phone number was Shilden Castle, they said, and if he wasn't there, and had left no details of his whereabouts, he obviously did not want to be contacted at all. Elise cried herself to sleep, moped about during the day, and did no work at all. On the fourth day Lorna came into her office and put a mug of coffee in front of her.

'Drink it,' she said. 'It's got whisky in it.'

'I don't want it,' Elise said wretchedly.

'Drink it,' Lorna repeated. 'And then I'll give you my news.'

'You've found out where Max is?' Elise brightened up immediately.

'No,' Lorna said. 'But I've got a clue.' She watched as Elise sipped the coffee. 'I've been making use of my contacts. That parcel Max received – it came from Petra Altham.'

Elise stared at Lorna. 'How on earth do you know that?'

'Never mind how I know,' Lorna said. 'It came from Petra. And you can bet that whatever was in it, it didn't do you any favours. I warned you, remember? Petra's a prize bitch. She's got back at you in a way she knew would hurt you – through Max.'

'But how? What could Petra send Max that would hurt me?'

'I've no idea,' Lorna said. She smiled. 'Perhaps you ought to go down to London yourself and ask her.

By the time she reached London that evening, Elise was so hyped up with her need to sort things out that, despite feeling tired after the long journey, she decided to go straight to Petra's mews cottage. It was in darkness when she arrived. She parked her car opposite, and settled down for a long wait.

Petra finally arrived by taxi. She stepped out of the cab wearing a figure-hugging dress and stiletto heels. A wide choker glittered round her neck. She had a full-length fur coat slung over her shoulder. As she went up the steps to her front door she appeared to sway. Elise gave her the chance to get inside and put the light on, then ran across the road and rang the bell.

'Dixie, is that you?' Petra's voice was slurred. 'Baby, I'm too tired for fun and games tonight.' She opened the door and saw Elise. For a moment she looked confused. Elise pushed forward. Petra was off balance and she stumbled; in a moment, Elise was inside.

Petra's bright red mouth made an ugly shape: 'What the fuck do you want?'

'An explanation,' Elise said.

Petra recovered a little of her poise. 'You're the one who should be explaining. Because you kicked up a stupid fuss about nothing *I* lost my job!'

'You didn't lose your job because of me,' Elise snapped back. 'You lost it because you got greedy.' She advanced on Petra. 'Just what did you send Max the other day?'

'Oh, so *that's* it!' Petra laughed harshly. 'Maxie got my little present, did he? And how did he like it?'

'If I knew where he was I'd ask him,' Elise said.

'So he's run out on you, has he?' Petra smirked. 'Well. I thought he would – just as soon as he discovered what kind of a two-faced bitch you are!'

Elise reached forward and grabbed the front of Petra's dress. 'Just tell me what you sent,' she said, with ominous calm, 'or I'll break your nose. And that's just for starters!'

'Big brave girl, aren't you?' Petra taunted. 'You touch me and I'll get some of my friends to pay you a visit. And they'll break much more than your nose, believe me.' She smiled. 'You're out of your depth, darling. Why don't you just go home?'

Elise let go of Petra's dress. She had an uncomfortable feeling that this was not an idle threat. The subdued lights glinted on Petra's diamond choker. She reached out a finger and touched it briefly.

'That's pretty,' she said sweetly. 'You like nice things, don't you? A cosy little mews cottage, a big Mercedes car. Jewellery and clothes. To get nice things, you need money. And to get money, you need to work.' Petra stared at her suspiciously. Elise went on: 'We both know the kind of work you do. What happens if your contacts start ringing up someone else?'

'If that snooty slut at Shilden thinks she can poach my clients, she's mistaken.' Petra's smile had disappeared now. 'And you can tell her so from me.

Elise knew she had touched a raw spot. She pushed home her advantage. 'What happens if word gets round that you're . . . indiscreet?'

'I'm not fucking indiscreet!' Petra snarled.

'Rumours spread fast,' Elise said. 'Especially nasty ones.'

'And who'd believe you?' Petra demanded. 'A trumped-up little arty farty designer!'

But Elise thought she heard a trace of nervousness in Petra's voice. 'Can you afford to test it?' she asked, sweetly. 'You haven't left many friends back at Shilden. You called me a bitch, and you're right. I can be the biggest bitch you've ever known. Try me!'

'I just told you, darling,' Petra threatened. 'I have some friends you wouldn't like to meet. Want to risk it, do you, just for that screwed-up boyfriend of yours?'

'Hurt me and it just makes you look guilty,' Elise countered.

'Listen, little miss look-don't-touch,' Petra said harshly. 'I'm not guilty of anything. You are! I cared about my job at Shilden, and you fucked that up for me properly. So I sent your screwed-up boyfriend some pretty pictures. Pretty *moving* pictures. Taken in the castle gym. Remember that, do you?' Her mouth stretched into a smile. 'I had a camera running for a little film I was making. Something for a friend of mine. I forgot to turn it off, and the tape hadn't finished. So when I played it back, there you were, with your sexy riding instructor, having fun.'

So that's why Petra's performance had sounded so

theatrical, Elise realised. She was playing out a fantasy for someone. A private client, probably.

'I thought Maxie might like to see you in action,' Petra sneered. 'Although I don't think he was really into watching sexy films. He had some funny ideas about women. I think he wanted us all to have wings and a halo. Perhaps my little bit of film proved to him that you weren't quite as perfect as he hoped. You were just another woman two-timing him, like his ex-wife. No wonder he walked out on you!'

In a way, Petra's explanation made Elise feel better. A misunderstanding could be sorted out – if only she could find Max Lannsen. The one place she knew she would not find him was Shilden Castle, at least as long as he suspected she was still there. She rang Lorna and asked for a few days off.

'I'll fix it for you,' Lorna promised. She rang back a couple of hours later. 'Fixed it,' she said brightly. 'But you've got to go and see George Farrow.'

'George?' Elise repeated. 'Whatever for?'

'In Max's absence he's more or less your boss,' Lorna said. 'Dress up and go and be nice to him. He likes you, remember. You might even get some more time off. He's got a house just outside London somewhere. I'll find you the address.'

Elise borrowed one of Jannine's newly acquired suits – a grey tailored jacket and slim skirt. She twisted her hair into a neat bun, and tucked any stray curls back out of the way. A pair of Jannine's medium-heeled grey shoes completed her outfit. They were half a size too large, but she padded the toes with cotton wool. Because the outfit made her feel almost frumpy, she wore some sexy panties; triangles of silk and lace held together with narrow ribbon ties.

George Farrow's London house was surprisingly unpretentious, set well back off the road, and in a quiet

212

residential area. A smiling young woman in a plain black dress answered the door.

'Miss St John? Please come in.' She led Elise to a room that was tastefully, if unexcitingly, furnished, and gave Elise the impression that it was little used. In fact, the whole house gave a similar impression. 'I'm leaving now,' the girl told Elise. 'But someone will be in to see you shortly.'

Mystified, Elise wandered over to a window and stared out. The garden was as neat, tasteful and, she thought, as boring as the house. The door opened. Elise turned. Max Lannsen walked into the room; a dark figure in a dark suit, and as attractive as ever. For a moment they both stared dumbly at each other, both equally startled. Then Lannsen said abruptly: 'What the hell are you doing here?'

'I might ask you the same thing,' Elise retaliated.

'I came because George Farrow asked me to.'

'So did I,' Elise said. They both heard the sound of a door shutting.

'The housekeeper's gone now,' Lannsen said angrily. 'We should have asked her what's going on.' He looked at his watch. 'Well, I'll give George five minutes, and if he doesn't turn up, I'm going too. I have things to do.'

'Max,' Elise said. 'I went to see Petra. I found out about the video. I didn't know it existed until she told me.'

He stared at her for a minute, then turned away. 'I'm sure you didn't,' he said coldly. 'And if you don't mind, I'd rather not discuss it. I don't want to hear your excuses. I've heard enough excuses in my life. Women are pretty damn good at them.'

'I'm not making excuses. I don't *need* to make excuses.' His attitude suddenly made her want to hurt him, to anger him, anything to break the glacial shell he had built round himself. She walked over and confronted him. 'Don't you think you over-reacted? You knew

213

about my affair with Blair Devlin. You knew you weren't getting a virgin.'

'Maybe I did,' he agreed. 'But I didn't expect to get another slut!'

She had slapped his face without thinking. Her palm stung from the force of the blow. He caught her wrist and spun her round. His body was tense with anger, but as soon as he touched her she also felt an erotic thrill.

'Bitch!' He pushed her forward to the pale-covered settee.

'I'm not!' she gasped. 'And you're hurting me.'

'No one slaps me and gets away with it,' he said. 'If you were a man, I'd flatten you.'

'Well, I'm not!' She was still struggling.

'You still don't get away with it,' he said.

He upended her over the arm of the settee and held her down with one hand. The other undid her skirt band and tugged the slim skirt to her knees and then her ankles. She felt the silk ties being pulled undone and her panties followed her skirt to the floor. In the brief pause that followed she said, in a small voice, her face half muffled in a cushion: 'Don't you *dare*!'

But she knew that he would dare and, what was more, she wanted him to! The flat of his hand landed on her bottom and she yelled, kicking out at him. Her shoes quickly came off. He avoided her flailing feet and carried on spanking her, holding her down easily with one hand. Her neat bun uncoiled and her hair fanned out over the cushion. The sound of his palm landing on her upturned bottom was interrupted only by her noisy protests, which finally subsided into gasps, prompted as much by an intense feeling of sexual delight as by the warm stinging sensation his descending hand had caused her. He finally stopped spanking her, but he still held her down.

'Did you like it better with him than me?' he asked,

his voice not quite steady. 'Is that why you did it?' She lay with her legs slightly apart. He pushed her even further forward.

'Don't be an idiot,' she said. 'I didn't know what it was like with you when I was with Blair Devlin.'

'I know when the cameras were fitted in the gym,' he said. 'I know when that tape was made.'

'You think you do!' She wriggled under his strong grasp. 'Hasn't it occurred to you that someone else could have been filming with their own camera? And that same person could have lied to you about when they found the tape?'

'Why should Petra lie?' he asked.

'To get back at me,' she said. 'You may not have noticed it, but dear Petra didn't like me at all – especially after she got the sack.'

'She deserved the sack,' he said. 'I would have got rid of her sooner, given the chance. She had her fingers in quite a few dishonest deals, and she was using our facilities to line her own pocket.'

'That's what she was doing when her camera filmed us,' Elise said. 'Acting out a scene with a girlfriend.'

'And then you acted out a scene with your boyfriend,' Lannsen accused.

'Yes,' she said, simply. 'But I was a free agent then. I hadn't made a commitment to you.'

'And now you have?'

'You know I have,' she said.

There was a long pause. She knew he was looking at her, and the thought of it turned her on. She deliberately parted her legs a little more.

'Do you know the worse thing of all?' he said, huskily. 'When I was watching that damn tape, watching you with Devlin – I wanted you. It hurt to watch, but I kept on watching – and I still wanted you.' His hand slid up suddenly between her legs. She needed his touch so desperately that she wriggled against him, encouraging

215

him to probe deeper. 'I wanted you,' he repeated. 'Badly. As badly as I want you now.'

Suddenly he turned her over and pulled her to her feet. He unzipped himself and entered her so quickly that she gave a gasp of surprise. But she was wet and relaxed, and she tightened her internal muscles, pulling him closer. She felt his hands on her still tingling bottom, supporting her, then lifting her. She hooked her legs round him. Carrying her like that he took her to the centre of the room where, still intimately joined, he lowered her on to the thick carpet, held her shoulders to the ground, and began to thrust strongly.

'You don't know what it did to me,' he muttered, close to her ear. His movements grew more powerful. He filled her and excited her, and she felt herself slipping deliciously out of control. 'I just wanted to take you, and beat you, and make love to you.'

She felt her climax approaching but hoped it would coincide with his. His movements were shorter and faster now. His body began to shake. She clung to him, and they rolled on the carpet in a tangle of legs and arms.

'Now,' she gasped. 'Now, please . . .'

His climax came with a sudden violent spasm of pleasure, and hers followed so closely that their bodies shook and then grew calm together, and then she felt totally relaxed, totally happy, and totally fulfilled. He lay half on top of her. She felt his weight, but did not want him to move.

'Don't ever do it again,' he said.

'Do what?' she teased. 'Make love?'

'Give me any reason to distrust you,' he said. 'All right, I over-reacted to that tape. I should have talked to you. Listened to your explanation. But you don't understand what Jeanette did to me. She always had an answer. She tied me up with lies. In the end I didn't believe anything.'

216

'I won't lie to you,' Elise said. 'Trust me.'

'I'm learning to,' he said.

Suddenly she sat up. 'My God, Max. George Farrow!'

He too pulled himself into a sitting position. 'What about him?'

'I was supposed to meet him here.' She jumped to her feet and grabbed her skirt. 'We've been rolling about on his carpet, making love. He could have walked in at any time.'

'And probably thoroughly enjoyed the show,' Lannsen grinned. He zipped himself up lazily. 'Although I'm not sure I would enjoy performing for an audience.'

She pulled on her skirt and tried to twist her hair into a loose bun again. 'For heaven's sake, Max,' she said. 'Tidy yourself up.'

He looked down. 'I am tidy.'

'Your hair isn't, and neither is your tie.'

'Stop worrying,' he laughed. 'George isn't going to walk in on us.'

'How do you know?' She checked her stocking seams.

'He asked you here, didn't he? And he asked me. Why do you think he did that?'

She realised that she hadn't thought about the coincidence before. 'I've no idea,' she said.

'I suspect that he heard about our little difference of opinion,' Lannsen said. 'And he wanted us to sort things out.'

'George Farrow doesn't know anything about our private life,' she objected. She thought about what had happened. 'Does he?' she added, no longer sure.

'Ask him,' Lannsen said. He took her hand and pulled her towards the window. Her Mini was parked outside. A large Daimler stood next to it. 'That's his car. Well, one of them. I came by taxi.'

They went outside. George Farrow climbed out of the driving seat of the Daimler. 'Hello, my dear,' he greeted Elise. 'I'm delighted to see you again. And you, Max.'

'Congratulations, George,' Lannsen said. 'Whatever you intended, it worked.'

'I'm delighted to hear it,' the older man said. 'You're terrible company when you're crossed in love. I had to do something.' He smiled at Elise. 'I take it you're responsible for cheering him up?'

'I hope so,' Elise smiled back.

'Lucky man,' Farrow said. He turned back to Elise. 'And you're lucky, too, you know. If your friend Lorna hadn't told me what was going on, you two would still be avoiding each other. And that wouldn't have done you, or our project at Shilden, any good at all.' He turned to Lannsen. 'Miss Chorley-Smythe is an asset. A much better type than Petra Altham.'

'I suppose so.' Lannsen sounded unconvinced.

'Come on now, Max,' George Farrow said jovially. 'I know you'd rather run Shilden as a straightforward country club, but if you want to make money you've got to supply the services. And we all need to make money, eh?' He patted Lannsen on the shoulder. 'But now you've got together with your lady again, why not enjoy yourself for a few days before going back up north? You've got the use of Phillip's flat for the rest of the week. He won't mind Elise moving in. There's a charity do at the Grange. Why don't you both go? I'll make sure you get invitations.' He smiled at Elise. 'You'll like it. It's an annual event, run like a fair, with side shows and tents and lots of artists and theatre people helping out. You might make some good contacts.'

'We haven't time,' Lannsen said.

'Max, we have,' Elise protested. 'It sounds fun.'

'Take her, Max,' George Farrow said. 'That's an order.'

'You don't really want to go to this charity thing, do you?' Elise said, watching Max Lannsen pulling a cream polo-necked jumper over his head. She loved watching him dress. In fact, she thought, I just love watching him.

'I'm not the party type,' he said, abruptly. 'I don't like small talk. and I don't like gossip.' He glanced at her. 'I've heard about these parties at the Grange. They can get . . . out of hand.'

'You mean we're really going to an orgy?' she teased.

'Would that bother you?' he asked.

'Oh, come on Max!' She stopped buttoning her silk blouse and walked over to him. 'I'm not about to share you with *anyone*.'

He put his hands inside her blouse and cupped her breasts. She felt his fingers tighten. 'Just keep it that way,' he said.

She put her fingers on his nipples, clearly visible beneath his cotton shirt, and felt him react. Leaning forward she covered one nipple with her mouth, keeping her fingers on the other one, manipulating it gently. After a moment he said, huskily: 'You're making my shirt damp.'

For an answer she pushed his shirt up and continued her caresses. 'Better?' she murmured, still tonguing him. 'The only thing that's getting damp now is me.'

'I could do something about that,' he said.

'I'm ready and willing,' she invited, still caressing him.

'Go upstairs,' he said, 'and strip.'

'Max?' She had expected him to take her quickly, right there. 'We haven't time.'

'Do as you're told,' he said.

She went up to the bedroom, peeling off her clothes as she walked. It did not take her long; she had not been wearing much to start with. She stretched out on the bed, on her back. The submissive female, she thought, waiting to be serviced by her man. Surprisingly she felt quite turned on by the idea. As long as the man is Max Lannsen, she thought, contentedly.

219

'What are you smiling at?' He had come upstairs without a sound.

'Nothing,' she said, demurely. 'Yet. I'm practising. Aren't you going to give me something to smile about?'

She watched him strip and when he finally stepped out of his briefs she thought once again that his body was every bit as attractive as she had always imagined. He was built like a runner, slim and muscular, with narrow hips and long legs. The black hair on his chest and between his legs emphasised his natural tan. He was partially erect, his cock moving enticingly as he walked towards the bed.

'Turn over,' he said.

She turned obediently and he knelt behind her. His hands slipped under her hips and he pulled her on to her knees. Reaching forward, he let her breasts fall into his cupped hands. He teased her nipples, holding her. She felt his stiffening cock press against her. Then she spread her legs slightly and he entered her, grasping her thighs and holding her while he thrust, slowly at first, and then with increasing speed and strength. Holding her in that position enabled him to enter her deeply, which she knew excited him, but also made her breasts and clitoris easily available to his searching hands, so that he could give each part of her an equal amount of varied pleasure. She came with a shuddering cry that he matched a moment later. When he withdrew she lay on her front, sleepy and satisfied. He lay beside her for a few moments, then reached out and stroked a strand of hair from her face.

'I'll get you a drink,' he said.

'As long as you don't have one,' she murmured. 'You're driving, remember?'

'Am I?' he said.

She turned and sat up. 'Yes, you are.' He was standing by the door. 'Max,' she accused, 'you did that to try and put me off going to the party.'

'I did it because I enjoy fucking you,' he said bluntly. 'But if we don't go to the party, I'll be able to do it again.'

'You can do it again anyway,' she said. 'After we come back.'

The Grange was a large house on the outskirts of London, set well back from the road and surrounded by trees. They pulled into the drive and Lannsen parked his Mercedes next to an old, but immaculate, Rolls-Royce. Some of the other cars were less impressive. Elise spotted a battered Ford escort and a Mini standing side by side.

The house was open, but most of the activities were obviously occurring in the extensive grounds. Music filtered through the trees. Coloured tents had been erected on the lawns. Brightly-dressed men and women wandered about carrying trays of drinks and food. A juggler walked by, tossing balls in the air. He smiled at Lannsen and Elise.

'Don't miss the Amazing Antonio,' he invited cheerfully. 'Illusionist Extraordinary. In the blue tent.' He winked at Lannsen. 'You should go and watch. You'll like it.' He turned to Elise. 'And so will you. There's something for everyone.'

'Come on,' Elise tugged at Lannsen's arm. 'I love magic shows.'

A few minutes later, they went into the crowded tent. The Amazing Antonio, gaudily dressed in a glittering suit and top hat, had already begun his performance. A large twin-doored cabinet stood on a stand. The doors were open to show an attractive young lady in an evening dress. She was smiling politely.

'Nothing underneath the cabinet,' Antonio insisted, waving a long wand under the stand. 'Nothing above it. Nothing behind. A few words from me and the lady will disappear.' The cabinet doors closed. The Amazing

Antonio muttered something and waved his wand again. 'Voilá!' he announced. The doors sprung open. The lady was still there, minus her dress. She was wearing sexy black lace underwear and looked startled. The crowd whistled and cheered. The Amazing Antonio looked equally surprised. He slammed the doors shut.

'That's never happened before,' he apologised. 'Allow me a chance to redeem myself.' He waved his wand again 'This time,' he promised, 'the lady will have disappeared.'

The doors sprang open. The woman in the cabinet gave a little shriek. She was now totally naked. She made an inefficient attempt to cover herself with her hands, while the crowd applauded.

Once again the magician slammed the doors shut. 'This time,' he promised, wiping imaginary sweat from his brow. 'She *will* disappear. I promise you.'

He took longer over his magic incantations. He waved his wand up and down, forwards and backwards. The doors opened – to reveal a young man in a smart evening suit.

'Well,' the Amazing Antonio shrugged. 'That's better than a naked lady, I suppose.' There was a chorus of male disapproval from the audience. Antonio smiled. 'Maybe I'll be more successful at making a gentleman disappear.' A flurry of wand waving followed. The cabinet doors opened again and, as Elise expected, this time the young man had been stripped of everything except a bulging posing pouch.

'I know what you ladies are hoping for,' Antonio guessed, slamming the doors shut again. 'But you're going to be disappointed. I've got the knack of it now. This time the cabinet will definitely be empty!' He threw open the doors with a flourish, revealing the young man displaying a sizeable erection and a charming smile.

Antonio shut the doors again. 'Now I'm as mystified as you,' he said. 'What next?'

He flung open the doors. The original lady, still naked, was now enjoying the attentions of the naked man. The crowd hooted and clapped as the man began to suck her nipple enthusiastically. She moaned and encouraged him, sliding her hands over his muscular buttocks and pulling him close. Antonio made a great show of trying to close the doors on them, without success. The couple began to get more amorous. The woman knelt and took her companion's now stiffly erect cock in her mouth, working on him expertly. He made a good pretence at modesty, trying to push her away, reminding her that people were watching, but she held him by grasping his balls, and carried on with her teasing. Antonio tried to free the supposedly jammed cabinet doors while the lady's head moved faster. Just as the young man was about to come, Antonio was successful. The young man's orgasmic shout of relief coincided with the banging of the doors. The crowd applauded. The Amazing Antonio bowed.

'Please show your appreciation when you leave,' he said. 'And I mean your financial appreciation, please. I don't want any thank-you notes. It's all for a good cause. All for local charities. Be generous'.

'I wonder what the dear old ladies on the charity board would say if they knew exactly how their donations were being raised?' Elise said, as they walked away.

Lannsen grinned briefly. 'They might wish they'd been here to watch,' he suggested.

'Well,' she said. 'You're thawing at bit, aren't you?'

He stopped and turned to her. 'I'm not chiselled out of ice. That's half my damned problem. If I'd been less sensitive, Jeanette couldn't have hurt me so much.'

'I won't hurt you,' she said. 'Trust me.'

'I do,' he smiled. 'Or maybe I should say, I'm learning to.'

'Come on,' she said. 'Since we're here we may as well eat their food.'

They passed several other tents, and resisted invitations to come in and sample the delights of a massage, to watch a rare exotic dancer, or to view a series of tableaux re-creating famous scenes from mythology and history. Then Elise saw a tent decorated with Tarot cards. The poster outside claimed that if you were at a crossroads in your life, or worried about love, Madam Khati would ask the ancient and mystical tarot to advise and help you with your problems. 'A fortune teller,' she said in delight. 'Just what I need.'

'You don't need,' he objected. 'You're not worried about love.'

'I'm at a crossroads,' she said. 'I could do with some advice. What happens when my job at Shilden is finished? Will I ever work in the theatre full time?' She glanced at him. 'Will I be lucky in love?'

'I can answer most of that,' he said.

'But you're not impartial,' she teased. 'The tarot is. You go and find some food. I'll check out my future.'

The interior of the tent smelled pleasantly of incense. Madam Khati, far from being an ancient old crone with gold earrings and a scarf round her head, was a good-looking woman of about forty, with a heavy fall of straight black hair. The hair and her dark eye make-up made her look ancient Egyptian. The effect was heightened by the heavy silver ankh cross she wore round her neck. She sat behind a small table. Behind her stood a statue of Bast, the Egyptian cat-goddess. The tent walls muted any outside noise. Madam Khati gave Elise a long, level stare, then picked up a pile of cards with pale grey backs, shuffled them and placed them face down on the table.

'Cut the cards.' Her voice was cultured and deep. 'Three piles.'

Feeling slightly intimidated, Elise did so. 'What I want to know is – ' she began.

'The cards will not answer specific questions,' Madam Khati said. She smiled briefly. 'You will not get the winning lottery numbers from the tarot, I assure you. The tarot guides. It suggests. It will tell you what you need to know. No more, no less. I use a modern, non-traditional pack. The Elemental Tarot. There is no special merit in ancient designs.' She gazed at Elise. 'You have cut. Now choose again.'

Elise tapped one pile, almost nervously. Madam Khati picked up the cards and began to deal them out, face down on the table. The first two cards were placed one on top of the other, the next four formed a cross, with another four in a close group on the right, and one extra card on its own.

'This is my own spread,' Madam Khati said. 'I use it for short readings. The pattern is a tool, nothing more.' She sat for a moment, then began to turn the cards over, all except the final one. The designs were modern and colourful without being garish. The cards contained both pictures and words. Madam Khati looked at them for a long time. 'Interesting,' she said at last. 'These,' she passed her hand over the cross and the square, 'tell me of your past and present situation. You will see that the symbols of earth and water, the square and the crescent, predominate in this spread. They represent the material world and the emotions. You have had recent changes in both these spheres. You have made one major emotional decision. But this,' she tapped the card that stood alone and unturned, 'is the key to your immediate future.'

She turned the card over. Elise saw a dark, faceless figure, surmounted by wings and a snake; a figure decorated with a cross similar to the one around Madam Khati's neck. The title of the card was Death. Despite herself, she gasped. But Madam Khati did not look in the least dismayed.

'Interesting,' she murmured. 'A card from the major arcana. The first in your spread so far. Another decision to be made. One that could transform your life.'

'But it says death,' Elise protested.

Madam Khati tapped the card with a long finger. 'It also says transformation.' Elise had not noticed the second word. 'In the tarot the death card means change.' Her finger traced the outline of the snake. 'A serpent sheds its skin. It renews itself. Do you see the green shoots in the ground? Renewal again.' She stared at Elise. 'You will have to make a decision. The other cards also speak of it. A decision that will involve your emotions, and those of others round you.' Her dark eyes surveyed Elise. 'It will be an important decision. One that could alter many lives. Choose wisely.'

Elise put some money in the charity box and left the tent. Lannsen was waiting for her with a tray of food.

'Well?' he said. 'Sorted out your future?'

She told him what had happened. 'It was very accurate,' she added.

He laughed. 'Changes? An emotional decision? It would have been accurate for me too. And just about three-quarters of the population of England.'

They found a place to sit and eat, hidden among the trees. 'It gave me a shock to see that death card,' she admitted.

'Forget it,' he said. He leant over and put a piece of fruit in her mouth. She ate in silence. 'It's not worrying you, is it?'

'Not really,' she said.

'You don't need a pack of fancy cards to look at a beautiful young woman and predict that she's going to make a few emotional decisions,' he said. 'And you're not supposed to take these side shows seriously, anyway. They're just here to make money for charity.'

'I know,' Elise said. 'It's just that Madam Khati seemed genuine.'

'Good acting,' he said. 'After you've eaten we'll go home and I'll give you some special therapy I've perfected that's guaranteed to make you forget all about death cards and gipsy fortune tellers!'

At times Elise felt it was too good to last. She finished her designs for staging the space-age striptease, and gave them to Lorna, who had taken over effortlessly from Petra Altham. Now her main priority was to work on the old master's rooms. It was a project that she knew she would enjoy, although it hurt her to have to take down the photographs, push aside the furniture and roll up the carpets. She was acutely conscious that someone had lived there for years, and now she was removing all trace of their existence.

'Then use some of the stuff,' Lannsen had suggested, when she told him her feelings. 'You don't have to make the place look like the Ritz hotel. Keep the style simple. Why not keep the old photographs, and renovate some of the old man's furniture.'

'But is that what your people want?' she asked.

'You're the designer,' he said. 'You give them what *you* want. Make it quirky. Old fashioned. Keep to the spirit of what's there.'

He had changed so much since they had returned from London that she joked about him being a Jekyll and Hyde.

'A split personality? Well, I could be,' he threatened. 'Jekyll is charming and tolerant – in other words, exactly like me. But Hyde might be a little more ... demanding.' He gave her a speculative look. 'Maybe you'd like that?'

'Maybe I would,' she agreed.

Their sexual relationship changed from then on. Sometimes they just made love, lazily learning about each other, getting comfortable with each other, but at other times he suggested new techniques and fantasies, delighting her with his inventiveness. She felt there were many sexual games he wanted to try, but was wary of suggesting. She knew now that he enjoyed spanking her, either holding her over his knees or tying her wrists and ankles to the bed posts, and she often tempted him into threatening punishment during the day, knowing that in the evening he would carry out his promise. She loved the feeling that he was in control; loved the knowledge that she was turning him on. Once, he tied her hands behind her back and ordered her to make love to him using just her mouth. Sometimes he would relax in his large armchair while she stripped for him. He would reward her by pulling her into his lap, or lifting her and carrying her to the bed. Other times he would order her to pose, lying nude on the sofa or in a chair, while he sketched or painted.

During these sessions it became a game for her to try and tempt him to make love to her before he had finished working. She did it by talking, by suggestion, by detailing what she would like to do to him, and what she would like him to do with her. Sometimes he resisted her, but often he would fling the sketch pad or board aside and take her, very fast and without preliminaries, or just work on her body with his hands and his tongue, until she begged him to end the torment and satisfy her. He often claimed that the more uncomfortable he became, the better he worked. When she saw some of the finished drawings, she was inclined to believe him. She found it difficult to accept that these seductively beautiful women, depicted with boldly flowing lines, were portraits of her.

'You've such a lot of talent,' she told him one day, 'I just can't understand how you shut yourself away from it for so long.'

'I need inspiration,' he said. 'Someone like you.'

It inspired her too, knowing that he was waiting for her at the end of the day. Waiting to eat, to talk. And to make love.

It was while she was rummaging through the old master's cupboards that Elise found the case full of scrapbooks. There were dozens of them, filled with newspaper cuttings detailing the successes of the local cricket team. Old Mr Bennett seemed to have lovingly collected every report of every match the team had ever played, both in Shilden and the neighbouring villages.

As she leafed through one of the books, a name caught her attention: Blair Devlin. She studied the picture and realised that one of the blurred faces in the team was indeed Devlin, probably aged about fourteen. Well, she thought, amused, he actually played cricket. And I imagined he spent all his free time on a horse. She leafed through the scrapbook, and realised that Devlin appeared in nearly all of the cuttings, which spanned about two years. She wondered if he had joined the cricket team because he liked the game, or to please the old master. Or maybe because, as heir apparent to Shilden Castle and all its traditions, he thought it was expected of him.

As she turned the pages a piece of paper fell to the floor. A letter, she thought. She picked it up and looked at it without much interest. *I, Arthur James Edward Bennett*, she read, *hereby bequeath my estate in its entirety to* ... She read the words without believing them. She could not believe them. An ordinary sheet of paper, neatly set out in an old-fashioned but firm hand. Signed, witnessed, and dated ... *to Guy Arthur Blair Devlin*.

Her first thought was, why didn't anyone look through these scrapbooks before? But then, she reasoned, why should they? A dusty case full of cuttings? Why should anyone bother? Especially if no one believed the old master had ever made a will, anyway.

She stared at the piece of paper in her hand, hating it. She remembered Madam Khati's words: a decision that could alter many lives. She had assumed it meant alter them for the better. Instead, fate had given her the chance to offer Blair Devlin the one thing he wanted most in the world: Shilden Castle. And the means to ruin the life of the man she loved.

Later that evening Elise lay on her bed staring at the ceiling. I don't need this, she thought desperately. Why didn't the old master lodge his will with a solicitor, then I wouldn't be in this position. She tried to convince herself that the will wasn't legal, so it was all right if she simply destroyed it. But she knew that it was signed, witnessed, and dated, which made it as legal as anything could be. What was she going to do? Hand over Shilden to Blair Devlin? Whatever Devlin did with the castle, it would not involve Max Lannsen, or the investors who had entrusted him with their money. The two men hated each other. Devlin would surely relish the chance to destroy Max Lannsen.

The phone rang. She jumped nervously and looked at her clock. Oh my God, she thought, I was supposed to meet Max half an hour ago. I can't go. Not now. The phone rang again, insistently. She picked it up.

'So you are there?' Even his voice turns me on, she thought. 'You were coming over. What's happened?'

'I'm sorry, Max,' she improvised. 'I've got this terrible stomach ache. I feel really bad. I've just taken a couple of painkillers.' She knew it sounded false and she suspected that he did not believe her.

'You could still come over,' he said.

'I'm sorry,' she repeated. 'I fell asleep. The painkillers affect me like that.'

There was a pause. 'You don't want to come?'

'I do,' she said. 'It's just that I don't think I'd be very good company at the moment.'

Another pause, longer this time. 'I'd be quite happy just to sit with you,' he said, and there was a frosty edge to his voice.

Now I've insulted him by implying that I think all he wants is sex, she thought miserably. 'You don't understand,' she began.

'I think I do,' he said, abruptly. And put the phone down.

Under any other circumstances she would have gone straight to him. But she knew she needed time and space to sort herself out. How could she explain how she felt? I can't even discuss this with him, she thought, because I can guess what he'll say. He'll remind me that all his remaining money is tied up in Shilden. If Blair Devlin takes over, he'll be ruined. Bankrupt, probably, if the investors have any claims on him.

And what about Devlin? She remembered him telling her that inheriting Shilden would have changed his life in more ways than she could imagine. What ways, she wondered? What was wrong with his life as it was? He was rich, wasn't he? He was part owner of a riding school. Did an old castle and an obsolete local title like Master of Shilden mean so very much to him?

She knew that it did. And it had meant a lot to old Mr Bennett as well. Although she had never met him, spending time in his rooms had made her feel quite close to him. Finding the will almost made her feel as if he was entrusting her to help him. He intended Blair Devlin to have the castle. She could not ignore that.

She lay back on the bed. Her need for Max Lannsen was suddenly so strong that it was painful. She wanted to feel the warmth of his body next to her, feel his hands moving over her skin. She wanted him to make love to her, roughly, even brutally, as a kind of punishment. She ran her hands over her body, cupping her breasts. But it failed to arouse her. Her mind was in too much turmoil. I'll talk to him, she thought. I'll explain. He'll understand. We'll work out a plan together. Tomorrow.

But she did nothing about the will. She carried on working and the will stayed in her drawer. And it was destroying her. She could not relax. She was tense and nervous. Her relationship with Max Lannsen began to suffer. Sometimes, when she made love, she wanted the physical action to blot out her thoughts. She clung to him with a desperate intensity. At other times she felt that she could hardly bear him to touch her. Each caress reminded her that she had considered – and was still considering – a betrayal.

If he noticed the change it her – and she could not see how he could avoid noticing it – he said nothing. But she felt him gradually withdrawing into himself, becoming wary. He reminded her of a cat who permitted certain physical liberties, but was always tense and ready to run. When she talked, he responded, but their conversations became increasingly stilted. They discussed work, and nothing else. Then their evening meetings ceased. There was no real decision made. Neither of them commented on it when they met. They were polite to each other, but no more. It was as if their physical relationship had never existed. It was like the closing of a door.

Elise spent all day and most evenings working on the designs for the old master's rooms. When she needed to relax she drove out into the country and sat in her car, listening to music. She avoided Lorna, who was now constantly busy anyway. Lorna had tried to sound her out about her private life, but Elise had refused to be drawn in. She knew what Lorna would say about the will. The same as Max Lannsen. Destroy it. When she finished the designs for the old master's rooms she took them to Lorna.

'You should give these to Max,' Lorna said. 'They're nothing to do with me.'

'It'd like you to give them to Max,' Elise said. 'Please. But not until tomorrow morning.'

Lorna gave her a critical look. 'OK. And you look terrible. Do you know that?'

Elise brushed a few strands of red hair out of her eyes. 'I love the way you always try and give me confidence.'

'You don't need confidence,' Lorna said. 'You've always had plenty of that. You need a good night's rest.' She paused. 'Or maybe a good night with a good man?'

'You're wrong on both counts,' Elise said. 'I know exactly what I need right now.'

I need to get away from Shilden, she thought, as she packed her case. I need to get this awful weight off my conscience. And I need to be in a place where I know there's no chance I'm going to see Max Lannsen. If I don't see him, maybe the pain will go away. Eventually. Half-way down the A1 she branched off on to a slip road and ended up in a small village. She found the sub-post office, sent an envelope by recorded delivery to Mr Blair Devlin at White Gates, Shilden, and then got back into her car and headed for the dual carriageway again. That evening she was back in London.

Chapter Eight

'*I* just don't believe it,' Jannine said. 'You've ruined him and you've walked out on him? Is this my best mate, telling me these things? The love of your life, and you've done *this*?'

'What else could I do?' Elise asked.

'Well, for Christ's sake!' Jannine got up and began to pace about. 'You could have talked it over with me.'

'I knew what you'd say.'

'Too right,' Jannine agreed, swinging round. 'Burn the bloody will!' She sat down again, facing Elise. 'Look, babe, I'm sure Blair Devlin was sexy as hell, and a real regular guy, and he was miffed at not getting his hands on the old ancestral pile and being the master of all he surveyed, or whatever, but so what? He wasn't starving in a garret, was he? Sounds to me as if he had a pretty good life, what with the locals tugging their forelocks, and the village virgins queuing up for their riding lessons.' She reached out and took Elise's hands. 'What the hell came over you, baby? Mr Devlin is going to have a field day now, destroying the man you say you love.'

'It just seemed the right thing to do,' Elise said, wretchedly.

'Right?' Jannine exploded. 'It's as wrong as anything could be!'

'Well, honourable thing then,' Elise amended.

'Oh, Jesus,' Jannine said. 'Who writes your lines?'

'Look,' Elise said. 'I don't understand why I did it, either. All I know is that if I'd done anything else I would have felt guilty for the rest of my life.'

'And what do you feel now?' Jannine asked.

'Miserable,' Elise said. 'Empty. Lost.'

'Guilty would have been better,' Jannine said. 'And it would have worn off as soon as you hopped into bed with Max. Now all you've got is the loan of my second best teddy bear. And your precious honour. I just hope they keep you nice and warm at night.'

Apart from buying her car Elise had spent hardly any of the money she had earnt at Shilden. But she wanted a job. Sitting in Jannine's tiny flat was depressing. She was further depressed to find that many of her college friends were either on the dole, or had taken jobs unrelated to their art school studies.

'Talent isn't enough,' Jannine said. 'You need contacts. You want commissions? You gotta be where it's at, baby.' Dressed in a smart but revealing evening gown, she was putting the finishing touches to her piled-up blonde hair. 'Take me. I wouldn't be going to this classy shindig tonight if I hadn't pushed it with some of Lorna's mates. They certainly mix with the toffs – but then some of them *are* toffs, so I suppose it's all pals together.'

'It hasn't got you any acting jobs yet,' Elise said, rather tactlessly.

'But I'm making money,' Jannine said, unoffended. 'Pretty soon it'll be good-bye to this dump. You could do it too. You've got the face and the figure.'

'But not the inclination,' Elise said. She added: 'Have

you heard from Lorna?' and hoped it sounded as if she wasn't really interested.

'If you mean have I heard what's going on at Shilden, or what's happened to Max Lannsen,' Jannine interpreted, 'no, I haven't. There's no reason for Lorna to phone me now that you've probably caused her to lose her job.' She glossed her hair with a quick spray of lacquer. 'Is that taxi outside yet?'

Elise looked out of the window. 'It's waiting,' she said.

Jannine walked over to the door. 'Well, have fun watching telly, darling. And don't stay up. I'll be late. Maybe very late.'

After switching through several boring programmes, Elise turned the television off. She was dozing in her chair when the doorbell rang. Jannine's door had a spyhole fitted. Elise put her eye to it and peered out. Two men stood outside. She would have placed them in their early thirties. They had neat haircuts and wore dark, expensive-looking overcoats. They looked respectable. They could have been insurance salesmen, or missionaries from the Church of the Latter Day Saints, but somehow she knew they were not cold callers. They rang the bell again. She suddenly remembered Petra's threats. I'm not going to answer, she thought. I don't have to answer. Maybe they'll go away.

'Miss St John?' It was a cultured voice. 'We know you're in there. Please open the door.' She kept quiet. The voice continued, 'Either you come out, or we'll come in and get you.'

'If you try to force the door, I'll call the police,' she threatened, wondering if this could really be happening to her.

'Isn't that rather extreme?' the voice asked politely. 'We've come from a friend of yours. A very good friend.'

'It's rather extreme to threaten to force an entry,' she

236

said. 'And I don't have any very good friends who would expect you to do that.'

There was a pause. 'If we told you Max Lannsen wants to see you, would that make a difference?'

'No,' she said. She wondered briefly if it was possible, and then decided against it. 'Max wouldn't send two heavies to kick my door down,' she added. 'If he really wanted to see me, he'd come himself.'

Another pause. 'Good point. Actually, we want you to see *him*.'

'I don't want to see him,' she lied. 'I just want you to go away.'

'Too bad.' The man laughed softly. 'Because when we go, you're coming with us. Like it or not.'

She heard something click in the lock. There was a few seconds pause and then, to her horror, the door swung open. The two men walked into the room, smiling. One of them swung something like a small pencil in his hand. 'The wonders of modern technology,' he said. 'Tell your friend Jannine she should really get some bolts fitted. There are some dodgy characters about these days.'

'I'm not going with you,' Elise said.

'Of course you are,' the first man said, politely. 'You want to see Max, don't you? If you try to be awkward we can make you a little groggy and carry you out. But we don't really want to do that. It's rather uncivilised. It would be a lot more sensible if you'd co-operate. We're your friends, you know. Do you want to get a coat?'

'Yes,' she said. She turned for the bedroom, with a vague and wild idea of escaping through the window, but one of them followed her and stood by the door, watching as she took her cloak from the wardrobe. She had a feeling that he could have crossed the room and grabbed her before she had taken a step towards the window, which was closed anyway. She wrapped the cloak round her shoulders. 'All right,' she said. 'I'm ready.'

'Very sensible,' the man nodded. When they went outside he told her: 'Lock the door. There are a lot of thieves about.'

'And they're very well equipped,' she observed tartly.

He laughed. 'The genuine ones would give a lot for the little gadget I used.'

'So you're not genuine?' she parried.

'We're not thieves,' he said.

Elise had another twinge of doubt when she was hustled towards a large Rover saloon. But even if she had wanted to escape she knew that she was no match for even one of these men, let alone two. Despite their gentlemanly politeness they gave an impression of dangerous efficiency. Just like Max, she thought suddenly.

The car sped through the dark London streets. Elise gave up trying to guess where they were going. One man sat next to her on the back seat while the other drove. When they finally reached the wider roads of the suburbs the car slowed, turned into a drive and halted. Elise saw a large house with a welcoming yellow glow in several windows. The front door had fancy iron hinges and an iron knocker, but the two men walked straight in.

A light hand on her arm guided Elise down the hall and into a spacious room. She briefly registered the expensive, dark wood furniture, and the polished floor carpeted with Oriental rugs. A French window opened on to the garden. A man was standing beside it. A tall slim man in a dark suit. She knew at once that it was Max Lannsen. Absurdly, all she could think of was this is how she first saw him. Standing by a window.

'Visitor for you, Max,' the man with Elise said cheerfully.

Lannsen turned. His surprise was so genuine that

Elise knew at once that he had not engineered this meeting. His startled gaze moved from her to the man next to her. 'What the hell is this, Peter?'

Peter smiled. 'Payment of a debt,' he said. 'You saved me from making a fool of myself over a woman once, remember, when I was just a young and impressionable Lieutenant? My army career would have probably ended right there if you hadn't straightened me out. I'm just returning the favour.'

'You're not returning any favours,' Lannsen said angrily. 'You should have minded your own damn business. Miss St John and I have nothing to say to each other.' Another thought struck him. 'Who the hell put you up to this, anyway?'

'No one,' Peter said. 'Well, your friend Lorna mentioned that you and your lady-love had split, and we realised that explained why you were such rotten company when we took you out for a drink the other day. Since we both knew what a stiff-necked obstinate bastard you are, we guessed that you'd go on suffering in silence unless we did something. So we applied for a little extra leave, and worked out this plan to bring you both together.'

'You needn't have bothered,' Lannsen said ungraciously. 'I'm sure Miss St John doesn't want to talk to me.'

'I didn't think you'd want to talk to *me*,' Elise said.

'Why not?' he asked. 'You walked out on me, remember? Took off without a word. Not that it surprised me. You'd been making it quite obvious that you didn't want my company.' He rounded on her suddenly. 'Why didn't you just tell me it was over? And where were you going in the evenings, anyway? Seeing Devlin, I suppose?'

She hardly noticed the two men leaving, closing the door softly behind them. 'No, I wasn't seeing Devlin.' Anger helped her explain. 'I haven't seen him since we

239

parted. I just wanted to be on my own – to sort myself out.'

'Couldn't you have let me help? Am I that unapproachable?'

'How could I talk to you?' She turned away from him. 'Don't you realise what it was like for me, knowing that I was going to ruin you?'

'Ruin me?' he repeated. 'How the hell could you ruin me?'

'The will,' she said. 'I found it. The old master's will, leaving Shilden to Blair Devlin.'

He was silent for such a long time that she began to wonder if he had heard her. 'You found the will?' he said at last. 'You were the one who sent it to Devlin?'

'It was in an old scrapbook,' she explained. 'I didn't know what to do. I didn't even know if it was genuine. I was going to destroy it, but I couldn't.'

'Why not?' His voice was cold. 'You knew that if it was genuine, Devlin would claim Shilden.'

'Yes,' she said.

'But you sent it to him anyway.'

'I had to,' she said.

He walked over and stood in front of her, his face a blank mask. She realised that his physical effect on her had not lessened. She still felt herself responding to his closeness.

'Why did you do it?' he demanded. 'Because you still fancied Devlin?'

'Don't be so ... so stupid!' It sounded inadequate but she could not think of any other word. 'If I fancied him, would I have left Shilden?' She went on in a sudden rush of words. 'It wasn't what I wanted, it was what the old master wanted. I know it sounds ridiculous, but I felt responsible. I did it because it was the right thing to do. The honourable thing.'

He stared at her for a long time. 'Honour?' he said, softly and surprisingly gently. 'I thought that word was

240

obsolete.' Then he laughed, startling her even more. 'Well, you certainly put the cat among the pigeons, didn't you? Devlin waited until he knew the will was legal before he contacted me, but Mrs Stokes got there first. I'm sure it was the high spot of her life, telling me that the Master of Shilden was coming home at last.'

'But aren't you angry with me?' she asked, in a small voice.

'Angry with you?' he repeated. He thought about it for a moment. 'I certainly should be. For walking out on me. For not trusting me. For not confiding in me.'

'I expected you to hate me,' she said. 'Don't you feel that I've betrayed you?'

'You want to know how I feel?' He caught her hand and pressed it against his bulging erection. 'That's how I damn well feel! Most of the time I'm with you, that's how I feel.' Then he bent his head and kissed her, a deep and almost brutal kiss, pulling her towards him.

'But I've ruined your life,' she said breathlessly, when his mouth released hers.

'You've ruined my self-control,' he said.

His fingers undid the buttons of her blouse. He kissed her again and pushed her back towards the wide settee. She felt his weight above her, holding her down. He massaged her breasts, and then used his mouth to arouse them even more. But this time he gave her the minimum of foreplay. His breathing quickened and he grasped the waistband of her pants, ripping the buttons in his haste to drag them down to her knees, then to her ankles. She kicked them off, and let him overpower her. Let him force her legs apart, and enter her.

'It's been so long,' he muttered. 'Too long.'

He thrust strongly and she moved with him. Despite the speed at which he had taken her she relished the close warmth of his body as it covered hers. His hands held her prisoner. She felt him beginning to shake as his climax overtook him. She felt him stiffen with orgasmic

241

pleasure, and his fingers dug painfully into her flesh. But she did not care. When he groaned in the final spasm of satisfaction she felt as happy as if she had experienced a marvellous orgasm herself. He lay close to her for a long time, and although her position was not very comfortable, she was disappointed when he finally moved.

'I'm hurting you,' he said, disentangling himself.

'You're not,' she said.

'Liar,' he touched her face briefly. 'And I don't suppose that was very good for you, either.' He paused and then laughed softly. 'But it certainly was good for me.'

She lay next to him. 'Whose house is this?' she asked. 'Yours?'

'A friend's,' he said.

'Did Blair Devlin throw you out of Shilden?'

He looked at her for a moment, and she could see the amusement in his eyes. 'No, he didn't. What a poor opinion you have of Mr Devlin.'

'You two weren't exactly friends,' she reminded him.

'He can afford to be generous now,' Lannsen said. 'He holds all the aces. No, all my stuff is still at the castle.'

'So you've got to go back?'

'Yes,' he said. 'And so have you.'

Elise did not want to return to Shilden. She was afraid that Blair Devlin might have gained the wrong impression from her actions. Afraid that he would think she wanted to resume their relationship. Afraid that she would have to hurt him again. As Lannsen's Mercedes ate up the miles on the motorway she wondered if Devlin would be waiting at the castle to greet them. But the first person they saw when they arrived was Lorna.

'Super to see you!' Lorna hugged Elise with what seemed like genuine enthusiasm. 'What an idiot you were, running off like that. Dev is around somewhere, sorting out the horses. He's in his element now. You'll see him later, I expect.'

Lannsen took her case out of the boot and went ahead of them up the steps. Lorna watched him.

'I still think he's got the sexiest bum ever,' she said. 'But I suppose thinking is all I'm ever going to do about it now.'

'Lorna,' Elise said. 'Do you feel too badly about me?'

Lorna looked surprised. 'Why should I?'

'I've ruined your career.'

'As a Madam?' Lorna smiled. 'Well, don't lose any sleep over it. If I wanted to carry on in the escort trade I'd go back to London. But I don't. I'm staying here. In fact I've got my old job back. I'm a dogsbody again, only this time I'm doing it for Dev.' She linked arms with Elise, walked to the steps and sat down. 'It's going to be great fun. I'm helping Julia with the riding school, too.'

'At White Gates?' Elise asked, still mystified.

'And here,' Lorna said. 'Dev's still going to run this place as a hotel, although I don't think he's planning to let the east wing pleasure house out to the public anymore.' She glanced sideways at Elise and grinned. 'But he might decide to spend his honeymoon in there – with Julia.'

'He's marrying Julia?' Elise was amazed.

'Next year,' Lorna nodded. 'See what you've done. You've changed things for everyone.'

'But I thought Dev saw Julia as a kind of substitute sister?'

'Didn't we all?' Lorna said. 'And I'll bet you thought Dev was pretty well-off as well?'

'Well, yes,' Elise agreed. 'You have to be, to own a riding stables.'

'He doesn't own White Gates,' Lorna said. 'Julia's filthy-rich daddy owns it. Dev's just an employee. He's got no money of his own, so he just accepted that Julia was out of reach, although it seems he's fancied her for ages. Mind you, I don't think Dev's finances, or lack of them, worried Julia or her father, but Dev's too proud to go cap in hand to anyone. Now, of course, he doesn't need to, thanks to you.'

'The old master left money as well?' Elise was surprised. 'Max always said there wasn't any.'

'The old master didn't have a bean,' Lorna said. 'But Shilden will make money now, thanks to Max. Most of the original investors are staying in, and the ones who were mainly interested in the pleasure house aren't about to make any public protests. Julia's daddy is talking about building an equestrian centre here, which means we'll definitely get it, because Julia wants it. Even dear old George is pleased. Apparently he's thinking of putting more money into the venture. Pretty soon Shilden is going to be so bloody respectable he'll be able to come here with his wife.'

Elise had a pleasant meeting with Blair Devlin. His attitude was almost formal, and it was clear that their previous brief affair was now just a pleasant memory.

'I can't tell you how much you've done for me,' he said. 'You've given me back my self-respect. My place in the community. Does that make sense to you?'

'I think so,' she said.

'I hope you'll stay on at Shilden,' he added. 'And Lannsen, of course. We could use his talents. We need an astute businessman to help run this place and make a profit.'

'So you're friends with Max now?' she teased.

'Not exactly,' Devlin admitted. 'Let's just say we stalk round each other, but with a bit more respect than before. But I think he's happier now that Shilden will be run as a legitimate hotel, without the added attraction of the pleasure house. I gather he never liked that aspect of the deal. It was forced on him by some of his investors. He couldn't really object.'

'I don't remember you objecting, either,' she said, demurely.

She was amused to see that he looked distinctly embarrassed.

'Well, maybe not,' he agreed. 'But that's past history now.' He smiled. 'We're all entitled to sow a few wild oats. But pretty soon I hope to be a respectable married man.'

'And the Master of Shilden,' she added.

'Thanks to you,' he said.

Elise fitted easily into an undemanding job as Lorna's helper. It was not exactly what she had wanted out of life, and sometimes she found herself dreaming of plays and theatres, and set designs. Then she reminded herself of the limited opportunities in her chosen field, and told herself she was lucky to have a job, a place to live, and the man she loved in bed with her at night. She and Max had generous wages and a pleasant suite of rooms overlooking the castle's private grounds. Being resident at the castle, their living expenses were low.

She knew she should have been completely happy. But she was not. She could have dealt with her own niggling feelings of frustration, but there was a deeper edge to her unease. She knew that Max Lannsen was not happy. He worked hard during the day managing the business side of Shilden, but at night he seemed tired and abstracted. He made love to her, and it was always fulfilling. They usually climaxed together, then lay in sleepy companionship. But his inventive sparkle had disappeared. He did not suggest any fantasies or games. The scarves he had used to tie her wrists and turn her into his willing slave stayed unused in the drawer. The short flexible riding crop he had bought to add spice to her erotic punishment, and which had stimulated her almost to orgasm the first time he had held her down on the bed and used it on her bottom, now hung untouched on its hook. She sometimes had the horrible feeling that he was making love out of a sense of duty, rather than with the enthusiastic sexual delight he had obviously felt in the past.

She believed he might be finding it difficult to adjust to working for Blair Devlin. She guessed he would find it harder to accept than she did. But she did wonder how long it would take him. And sometimes she wondered if their relationship would survive the wait.

Lying beside him in bed, with their love-making over, she glanced sideways at his profile. He looked as remote and untouchable now as he had when she first met him. This is getting worse, she thought. I have to do something about it.

'Max?' She propped herself up on one elbow, and looked down at his impassive face. 'What's bothering you?'

'Nothing,' he said.

'That's a blatant lie,' she challenged.

He managed a smile. 'You guessed? I never was very good at it.'

'You told me off once,' she said, 'for not confiding in you. Keeping our worries to ourself has caused us to split up twice. I couldn't bear it to happen again.'

He looked up at her for a long minute. 'Are you happy here?'

'Well, yes,' she said, mystified.

'Completely?'

'Is anyone completely happy?'

'Don't wriggle.' He lifted his arms and linked his hands behind his head. 'What would make you completely happy?'

'Oh, Max,' she said, 'what a question. Does anyone know the answer to that?'

'Try and find one,' he suggested.

She thought about it for a moment. 'Having a resounding success in the theatre, I suppose. Having all the critics rave about the wonderful, marvellous, imaginative set designs. Something like that.'

He was silent for so long that she thought the subject was closed. 'That's what I thought,' he said at last. He turned his head slightly. His eyes strayed from her face down to her breasts. His look still made her flesh tingle with anticipation and her nipples tighten. But he did not touch her. 'This meeting with George tomorrow,' he said. 'You know what he's going to offer me, don't you?'

'He's going to ask you to run the business side of the equestrian centre,' she said. 'You can do that.'

'I could,' he agreed. 'Easily.' He sat up suddenly. 'Get out of bed. And walk. Walk round the room.'

Totally mystified she did as he instructed. He watched her intently. 'Come here,' he said at last. She walked to the bed. 'Up here.' He patted the bed next to him. When she climbed back on the bed he threw back the covers and once again she admired his lean body, his dark tan contrasting with the white sheets. She was surprised to see that he was semi-erect. They had often made love several times a night, but not since returning to Shilden.

She reached down for him. 'That's better,' she said. 'You still like me.'

'Did you doubt it?' he asked.

'I was beginning to,' she admitted.

He removed her hand, but gently. 'Kneel across my face,' he said. 'I want to tongue you, and watch you, and lay here while you do all the work.'

She straddled him and gripped the headboard, lowering herself down towards him until she felt the warmth of his tongue exploring her. She wriggled her hips enticingly, encouraging him to touch her smoothly and lightly, but as she felt the sensations begin to build she moved faster, and lowered herself closer to his mouth. As always he knew just how to tease her into a climax. She felt herself come in a rush of pleasure and rolled away from him before she collapsed. After a few minutes he said huskily: 'Now me.'

She slid down to take him in her mouth and felt him growing larger as she did so. She closed her lips round him and sucked hard in the way she knew he enjoyed. His body stiffened as his pleasure mounted. She moved from his penis to his balls, tantalising them with her mouth and tongue, then moving back to his fully erect cock. His pushed himself into her, seemingly oblivious of her comfort, but she did not care. It was the first time for weeks that she felt the once familiar sexual excitement sparking between them. He came suddenly, with a groaning cry.

'Good?' she asked, after a moment.

'Yes,' he said shortly. He lay back, staring at the ceiling and then, equally abruptly, he said, 'I'm not taking it.'

Mystified she asked, 'Taking what?'

'The job,' he said. 'Manager of the equestrian centre, or whatever George decides to call the position. And I'm not staying at Shilden. I'm leaving next week.'

'You've quarrelled with Dev?' she guessed.

'No,' he said. 'Devlin's been very generous. I haven't quarrelled with anyone. I just can't take this anymore.'

'Max,' she said, 'you're not making sense.'

He pulled himself into a sitting position. 'I'm making as much sense as you did when you told me what would make you happy. I hoped you'd say something like that, because it means you probably understand the way I feel. It's to do with fulfilment. I don't want to be a businessman. I want to know if I'm really a painter. I want to know before it's too late. So I'm going back to London to find out. It'll be hard, but I don't care.' He looked at her with the kind of smile she had not seen for a long time. 'Coming?'

'You bet I am,' she said.

'Damn it, Max,' George Farrow said. 'Surely you can paint in your spare time?'

'If I take on the equestrian centre,' Lannsen said, 'I won't have any spare time.'

'I'll get you an assistant,' George promised. Getting no response he persisted. 'Two assistants?' Lannsen shook his head. 'More money?' Another shake. 'You're a fool, Max. Artists starve. Even good ones. What happens when your savings run out?'

'Elise will be working,' Lannsen said.

'You'd live off a woman?'

'Certainly,' Lannsen grinned. 'It's what dissolute artists always do.'

George Farrow turned to Elise. 'I suppose you approve of this madness?'

'Yes,' she said. 'Because I understand it. We both need to prove ourselves. The longer we stay here the harder it would be to make the break. In the end we probably wouldn't manage it. We'd be trapped.' She turned to the older man. 'I know you find it difficult to understand, but we need the creative challenge. We need to know we tried, even if we end up as failures.'

'You're both totally insane,' George Farrow said. 'There's obviously no point in arguing with you.' He smiled suddenly. 'So I'll work on the theory that if you can't beat 'em, join 'em.' He turned to Elise. 'Do you remember me offering to help you make some theatre contacts? The offer still stands, if you want to take it up. I can't make anyone employ you, but judging from the work you've done here you've got talent and imagination. You deserve success. And as for you, Max, I'm willing to act as your sponsor for a year. Get some work together and then we'll approach the galleries.'

'I don't want charity,' Lannsen said.

'I not offering charity, damn it,' George Farrow said. 'This is a business proposition, and a business risk. If you're successful I'll be taking a cut. We'll work out the details later.' He sat back and smiled. 'How does that sound to you both?'

'It sounds generous,' Elise said quickly.

'You were generous,' George Farrow said. 'Generous to Blair Devlin and to me.' He looked at her speculatively. 'I believe the Victorian bathroom is still intact. You wouldn't like to be generous one more time, would you, and make an old man very happy? Just one more little show, for old time's sake?'

'No, she wouldn't,' Lannsen interrupted. His dark eyes fixed on Elise. 'Sorry George, but from now on my future wife only strips for me.'

BLACK LACE NEW BOOKS

Published in January

NADYA'S QUEST
Lisette Allen

Nadya's personal quest leads her to St Petersburg in the summer of 1788. The beautiful city is in a rapturous state of decadence and its Empress, well known for her lascivious appetite, is hungry for a new lover who must be young, handsome and virile. When Nadya brings a Swedish seafarer, the magnificently-proportioned Axel, to the Imperial court, he is soon made the Empress's favourite. Nadya, determined to keep Axel for herself, is drawn into an intrigue of treachery and sedition as hostilities develop between Russia and Sweden.

ISBN 0 352 33135 6

DESIRE UNDER CAPRICORN
Louisa Francis

A shipwreck rips Dita Jones from the polite society of Sydney in the 1870s and throws her into an untamed world where Matt Warrender, a fellow castaway, develops a passion for her he will never forget. Separated after their eventual rescue, Dita is taken back into civilised life where a wealthy stud farmer, Jas McGrady, claims her for his bride. Taken to the rugged terrain of outback Australia, and a new life as Mrs McGrady, Dita realises her husband has a dark secret.

ISBN 0 352 33136 4

Published in February

PULLING POWER
Cheryl Mildenhall

Amber Barclay is a top motor racing driver whose career is sponsored by Portia Lombardi, a professional dominatrix with a taste for control as forceful as Amber's driving. In the run-up to an important race, competition is fierce as Marie Gifford, Portia's financial dependent, sparks a passionate sexual liaison with the dashing Lawrie Samson, Amber's only rival. But what will happen when Lawrie discovers an astonishing link between the three women?

ISBN 0 352 33139 9

THE MASTER OF SHILDEN
Lucinda Carrington

Trapped in a web of sexual and emotional entanglement, interior designer, Elise St John, grabs at the chance to redecorate a remote castle. As she sets about creating rooms in which guests will be able to realise their most erotic fantasies, her own dreams and desires ripen. Caught between Max Lannsen, the dark, broody Master of Shilden, and Blair Devlin, the sexy, debonair riding instructor, Elise realises that her dreams are becoming reality and that the future of these two men suddenly depends on a decision she will be forced to make.

ISBN 0 352 33140 2

MODERN LOVE
An Anthology of Erotic Writings by Women
Edited by Kerri Sharp

For nearly four years Black Lace has dominated the erotic fiction market in the UK and revolutionised the way people think about and write erotica. Black Lace is now a generic term for erotic fiction by and for women. Following the success of *Pandora's Box*, the first Black Lace anthology, *Modern Love* is a collection of extracts from our bestselling contemporary novels. Seduction and mystery and darkly sensual behaviour are the key words to this unique collection of erotic writings from the female imagination.

ISBN 0 352 33158 5

To be published in March

SILKEN CHAINS
Jodi Nicol

Fleeing her scheming guardian and an arranged marriage, Abbie, an innocent young Victorian woman, is thrown from her horse. She awakens in a lavish interior filled with heavenly perfumes to find that Leon Villiers, the wealthy and attractive master of the house, has virtually imprisoned her with sensual pleasures. Using his knowledge of Eastern philosophy and tantric arts, he introduces her to experiences beyond her imagination. But will her guardian's unerring search for her ruin this taste of liberty?

ISBN 0 352 33143 7

THE HAND OF AMUN
Juliet Hastings

Marked from birth, Naunakhte – daughter of a humble scribe – must enter a life of dark eroticism as the servant of the Egyptian god Amun. She becomes the favourite of the high priestess but is accused of an act of lascivious sacrilege and is forced to flee the temple for the murky labyrinth of the city. There she meets Khonsu, a prince of the underworld, but fate draws her back to the temple and she is forced to choose between two lovers – one mortal and the other a god.

ISBN 0 352 33144 5

If you would like a complete list of plot summaries of Black Lace titles, please fill out the questionnaire overleaf or send a stamped addressed envelope to:-

Black Lace, 332 Ladbroke Grove, London W10 5AH

BLACK LACE BACKLIST

All books are priced £4.99 unless another price is given.

---------✂---------------------

Please send me the books I have ticked above.

Name   ....

Address   ....

          ....

          ....

          .... Post Code   ....

Send to: **Cash Sales, Black Lace Books, 332 Ladbroke Grove, London W10 5AH.**

Please enclose a cheque or postal order, made payable to **Virgin Publishing Ltd**, to the value of the books you have ordered plus postage and packing costs as follows:

UK and BFPO – £1.00 for the first book, 50p for each subsequent book.

Overseas (including Republic of Ireland) – £2.00 for the first book, £1.00 each subsequent book.

If you would prefer to pay by VISA or ACCESS/ MASTERCARD, please write your card number and expiry date here:

....

Please allow up to 28 days for delivery.

Signature   ....

---------✂---------------------

WE NEED YOUR HELP ...
to plan the future of women's erotic fiction –

– and no stamp required!

Yours are the only opinions that matter.

Black Lace is the first series of books devoted to erotic fiction by women for women.

We intend to keep providing the best-written, sexiest books you can buy. And we'd appreciate your help and valued opinion of the books so far. Tell us what you want to read.

THE BLACK LACE QUESTIONNAIRE

SECTION ONE: ABOUT YOU

1.1 Sex *(we presume you are female, but so as not to discriminate)*
Are you?
Male ☐
Female ☐

1.2 Age
under 21 ☐   21–30 ☐
31–40 ☐   41–50 ☐
51–60 ☐   over 60 ☐

1.3 At what age did you leave full-time education?
still in education ☐   16 or younger ☐
17–19 ☐   20 or older ☐

1.4 Occupation _____

1.5 Annual household income

under £10,000 ☐ £10–£20,000 ☐

£20–£30,000 ☐ £30–£40,000 ☐

over £40,000 ☐

1.6 We are perfectly happy for you to remain anonymous; but if you would like to receive information on other publications available, please insert your name and address

_____

_____

_____

_____

SECTION TWO: ABOUT BUYING BLACK LACE BOOKS

2.1 How did you acquire this copy of *The Master of Shilden*?

I bought it myself ☐ My partner bought it ☐

I borrowed/found it ☐

2.2 How did you find out about Black Lace books?

I saw them in a shop ☐

I saw them advertised in a magazine ☐

I saw the London Underground posters ☐

I read about them in _____

Other _____

2.3 Please tick the following statements you agree with:

I would be less embarrassed about buying Black Lace books if the cover pictures were less explicit ☐

I think that in general the pictures on Black Lace books are about right ☐

I think Black Lace cover pictures should be as explicit as possible ☐

2.4 Would you read a Black Lace book in a public place – on a train for instance?

Yes ☐ No ☐

SECTION THREE: ABOUT THIS BLACK LACE BOOK

3.1 Do you think the sex content in this book is:
    Too much   ☐   About right   ☐
    Not enough   ☐

3.2 Do you think the writing style in this book is:
    Too unreal/escapist ☐   About right   ☐
    Too down to earth   ☐

3.3 Do you think the story in this book is:
    Too complicated   ☐   About right   ☐
    Too boring/simple ☐

3.4 Do you think the cover of this book is:
    Too explicit   ☐   About right   ☐
    Not explicit enough ☐

Here's a space for any other comments:

SECTION FOUR: ABOUT OTHER BLACK LACE BOOKS

4.1 How many Black Lace books have you read?   ☐

4.2 If more than one, which one did you prefer?

4.3 Why?

SECTION FIVE: ABOUT YOUR IDEAL EROTIC NOVEL

We want to publish the books you want to read – so this is your chance to tell us exactly what your ideal erotic novel would be like.

5.1   Using a scale of 1 to 5 (1 = no interest at all, 5 = your ideal), please rate the following possible settings for an erotic novel:

Medieval/barbarian/sword 'n' sorcery ☐
Renaissance/Elizabethan/Restoration ☐
Victorian/Edwardian ☐
1920s & 1930s – the Jazz Age ☐
Present day ☐
Future/Science Fiction ☐

5.2   Using the same scale of 1 to 5, please rate the following themes you may find in an erotic novel:

Submissive male/dominant female ☐
Submissive female/dominant male ☐
Lesbianism ☐
Bondage/fetishism ☐
Romantic love ☐
Experimental sex e.g. anal/watersports/sex toys ☐
Gay male sex ☐
Group sex ☐

Using the same scale of 1 to 5, please rate the following styles in which an erotic novel could be written:

Realistic, down to earth, set in real life ☐
Escapist fantasy, but just about believable ☐
Completely unreal, impressionistic, dreamlike ☐

5.3   Would you prefer your ideal erotic novel to be written from the viewpoint of the main male characters or the main female characters?

Male ☐ Female ☐
Both ☐

5.4 What would your ideal Black Lace heroine be like? Tick as many as you like:

Dominant	☐	Glamorous	☐
Extroverted	☐	Contemporary	☐
Independent	☐	Bisexual	☐
Adventurous	☐	Naïve	☐
Intellectual	☐	Introverted	☐
Professional	☐	Kinky	☐
Submissive	☐	Anything else?	☐
Ordinary	☐	_____	

5.5 What would your ideal male lead character be like? Again, tick as many as you like:

Rugged	☐		
Athletic	☐	Caring	☐
Sophisticated	☐	Cruel	☐
Retiring	☐	Debonair	☐
Outdoor-type	☐	Naïve	☐
Executive-type	☐	Intellectual	☐
Ordinary	☐	Professional	☐
Kinky	☐	Romantic	☐
Hunky	☐		
Sexually dominant	☐	Anything else?	☐
Sexually submissive	☐	_____	

5.6 Is there one particular setting or subject matter that your ideal erotic novel would contain?

_____

SECTION SIX: LAST WORDS

6.1 What do you like best about Black Lace books?

_____

6.2 What do you most dislike about Black Lace books?

_____

6.3 In what way, if any, would you like to change Black Lace covers?

_____

6.4 Here's a space for any other comments:

_____

_____

_____

_____

_____

Thank you for completing this questionnaire. Now tear it out of the book – carefully! – put it in an envelope and send it to:

Black Lace
FREEPOST
London
W10 5BR

No stamp is required if you are resident in the U.K.